The leaves of the trees rustled in the cool breeze, and a shower of petals tumbled through the air, speaking to the world's transience. It was in that enchanting garden that Fourier found a shimmering bud—a girl.

Re:ZERO -Starting Life in Another World-

The only ability Subaru Natsuki gets when he's summoned to another world is time travel via his own death. But to save her, he'll die as many times as it takes.

CONTENTS

A Dream's Beginning
001

Felix Argyle Is a Pretty Boy
025

The Valkyrie of Duke Karsten's Lands
(Originally appeared in *Monthly Comic Alive*, nos. 106–107)
043

Felix Argyle's Curse
105

The Dream of the Lion King
187

Re:ZeRo Ex
-Starting Life in Another World-

VOLUME 1

The Dream of the Lion King

TAPPEI NAGATSUKI
ILLUSTRATION: SHINICHIROU OTSUKA

New York

Re:ZERO -Starting Life in Another World- Ex, Vol. 1
Tappei Nagatsuki

Translation by Kevin Steinbach
Cover art by Shinichirou Otsuka

This book is a work of fiction. Names, characters, places, and incidents are the product of the author's imagination or are used fictitiously. Any resemblance to actual events, locales, or persons, living or dead, is coincidental.

Re: ZERO KARA HAJIMERU ISEKAI SEIKATSU Ex SHISHIOU NO MITA YUME
©Tappei Nagatsuki 2015
First published in Japan in 2015 by KADOKAWA CORPORATION, Tokyo.
English translation rights arranged with
KADOKAWA CORPORATION, Tokyo through Tuttle-Mori Agency, Inc., Tokyo.

English translation © 2017 by Yen Press, LLC

Yen Press, LLC supports the right to free expression and the value of copyright. The purpose of copyright is to encourage writers and artists to produce the creative works that enrich our culture.

The scanning, uploading, and distribution of this book without permission is a theft of the author's intellectual property. If you would like permission to use material from the book (other than for review purposes), please contact the publisher. Thank you for your support of the author's rights.

Yen On
1290 Avenue of the Americas
New York, NY 10104

Visit us at yenpress.com
facebook.com/yenpress
twitter.com/yenpress
yenpress.tumblr.com
instagram.com/yenpress

First Yen On Edition: November 2017

Yen On is an imprint of Yen Press, LLC.
The Yen On name and logo are trademarks of Yen Press, LLC.

The publisher is not responsible for websites (or their content) that are not owned by the publisher.

Library of Congress Cataloging-in-Publication Data
Names: Nagatsuki, Tappei, 1987- author. | Otsuka, Shinichirou, illustrator. | Steinbach, Kevin, translator.
Title: Re:ZERO starting life in another world ex / Tappei Nagatsuki ; illustration by Shinichirou Otsuka ; translation by Kevin Steinbach.
Other titles: Re:ZERO kara hajimeru isekai seikatsu ex. English
Description: First Yen On edition. | New York : Yen On, 2017.
Identifiers: LCCN 2017036833 | ISBN 9780316412902 (v. 1 : pbk.)
Subjects: | CYAC: Science fiction. |
Time travel—Fiction. | BISAC: FICTION / Science Fiction / Adventure.
Classification: LCC PZ7.1.N34 Ref 2017 | DDC [Fic]—dc23
LC record available at https://lccn.loc.gov/2017036833

ISBNs: 978-0-316-41290-2 (paperback)
978-0-316-47907-3 (ebook)

1 3 5 7 9 10 8 6 4 2

LSC-C

Printed in the United States of America

A DREAM'S BEGINNING

1

When he saw her in the castle garden, Fourier Lugunica came to a screeching halt.

His large scarlet eyes went wide with curiosity as the wind tugged at his golden locks. One of his pronounced canine teeth poked out like a small fang as the breath rushed from his mouth. The young boy, not even ten years old, leaned out of the open-air gallery to peer into the garden.

Fourier was very much in the middle of running from one of his tutors and had no time to gawk. He could already hear the man's voice behind him in the hallway. If he was caught, he would be dragged back to his dangerously boring lesson—but even knowing that, Fourier couldn't tear his eyes away from the scene before him.

The gardens at Lugunica's royal castle were the work of crown gardeners who exercised every bit of skill and knowledge they possessed. The result was a fantastically rich tapestry, dizzy with flowers and different blossoms every season.

The leaves of the trees rustled in the cool breeze, and a shower of petals tumbled through the air, speaking to the world's transience. It was in that enchanting garden that Fourier found a shimmering bud—a girl.

Her verdant green hair was tied back as she struck a posture both refined and beautiful. Clad in a dress the color of fresh grass, obviously of fine make, the young, self-possessed girl wore it perfectly. Fourier saw little more than her profile from where he stood, but the pale white of her neck and cheek along with the amber of her almond-shaped eyes hinted at her brimming beauty.

And yet, had that been all, she might not have made such a firm impression on Fourier. It would have been no more than a momentary affair, a glimpse of a gorgeous young lady in the castle.

But it did not end there.

"—"

The girl stood in the garden, casting her eyes over the array of colorful flowers. If she had merely been taken with the vibrancy of the blossoms, it would have shown that her disposition was like that of any other. But instead of looking at the flowers in the center of the garden, she was inspecting a single bud in a far corner. Staring at it intently, as though she believed it might open then and there...

"Your Highness Fourier! So you heed me at last!"

His tutor, breathing hard, finally reached the spot where Fourier stood in the hallway. He regarded the boy with relief written on his face, but that was soon replaced with an expression of puzzlement when he noticed how Fourier was staring into the garden.

"Your Highness?" he said. "What has caught your interest ou—?"

"Nothing, sir! Nothing! Not a thing! Surely not something for you to worry about!"

Fourier rushed at the instructor as the man tried to discern what had the boy so intrigued. The hand Fourier held out in hopes of hiding the scene collided with the tutor's face, and the man stumbled back with a cry of "My eye!," but Fourier had no time to concern himself with that. He was more worried that the girl by the flowers might have overheard the commotion.

Anxiously, he looked toward the garden. That happened to be the exact same moment the girl, who had heard something going on, turned in his direction. Fourier scrambled to lower his gaze.

"Th-this isn't good. I feel really weird... Maybe I'm sick or something? My cheeks are all hot, and it's hard to breathe..."

Noting an ache in his chest and how he had a difficult time breathing, Fourier concluded that this was a bad place for him to be. He grabbed his writhing teacher by the leg and began fleeing back down the hallway in tremendous haste.

"Y-Your Highness! Ouch! That hurts!"

"Just grin and bear it! It's not like I'm strong enough to pick you up! But I can't just leave you in such a dangerous place. After all, I'm part of the royal family—pride of the people."

"I am moved by your concern for me, my prince, but—*yow!* Perhaps you could stop running and—*ouch!*" The tutor cried out, his head colliding with every wall and pillar they passed, but Fourier ignored him. He could still see that girl whenever he closed his eyes. She was clearly the cause of his pounding heart, yet for some reason he could not force her image out of his head, no matter how much time went by.

It was a mystery to Fourier why he felt so reluctant to leave as he dashed away from the garden.

2

Fourier Lugunica belonged to the royal family of the Dragonfriend Kingdom of Lugunica, a dynasty with more than a thousand years of history; he was the son of the reigning king, Randohal Lugunica. Consequently, he was a prince with the right of succession, and worthy of the highest honors.

"Yes, but I'm the *fourth* prince. My brothers all precede me. I don't see the kingship passing to me anytime soon. Doesn't it make all this effort, day in and day out, seem a bit pointless?"

"Ho-ho-ho! I see you've learned the art of impudence, Your Highness."

Fourier had finished his classes and was seeking respite in his personal rooms, where he was conversing with a visitor.

Fourier screwed up his face at the word *impudence*. The one laughing was an exceptionally old man, his long hair and beard both white from age. Miklotov MacMahon—a representative of the Council of Elders who was considered the brains of the kingdom. Miklotov was the one who wielded all the real power in the government. Truly deserving to be called a wise man. Fourier was well acquainted with the rumors that even if the king were to disappear, the kingdom would continue running smoothly so long as Miklotov was around.

Fourier was not enamored with the rumors that made light of his father, the king, but Miklotov was a loyal subject who served the realm without ambition. And it was true enough that the elder did his utmost serving a royal family that left something to be desired in the way of stewardship—so Fourier was hard-pressed to condemn such talk.

"If my father and brothers aren't up to the job, why don't you become king?" Fourier said. "Things would be much simpler that way. Don't you think?"

"You give this old man quite a shock," Miklotov replied. "Those are not words that one of Your Highness's station should speak so lightly. And in any event, it would be in violation of our pact with the dragon."

"Our pact with the dragon, right."

Miklotov gave a somber nod. Fourier laid his head on his desk and began to think.

The pact they spoke of was the reason the Kingdom of Lugunica was occasionally referred to as the Dragonfriend Kingdom: An oath sworn with the Holy Dragon Volcanica, whose protection had ensured the kingdom's prosperity for hundreds of years.

"The dragon handles everything," Fourier mused. "The kingdom's harvests and safety. And the only one who can receive its blessings is a blood descendent of the first King Lugunica, who forged a bond of friendship with it. It all seems a bit too good to be true."

"And yet we do have the dragon's blessing. This makes His Majesty the King, to say nothing of Your Highness, people of the utmost importance to this kingdom."

"So I've heard, enough times to make my head ache."

"Mm. And I have said it often enough to make my tongue sore."

Fourier pursed his lips, but Miklotov stroked his beard nonchalantly.

"That story is the reason I earnestly wish you would have a greater appreciation for your position, Your Highness."

"Hmm, then I guess I have no— Wait! If it's only our blood that makes me and my father so important, doesn't it mean that all this study isn't really necessary? What about that?"

"Ho-ho, impudence rears its head again. Think of it from your subjects' point of view. They may be obliged to respect whoever holds the office, but do you think they would rather serve under an ignoramus or brute—when they could have a man of intelligence? And the intellect does not blossom without proper cultivation. Nor does the blood of the Lion King."

"The Lion King? That dusty old name again?"

An unusual passion had entered Miklotov's voice, but Fourier regarded him with a wry smile. "Lion King" was a term for the first ruler to make a pact with the dragon—in other words, the first person to establish what was now the Kingdom of Lugunica. He had been called "the last Lion King."

"I understand how much you expect of the Lion King's descendants," Fourier said. "But it's lot to ask of those of us born so far down the line of succession. The sages are all but unparalleled, whether you search the world over or look back through history. I don't expect any to be born anytime soon."

"So you may say, Your Highness, but the blood has not run thin. It is a fact that once every several generations, a true master appears in the royal line. Two generations ago..."

Miklotov had been speaking fluently, but suddenly he stopped. His wrinkled face darkened, and he shook his head and murmured, "No."

After a moment, he went on: "My apologies. A slip of the tongue. Memory grows unreliable in old age."

"You losing your memory is about the worst thing that could

happen to this kingdom! Quit worrying about a delinquent like me and take care of yourself!"

"I hardly think Your Highness is delinquent..."

Miklotov put up some resistance as Fourier tried to hustle him out of the room. But his old bones were no match for a boy in the prime of youth.

"Now, then..."

Having chased off the garrulous elder, Fourier was alone. He began to strip off his clothes. He changed into whatever he felt like and wrapped his head in a bandanna that would disguise his conspicuous golden hair. Then, having prepared against every eventuality, he snuck out of the room.

No one was in the hall. Fourier set to running through the quiet castle in a great hurry. He was hoping to stay inconspicuous, it would not do for anyone to see him.

He was headed for the same place he had gone to every day recently.

—A gallery, where every day he looked out over the gardens, hoping to see that girl.

3

Fourier arrived in the gallery nonchalantly, making sure no one was around before he climbed up on the railing and began looking avidly through the garden for the girl he sought.

"Hmm. Not today, either, huh? I make such an effort to come here, and all for nothing. To do such a thing to a prince—that girl is fearless. Heavens."

Unable to find the one he so longed for, Fourier was full of regret. Ten days had passed since he first saw her there. That day, he had run away because the drumming in his chest had seemed dangerous, but now he hoped to see her again exactly because he wanted to experience that feeling once more.

The ache in his heart had never really gone away. In fact, it was renewed every time he recalled her face. He was convinced that the only way he could find relief was to meet her.

Fourier had never doubted the intuition that guided his actions. He would on occasion sense an answer emerge, for no particular reason, from among countless choices. What he discovered this way always led him down the right path. It had been the same whether in arithmetic and history class, or when deciding a move in Chantrange, a board game played with pawns. As an extreme example, several years earlier, he had even foreseen that a wheel would fall off the dragon carriage his father, the king, rode in.

But all of these were dismissed as mere chance; simple guesses that could not be repeated. He told his teacher, but the man grumbled something about nonsense. Fourier was not so ignorant a child as to press the issue of a insight that made him different from normal people.

"No matter. The girl is what's important now. If I only knew her name, at least, this would be so much easier…"

His only clue at the moment was that she must be the daughter of some family prestigious enough to be granted entrance to the castle. If he told them when and where he had seen her, the guards and serving girls might have been able to help him.

"But I hate needing things from people. I don't know why, but I feel it would be rather inconvenient if anyone knew I was looking for her. Hmm…"

The palpitations, the unusual sense that what he was doing was not quite acceptable—all of this mystified Fourier. He didn't even really know what he would do if he ever found her.

"I suppose I can figure out what I should do after we meet. I think I recall some important person saying that thinking too carefully is just another form of cowardice… Mm!"

As he stood there muttering to himself, suddenly something clouded the edges of his vision. Fourier leaned out over the railing, trying with his eyes to follow the silhouette of whoever was passing directly below the open hallway. He saw a hint of a sleeve the hue of fresh grass.

It was the right color, the one he remembered from that girl's dress.

"Oops…"

The moment the girl's image floated through his mind, Fourier felt his foot slip from the railing. He had pitched too far forward, lost his balance, and found himself tumbling out of the gallery. The garden was paved with flagstones. If he hit his head on one, it wouldn't be pretty.

He was going to pay for this little indulgence with his life…

"Hwah?!"

But as it turned out, no such thing happened. He felt his body sinking into something soft, breaking his fall.

"*Bff! Bfaaah! Pft! Bleh!* What is this? Is this—dirt?!"

Extricating himself from the soft pile of earth, Fourier spat leaves and mud out of his mouth. He had apparently managed to land in a flower bed instead of on the flagstones; miraculously, he was unhurt.

Looking up, he could see the hallway he'd come tumbling out of. Perhaps it was sheer chance, again, that had kept him from hurting himself despite a fall of nearly two stories.

"Wow. That's my luck for you. Just goes to show that a little good fortune can get you out of even the tightest spot," Fourier said with a touch of awe, looking at his muddy palms. He ignored the fact that if he had really been blessed with good fortune, he wouldn't have fallen in the first place. He jumped out of the flower bed and looked around, thinking that he would have to find a maid to ready a bath for him.

"—"

And there stood the girl, watching him with wide eyes.

She had the identical, beautiful green hair, still tied up, the clear amber irises he remembered, and she was wearing that grass-colored dress. She was exactly the same girl who had been burned into Fourier's memory.

"Oh… Oh! Ohhh…"

No sooner had this registered than Fourier felt his cheeks start burning, and he found he had lost the ability to speak. His confidence that he would know what to say when the time came had left him in this sorry state.

While Fourier stood there unable even to think, the girl, her eyes still round with surprise, slowly looked up. She looked back and forth between him and the railing—once, twice. Then he realized that she thought he had hurt himself.

"Aw, no need to worry about me! See? I'm not injured in the least! I can see I've upset you, but you needn't worry about it. My body is so tough it's practically a weapon!"

Fourier was still confused, but he held out both arms in an effort to prove he was unharmed. The girl showed no reaction, but she must have at least understood that he was all right.

Fourier very much wanted to continue the conversation, but he was also all too aware that she had witnessed him in a most unprincely moment, and his feet had a strong desire to carry him far away from that spot. Perhaps he would have to be content with having met her a second time.

"Well, I'm quite busy with a great many things, so excuse me! I bid you good day— Huh?"

He waved and was about to step out of the flower bed, when he found his path blocked. The girl was standing in front of him and fixing him with a sharp stare. She spoke sternly.

"—You think you can weasel out of this with such flimsy excuses, intruder?" Fourier noticed how clear and strong her voice was, befitting her appearance. But astonishment soon replaced that feeling—thanks to the dagger glittering in the girl's hand.

"W-whoa! A woman like you shouldn't be walking around with a thing like that!"

"My father doesn't like it, either, but as you can see, it's good to have around sometimes. Don't try anything funny. And don't underestimate me just because I'm a girl. Just wait until you find out what they do to people who try to break into the castle."

"Huh? Wha? Hrh?"

The girl's voice had become razor-sharp, and she showed no sign of responding to Fourier's attempts to calm her down. No hesitation appeared in her eyes. She really did think he was an intruder.

She couldn't have been older than he was, and yet she had such courage. No, there was something else.

"—"

Her grip on the dagger hilt was so tight that Fourier could see her fingertips turning white. She had no experience pointing a blade at a person. This was simply what she felt she had to do, while trying not to shake.

Fourier had certainly not expected to be spoken to this way. He had never thought that when he met the girl again, it might be like this, or that this was the attitude she would take toward him. But there was one thing he hadn't been wrong about—

"You are truly a good young woman, aren't you?"

It was that he cared about the girl in front of him even more than he had imagined.

The girl's expression wavered, thrown off by Fourier's murmur.

"...You can't trick me. My eyes can see right through lies and ruses."

"An upsetting response, when I've revealed my true feelings. What is it you dislike so much about me? I should like to know!"

"...Do you think I'd trust someone who hides his face, just because he asks me to?"

"Hmm...? Oh! Oh, I see, I see! That was my mistake."

Fourier finally realized that the reason for the girl's suspicion was his own fault. He touched his head and found the bandanna he had used as a disguise. He hurriedly removed it, and his golden hair fell around his face. At that, the girl's eyes grew even wider.

"I see I confused you," Fourier said. "As you can tell, I am no intruder. I am the fourth prince of this nation, Fourier Lugunica! You may gaze upon my visage."

Fourier wiped some sweat from his brow as he announced himself, trying to reassure the shocked young woman. Surely her suspicion would vanish, and that smile of hers would bloom like a flower...

"My deepest apologies, Your Highness! Even turning my own dagger upon myself would not atone for this!"

...but of course, nothing was ever that easy.

4

The girl with the dagger knelt in place when she realized who Fourier was. This would be an earth-shattering event for her. She had captured someone she thought was an intruder in the castle, and he turned out to be a prince. And she had even bared her blade—it would be too much for her poor heart.

"How could I ever ask you to take the blame? I disguised myself with the bandanna, well enough to make you suspect I was some dubious character. Am I a brute who would hold one of my subjects responsible for a misunderstanding that was my own fault?"

"But to have taken such a tone with Your Highness… It does not deserve forgiveness. Please, deliver judgment."

"You are strangely stubborn, aren't you? Your sense of duty is so demanding! Very well, then, do as I say. You feel guilt toward me and would do what you must to see my humor settled. Is that not so?"

Fourier was desperate to stop the girl, who seemed ready at that very moment to sheathe her dagger in her own belly. She replied, "Yes, my prince," and handed him her knife. "Please, Your Highness, do with me as you see fit. I will accept any punishment."

"Um—'as I see fit'? 'Any punishment'? Why is my heart pounding so…?" Fourier felt his heart racing in his chest at the sight of the severe girl before him. But he shook his head to clear his mind and took a deep breath to calm his heart. "Then I pronounce your punishment. You… Yes. I order you to help me pass the time for a while. Converse with me for my pleasure, until I have settled down some."

"I… Your Highness, how is that a punishment…?"

"Stay your tongue! I shall entertain no protests! Did you not say you would abide by my wishes? Well, my wishes are plain. You cannot refuse so this matter is finished. Yes?"

Arms crossed over his chest, Fourier brought the conversation to an abrupt end. The girl stared at him for a moment and then touched her hand to the corner of her mouth.

"Hee-hee!"

A giggle slipped out, though she tried to hold it back. It was the first time Fourier had seen her smile in a way expected of one her age. A girlish and lovely lifting of her lips broke through her stiff and somber expression.

"I was worried for a moment, but all for nothing, it seems... Hmm?"

As he uncrossed his arms, Fourier happened to catch a glimpse of the dagger he still held in his hand. That was when he noticed it. The dagger was an exceptional piece of work, yes, but the hilt and sheath bore a distinctive mark. It looked like a lion with its jaws open, and it was very familiar to Fourier.

"This insignia—a crest in the shape of a lion baring its fangs. You must be a member of the Karsten house... Wait. You must be Meckart's daughter! You are, aren't you!" he said, pointing to the dagger after he suddenly realized who the girl was.

The girl gave a resigned sigh and a somber nod. "Yes. It is as Your Highness discerns. I am the daughter of Meckart Karsten, head of the House of Karsten. My name is Crusch Karsten. It was terribly rude of me to not introduce myself first."

"It was my choice to give my name. And my choice to hide my face. There's no need to start that again. But imagine my surprise—the daughter of the famous Meckart Karsten."

Crusch. Fourier held the sound of her name in his ears, carved it into his memory.

Her father, Meckart, was a high-ranking nobleman of a ducal household. Though he gave a somewhat diffident impression, he was a thoroughly trustworthy servant of the royal family. It was simply hard to picture this girl as his daughter.

"Crusch. A fine name. It fits your gallant and noble bearing."

"Your Highness is too kind. But I thank you."

"D-do you take my words for flattery? Ah, yes. I must return this to you." Unaware that he was staring enamored at the self-effacing Crusch, Fourier coughed. His cheeks felt hot. He passed the dagger to her in an attempt to focus on something else. She took it reverently, clutching it gently to her chest.

"It looks like something of a treasure to you," he said.

"...It is a gift from my father. To celebrate my birthday, though he warned me to use it carefully." Her voice was hesitant; perhaps she was still flustered at her episode of mistaken identity. Fourier deliberately tried to change the subject so they wouldn't find their way back to that again.

"A dagger for his daughter's birthday? Even for Meckart, that seems a tad tone-deaf."

"I asked for it. Father asked what I wanted, and I said I wanted the crested dagger passed down by the heads of our house."

"Hardly tone-deaf at all! Yes, a dagger is a fine gift. Convenient to have around, daggers!"

"You need not bother yourself to spare my feelings, Your Highness. I understand that my tastes are not quite like those of other young ladies." She gave a somehow ephemeral smile at Fourier's furious attempts to change his opinion in mid-conversation.

Most girls Crusch's age might have requested jewelry with which to adorn themselves. It was indeed an unusual child who, given the choice, would pick the family's heirloom dagger for a gift. But, seeing how tenderly Crusch held the thing, Fourier sensed it would be superficial to rush to such a judgment.

"What's wrong with it? It might be one thing if a girl were fixated on the blade itself, trying desperately to obtain it. But that is not what was in your mind, was it? You were taken with the lion crest, weren't you? And how can I bear any ill will toward a girl like that? After all, I myself am a descendant of the Lion King!"

"—"

"Is something wrong?" Fourier asked. He had been so confident as he spoke, but Crusch simply stared at him. This girl had seemed so stoic at first, and now he had seen so many of her varied expressions—although he wished more of them were smiles.

"N-no," Crusch said. "It's simply... This is the first time anyone has thought I might have been interested in the crest, and I was surprised."

"Ah, I see. But is it not true?"

"Yes...it is."

Crusch seemed to want to understand why Fourier had made this guess with such confidence. So he stuck out his chest proudly and said, "So you know, there was no particular reason I thought that. No proof. Just my own certainty."

"…I can see Your Highness is serious. You surprise me more with every moment."

"Generally speaking, I am always serious. My eccentricities are of a kind not often detected by the common people, however. Heh-heh! Are you afraid of me now?"

"No, my lord. Only admiring." Crusch pulled in her chin, raising the dagger so that Fourier could see it. Her delicate fingertips ran across the seal, and her amber eyes sparkled. "Is Your Highness aware of the reason that the crest of my house—the Karsten house—is a lion?"

"Um—yes, yes, of course I am! But…just for form's sake, I wish to hear it from your own lips. I must see if we share the same understanding."

"Of course. As Your Highness knows, the lion crest was originally the insignia of the Lugunica royal family."

That had been four centuries earlier, before the pact with the dragon was made and the nation came to be known as the Dragonfriend Kingdom. In those days, the Kingdom of Lugunica had flown the lion crest, and its ruler had been called the Lion King.

Wise and strong, these lords provided guidance to all the people. The title was lost when the last Lion King made his pact with the dragon, and dragons became more revered than lions in Lugunica.

"By the dragon's good grace, the kingdom became rich and prosperous," Crusch concluded. "And with the Lion King no longer needed, the lion crest gave way to the one we have today, which bears the dragon."

"That's right—I remember now! The lion crest was not lost but gifted by the ruler to an especially valued subject. And the lion bearing its fangs—"

"—became the symbol of my family, House of Karsten."

Miklotov's endless chatter and those classes Fourier was always running away from had finally come in handy. But he had rarely heard the ancient title "Lion King" more than he had today.

"The Lion King..." he breathed.

"Indeed," she said, "the Lion King."

It was a title that had been all but forgotten by many. Fourier tried to speak it freely but found himself unable. The smile that played across Crusch's lips had brought him up short as she agreed with him. It was not the smile of someone faintly recalling an old and faded name from the past.

—Rather, it bespoke an admiration, indeed a fondness, for the forgotten king.

"Eeyowch!"

"Your Highness?! Wh-what are you doing to yourself?"

Fourier had been on the verge of breaking into a vacuous smile. To prevent it, he had given himself a forceful slap on the cheek, startling Crusch.

"Are you all right, Your Highness? Has something happened?"

"N-nothing at all. A trivial matter. A bug landed on my cheek. It is my burden to be loved even by creatures as small as that!"

Fourier's cheek was red and his eyes were watering, but Crusch looked suitably deceived and said, "I see..."

Convinced that the pain had been worth it, Fourier privately praised his own judgment. Then he tried to turn the conversation back to the subject of the Lion King.

"Crusch. I see you have an exceptional appreciation of the Lion King. Why is that?"

"No special reason. And is this something we should be discussing in the royal castle...?"

"What, would it become an issue if anyone overheard? Then let it be our secret, yours and mine. I, for one, certainly shall not tell anyone. I never betray a promise!"

He sounded so sure of himself. After a moment's silence, Crusch smiled again. She was speaking to one of the primary members of the royal household. There was no such thing as a secret. To her,

Fourier seemed to have forgotten that he was of royal blood. She looked at him, a little stunned.

"I have a thought sometimes. Even though, knowing the meaning of my house's crest, and knowing of the pact with the dragon that protects our kingdom, I think it might be too much for this small body of mine."

"What thought is that?"

"In the time of the Lion King, we did not have the stability we enjoy now. But they did not have this stagnation, either. The dragon's blessing makes our lives easy—perhaps too easy."

"—"

Fourier found himself swallowing heavily at her words. Seeing him fall silent, Crusch's lips curled into a smile again. However, it was not the affectionate smile of earlier but a detached expression that somehow seemed adult.

"Will Your Highness punish me now for disrespecting the kingdom?"

"In all honesty, I'm beginning to think it *is* best to keep this between us. You're right that this talk ought not to be shared with just anyone. And yet…"

Fourier could not quite see what Crusch saw. Call it a difference in intellect or in way of life. The young prince had only just begun becoming acquainted with her nature, and he was unable to offer an answer to what she pondered.

When she saw Fourier agonizing over what she had said, Crusch half closed her eyes, the strength draining from her shoulders. "Forget what I said, my lord. Think of it as the foolish mumblings of a girl who knows not her place. I have no brothers, but it remains that I am a woman. I am unable to choose a life befitting my house's crest…the path of a lion."

She spoke the words *unable to choose* in a tone of profound resignation. There was something she desperately wanted to do and couldn't. Surely that was what set the young woman Crusch distinctly apart from other girls. It was why she had captured Fourier's attention so completely.

He felt a rush of heat in his raging heart. He opened his mouth, revealing a fang-like tooth.

"Foolishness? Let others call it that. But you must never concede so yourself."

"...Your Highness?"

Fourier knew all too well the pain of misunderstanding and dismissals with words like *foolishness* or *nonsense*. It had caused him to give up in the past—but even if he had to admit as much, it was difficult to allow this. To see the woman who had grabbed his attention forsaking the very thing that had sparked his interest in her.

"I don't know what desires you harbor or what you wish to do. But I am sure that the girl standing here before me today is the result of her efforts to achieve that goal. It seems you now regard that time as wasted, but..."

He had been utterly captivated by the sight of her standing there—her face, the sound of her voice, and the time they had spent together. And all these things he had fallen for had surely come about because of her constant striving to realize her wish, the wish she was now about to abandon. And so his pushback came from the fire of his own deeply seated passion.

—To let that wish go would be a grave mistake. This, Fourier knew with every fiber of his being.

"I'm convinced you are more intelligent than I. But intelligence has little to do with me. You are wrong! I know you are!"

"Your Highness...? You mean what I seek is wrong, as well?"

"I don't know! I don't know what is wrong. But something is."

Crusch looked taken aback by Fourier's blunt pronouncement. Her ideas had been amply criticized in the past. She had been repeatedly told she was wrong, different from those around her, until she had finally begun to doubt her own thinking. At heart, Fourier's outburst was not the same as those other rejections.

"Don't give me that resigned smile! Perhaps your words are foolishness, but they belong to you. I will not laugh, and anyone who laughs does not have the vision to see where you are headed. You never know what might come of it—what flower might bloom. You are still just a bud! And who can say what wonderful blossom might emerge before it has fully come into itself?"

Fourier was rather proud of having come up with this metaphor. He turned to the flower bed and pointed to the immature bud in the corner.

"I do not know what you were seeing, but when you looked at that sprout I knew your heart. Because, I am sure, it is the same as mine!"

"—"

"S-so... So don't blame yourself for being different from others. It means nothing, and it is unimportant. We may have our differences, but if we see the same beauty in the same things, then all will go well for us!"

Fourier thrust his fist into the air, exclaiming, "How about that?" in a show of excitement. Crusch was wide-eyed, overwhelmed by his ardor. Silently, as if drawn along, she looked at the flower bed, too.

Then she said, "I came here today to see if that had flowered yet."

"I thought as much. You were observing it with such interest."

Crusch was confused. "Is this not the first time Your Highness has seen me here?"

"Oh! Uh, no, it is the first time! I was just…speaking on intuition! Yes, that's it!"

Crusch didn't press Fourier about these strange remarks, only smiled. Quietly, she said, "If you think we see the same beauty in the same things…" Her face relaxed. "Then, my lord, when this bud blooms, may I view it with you? To find out if someone as unusual as myself shares your sensibilities?"

"Oh? Oh! You may! You certainly may. I would enjoy that!"

Fourier answered in a fit of ecstasy, turning red from the neck up at Crusch's smiling invitation.

Only the flowers—and a single bud—bobbing in the wind stood witness to this odd but amusing exchange.

5

"So the source of young master Fourier's heartsickness is Crusch Karsten, is that it?"

In a room of the Lugunica castle lined with bookshelves, Miklotov was receiving a report. Standing in front of the old sage was the tutor tasked with Fourier's education. The prince had always been capricious, but lately he had been even less able to focus than usual. When the instructor told him what the problem was, Miklotov nodded and stroked his long beard.

"Mmm. I see. The daughter of the honorable Lord Meckart. I've heard that she's quite an odd girl... Perhaps that is precisely what drew His Highness Fourier to her."

"I am afraid I don't know, sir. But it appears to be fact that the young lady and His Highness are on familiar terms. The other day, I gather they went to the garden to look at a flower together..."

"How sweet. But if this causes him to neglect his studies..."

"Er, ahem, on that note, sir." The tutor interrupted Miklotov. The sage raised an eyebrow. "If anything, His Highness has been more focused on his studies than before. Perhaps his acquaintance with the young lady has..."

"...moved him to present himself as his best? Yes, how sweet, indeed." Miklotov finished the tutor's reluctant sentence.

The mood was somewhat awkward, but immediately after, Miklotov's gaze sharpened, and he straightened up. Fixed by the old man's stare, the tutor felt his throat go dry. Miklotov asked:

"And the young lord...? Has he shown any signs of the blood?"

"Ahem, he—no, he doesn't appear to... At least, not that I have seen."

Despondence crossed Miklotov's eyes. The old sage let out a long sigh.

"Is that so? ...Perhaps the second coming of the Lion King is only a dream..."

He could not hide his disappointment. The tutor, not quite able to sympathize with either the elder's thought process or his wishes, could only remain silent.

The sage wished for the second coming of a wise ruler who had held sway in the days of the Lion Kings. But the tutor wondered what meaning there could be in that. The kingdom was secure under its pact with the dragon and the blessings it provided. The royal family needed only to carry on the bloodline; no more was asked of it.

Thus, the instructor did not report to Miklotov the more peculiar aspects of Fourier's nature. Sometimes the boy would be seized by an unaccountable intuition. But the tutor had dismissed his flashes of insight into board games and arithmetic exercises as mere flukes. He was too much of a realist to consider these events as signs that Fourier was qualified to be the sage king.

And if he failed to sympathize with Miklotov's reasoning, he was also unable to understand Fourier's resourcefulness. This tutor was a gifted teacher, but no more than an ordinary citizen of the kingdom. He had reached these heights largely because there had not been enough officials to fill every vacant position.

"In that case, I hope His Highness will at least spend his days in good health. I shall exercise these old bones a little longer to be sure it is so..."

Sage though he was, Miklotov was not a mind reader. He could not know that, in his heart, the tutor actually possessed the account Miklotov longed to hear. And Fourier lived in ignorance of what others hoped of him.

It was a species of tragedy, but also one of the great ironies of destiny.

—But it would be far, far in the future before the true meaning of this would come to light.

6

After that, Fourier Lugunica found his days ever more fulfilling, never realizing that those who looked to him expectantly saw their hope slowly give way to despair.

Several days after he had made his promise to Crusch, they watched the bud bloom into a great flower. Her smile at the moment she laid eyes on the blossom was fixed clearly in Fourier's mind.

"—It's beautiful, isn't it, Your Highness?"

"Indeed, it certainly is! I believe I shall never forget this." Fourier decided to keep to himself what exactly he would commit forever to memory.

Their garden rendezvous continued frequently after that day. Crusch would visit the garden whenever she arrived at the castle, and Fourier would always be there. But Crusch was different somehow, ever since they saw that flower blossom together. As they saw each other more and more, something about her began to change.

"You no longer tie your hair back," he remarked one day.

When they had first met, her hair had been tied up, and she had worn a dress that was the very picture of girlishness. But lately, whenever he saw her, she let her long hair hang down, and the designs of her dresses grew more refined.

"I owe it to what Your Highness said," Crusch replied with a slight smile. But Fourier couldn't imagine what she meant. What had he said to her to inspire such change?

"You need not understand, my lord. But I thank you just the same."

"Hrm! But how will I be at peace without knowing? It weighs on me so!"

Crusch said nothing in reply to Fourier's outburst but only reached down to her hip. The dagger hung there, and Fourier realized she had developed a habit of touching the lion crest. He felt suddenly as though the Lion King had taken her from him, though she was standing right there.

"You're quite enamored with the Lion King, aren't you?" he said.

"You misunderstand, Your Highness. I'm simply proud of my ancestor, who diligently supported his country and was recognized as the greatest servant of the king...though I understand I do this quite often."

Her flushed cheeks betrayed her attempted excuse after noticing the prince's sullen demeanor. Less and less happy with the situation, Fourier eyed her dagger ruefully.

"But the Lion King is no more," he said. "Think of him as highly as you like; no one else will ever…"

"—"

"Er—no! I mean—I was speaking figuratively! I didn't—" His inadvertent words must have struck Crusch in the heart, for she retreated into oppressive and mournful silence while Fourier frantically tried to take back what he had said. Finally, he clapped his hands and said, "Very well! If that is what you wish for, then I shall make myself into the person you seek!"

"My lord?"

"Let us see whether your love for this kingdom approaches what the Lion King saw in your honored ancestor! Why not? The Lion's blood flows in my veins, does it not? I have every right to be the judge of this!"

Crusch's shock at these mental gymnastics gave way to a smile.

"Hmm! Do you laugh at me? I daresay, I've impressed even myself with my impeccable logic!"

"N-no, I…I apologize. It is simply… Your Highness is such an amazing person…"

"Ah-ha! You wonder, do you not, whether I am as worthy of a vow of loyalty as the Lion King? Very well. Watch me closely. I shall judge your loyalty as you shall judge my worthiness. Then, we resurrect once more the bond between the Lion King and his most devoted retainer!"

"Ah—ha-ha-ha!"

"Don't laaaugh!"

But her amusement was like a flower blooming, and soon Fourier joined her.

No one knows whether the vow they exchanged was made in seriousness. But the two of them remained dear to each other long after, and in time another young man was added to their number. When that happened, Fourier would dream a dream, inspired by the bond this vow had started.

So this was merely the beginning of a dream—the dream of Fourier Lugunica.

<END>

FELIX ARGYLE IS A PRETTY BOY

1

"This is terrible! They say I am to attend a matchmaking meeting!"

Such were the desperate words that rang through the Karsten manor one fine afternoon. The door to the parlor flew open, and a young boy with golden hair tumbled in, still breathing hard.

He had scarlet eyes, distinctive canine teeth, and fine clothing, including an extravagant fur robe. If he could have mustered a dignified silence and a smile, no doubt he would have captured the hearts of many a girl. But alas, no one had ever seen him act that mature.

The restless young boy was named Fourier Lugunica, and he was the fourth son of the king of the Dragonfriend Kingdom of Lugunica, a bona fide prince.

"Calm down, Your Highness. How can the rest of us maintain our composure when you are so frantic?"

The source of this admonition was a young woman who showed not even a hint of panic. She had long, beautiful green hair tied with a white ribbon, her still-growing body clad in men's clothes. Her almond-shaped amber eyes and firm features marked her as someone who would be a great beauty one day.

This was Crusch Karsten, the only daughter of the master of this house, Meckart Karsten. She would one day inherit her family's ducal estate and was sure to become a woman of great stature. But at this time, she was still a girl of fourteen—those around her had had scant opportunity to recognize her gifts.

"You expect me to be calm at a time like this?! They're trying to marry me off! Don't you think that should be of great concern to you? Shouldn't it be of great concern to her, Ferris?!"

"Ah? You're asking Ferri?" The person in question spun and pointed to himself. The thoroughly surprised speaker was a girlish boy flicking his flaxen cat ears—Felix Argyle.

It had been five years since Felix, for his own reasons, had taken the name Ferris, begun dressing in women's clothing, and become Crusch's attendant. The two of them were well acquainted with Fourier since long ago and had developed the capacity to enjoy whatever apparent crises the excitable young prince brought them.

Overcoming his initial surprise, Ferris tapped a finger to his lips and said, "Mm, you're right, Prince Fourier. But! But! You're fourteen now... You're not a child, so it makes sense they'd want to set up a meowtch for you."

Fourier paled at that; his balled fists trembled. "No, absolutely not! I shall not be party to any matchmaking! I refuse!"

"But, Your Highness. As a member of the royal family, it is your duty to take a spouse and continue the royal line. The problem won't go away simply because you don't like it."

"U-um, you're not wrong, of course. It's—I'm not objecting to the idea of marriage in general, you see. But, you know...I—I have the right to choose, don't I? I don't need a matchmaker to... Ahh, what are you forcing me to say?!"

"Ah, my loutish prince..." Ferris said.

As Fourier voiced his ardent resentment of the matchmaking meeting, Crusch replied with irrefutable logic. Fourier attempted to respond, but there was nothing he could say, and he soon resorted to a red-faced bout of temper.

Ferris could only shake his head and sigh. He felt the frustration born from five years of watching these two talk past each other.

Fourier's infatuation with Crusch was plain to see. It made sense he would have no interest in a matchmaking meeting when his heart had belonged to another for so long. If only he could bring himself to be honest about it. The fourth prince, Fourier, and the daughter of a duke. They were close enough in status; there would be no harm in it. But...

"Ferris, His Highness seems quite upset. Did I say something wrong? What do you think?" Crusch said, whispering to him so the prince couldn't hear. She was totally oblivious.

Crush was Ferris's lifelong master, the most loving girl in all the world—and she was utterly unable to discern anything more than friendly affection. There was no harm in Fourier's romantic interest, except that Crusch herself was his last and greatest obstacle.

He wished Fourier would hurry up and find the courage to confess his feelings...

"No, Lady Crusch, you haven't done *anything* wrong. It's all His Highness. He's made the meowstake. Lady, help me tell him to be less of a lout..."

"Hmm, very well. I suppose I can trust your assessment. Your Highness, I'm not entirely clear on this, but I offer my heartfelt request that you stop being such a lout."

"Hrk!"

There was no bite to the words, but Fourier clapped his hands over his chest and fell to his knees because it was his beloved who had spoken. Crusch's eyes went wide at this, and she looked reprovingly at Ferris.

"I'll punish you for this later, Ferris."

"Awww, but Ferri just wanted to get a smile out of you, milady!"

"Sheesh. Ever the smooth talker. I suppose you're the only one who could sneak something like that past my blessing of wind reading. It's just as well to be reminded that my protection isn't all-powerful."

"Yes! That's all Ferri was trying to do—to remind you of that, milady."

"I'll pretend to believe you. But I'm still going to punish you."

Crusch nodded sternly. Not once in her life had she ever failed to follow through on something she said she would do. *Punishment* was a fine-sounding word, but she didn't pull her punches when it came to handing them out, so anyone who wanted to play a prank on her had to be prepared for the consequences.

"Oh well! Ferri will keep making jokes, that's for sure! Just to see the lovely Lady Crusch wear that look of surprise on her face! Oh, what a rare treat!"

"Arrgh, that will be enough out of you two! When a person comes in agonized, tormented, is it not usual to comfort him?! Or do you enjoy leaving me to suffer? Oh, the loneliness!" Fourier broke in after growing quite tired of being left out.

It could be a challenge to pacify Fourier once he got into one of these childish tantrums. Crusch and Ferris turned to the task together.

It was perhaps a testament to the strength of the relationship among the three that neither of them seemed to consider this role a burden.

2

When Fourier's temper finally cooled, the trio stayed in the parlor discussing the details of the matchmaking interview.

"The prospective match is the daughter of some relation to the archbishop of Gusteko. They say she's nineteen! A whole five years older than me. This will not do at all. We must cancel the meeting." Fourier already sounded thoroughly convinced of his own conclusion.

"Your Highness! Your Highness, I'm telling you, you have no proof!" Ferris attempted to remonstrate without raising the young lord's hackles again.

The Holy Kingdom of Gusteko was one of the four great nations, known for its freezing temperatures and the blizzards it endured year-round. It was also famous for a religious outlook that could only have been produced by such harsh circumstances, a unique form of spiritualism. The archbishop Fourier had mentioned was a deeply revered person in that country.

"In Gusteko, the archbishop is almost as important as the Council of Elders is here," Ferris said. "A meowrriage alliance with that family would be very important for Lugunica…"

"Such a match would be of tremendous import for both nations, Your Highness," Crusch added. "This is an essential duty."

"Wait, wait, wait, wait! We're just going in circles. When did the both of you start siding with the Holy Kingdom? What I'm saying is I don't want to make *any* matches! Help me!" Fourier clung to Ferris's knees, nearly in tears. Ferris couldn't help thinking how unbecoming this scene would look if anyone were to bear witness, but nonetheless he gave the crybaby prince a pat on the head.

"If you're that upset, Lord Fourier, then they probably won't go through with it…but unfortunately, being bothered probably isn't a good enough reason to turn down the meeting itself."

"Mm, yes, I realize that myself. By which I mean, when I said as much to Miklotov, I was subjected to one of his rare fits of anger. I had no idea he could work himself into such a fury…"

Miklotov of the Council of Elders was known for his wisdom and his level head. The news that Fourier had already managed to upset the great adviser caused Ferris to put his head in his hands, then shoot a desperate look at Crusch.

"Lady Cruuusch… What should we do?"

"Good question. For the good of the kingdom I would have His Highness simply resign himself to this meeting, but as I owe a great debt to him, I am obliged to do all I can when he comes to me for help. Incidentally, Your Highness, if this marriage were to go ahead, would the young lady be coming to Lugunica?"

"No—Miklotov told me I should prepare to continue my studies somewhere chilly… I can't do it! I hate being hot *and* being cold, but cold is definitely worse! You know me—even on a warm day like today, I never let my robe out of my sight."

Fourier couldn't bring himself to have any interest in the meeting, and he was certainly concerned about what life would be like once he was wed. He would feel bad for a young woman stuck with someone who had resisted the match so fervently. Then again, if she was anything like Fourier, it was possible she was also being forced into this.

"And that means it's possible neither of the parties to this marriage would be happy..." he moaned.

It would have been simple enough to point out that many marriages were similar, and let the matter end there. But just as Ferris loved and respected Crusch, he felt a deep affection for Fourier as well. If it could be done, he wanted to see them both enjoy the greatest possible happiness in this life. Even if, at the worst, it left Ferris himself without a place to belong.

"Okay, Your Highness, mew've made yourself perfectly clear. We must find a way to scuttle this meeting. I guess your reputation can't get any worse, anyway!"

"Oh! You've come around? Now, that's encouraging, Ferris! So, what's your plan? Shall we pretend I'm already betrothed? You know, to...someone?"

"Mew would have to show more courage than you've ever shown in your life to pull that off, Your Highness!"

They would need more than enthusiasm. Even as he chastised Fourier for his lack of spine, Ferris took Crusch's hand. She was looking very put out. Then he placed it over another hand that was still clinging to his knees—Fourier's hand.

"This is how it works," Ferris said. "As sorry as I feel for the young lady, at the meeting you have to declare that your heart already belongs to another...and that's how you'll make it through!"

"Th-th-that's your plan?! But...but Crusch and I aren't lovers...!"

"You're right, you're not! But all you have to do is get the other side to believe you are and back out of the match. After that, the two of mew just have a big fight and 'break up' or something. No more problem!"

"Ferris! My heart hurts for some reason! And my chest and my back! Please, cast healing magic on me!"

"Healing magic can't fix the kind of pain you're mewling right now, Your Highness. Sorry!"

Fourier found himself caught up in the momentum of Ferris's

idea. The trio's hands were still joined, and Fourier slowly turned red as he came alive to the realization that he would get to pretend to be Crusch's lover.

After that epiphany, he was quick to jump on board. He stood with no small amount of confidence and said, "Heh-heh! Very well, then! I expected no less of you, Ferris... I applaud you for detecting my natural talents as an actor!"

"No, no, it's all down to Your Highness's pliant personality. Ferri didn't do anything!"

"Ha-ha-ha! You needn't praise me so! Yes, I've started to feel quite good about this. The cloud that hung over me has vanished like it was never there! Very good—now, Crusch!" With a great guffaw Fourier returned to his usual self. He held out his hand to his beloved Crusch, flashing a smile that showed his teeth like a child playing a mischievous trick. "Work with me to reduce this meeting to nothing! I request this cooperation of y—"

"Your Highness, I'm afraid there is something I must tell you."

"Um...and what would that be?"

Fourier looked less than pleased to have been interrupted at the climactic moment of his speech. Crusch gave him a knowing look, but at the same time, she furrowed her well-formed eyebrows.

"It so happens that my father has already asked me to attend to some business on the same day as your meeting. It's no less than a summons to the palace from Miklotov..."

"Mrrow?!"

Fourier was taken aback, and Ferris couldn't hide his surprise. But unlike Fourier, who had already stopped thinking, Ferris suspected such an inconvenient turn of events was entirely intentional.

"Do you think they deliberately arranged a conflicting engagement so you couldn't mess with the meeting?" Ferris asked.

"Knowing my father and the esteemed Miklotov, such a ploy is possible. Then again, it might really be just coincidence... So, Your Highness, I'm very sorry to say I will not be able to lend you my aid."

"I—I see. Th-that's fine. Ha-ha. That's... Yes, completely fine."

Fourier sat down broodingly, not quite able to hide his disappointment, despair, and shock. He looked absolutely pathetic, and Ferris rushed to comfort him.

Seeing Fourier's expression, Crusch cocked her head and nodded. "My lord, I don't suppose it matters whether I am the one you're allegedly in love with?"

"—Huh?"

Ferris and Fourier both looked up and spoke at the same moment.

Seeing their perfectly synchronous reactions, Crusch gave one of her rarest smiles: the grin of a refined young woman who had something naughty in mind.

3

The long awaited day had arrived. The meeting was held in a mansion close to the border between the Kingdom of Lugunica and the Holy Kingdom of Gusteko. Specifically, it was the manor of Viscount Misère, who oversaw the whole northern region of Lugunica; when informed of the scheme they were planning, he had been surprisingly eager to participate.

"That Holy Kingdom lot are frankly eerie. I don't want to imagine the royal blood of Lugunica being mingled with the line of those dreamers. The young lady you'll be meeting today is especially bad. By all means, bring things to a screeching halt!"

Although he couldn't raise too much hell about it, being on the border caused no end of trouble for the local lord. He was more than willing to overlook a little mischief in order to obtain some relief for himself.

"Meowbe you have to be a bit weird to get an important job like this. Lord Meckart is the same way."

Viscount Misère reminded Ferris of a certain troublesome master of a noble house. Meckart hardly seemed the image of a nobleman, but when Ferris thought back on all the people he had seen in the castle, it seemed very few of them looked quite the way one expected when imagining the aristocracy. He also recalled the time when he had gone for training in healing magic several years before. There was a distinct impression that none of the nobles were very, well, noble.

"Well, that's not true of the ones I'm closest with, though," he mused. Neither Crusch and Fourier nor Meckart offered anything to complain about on a personal level. They weren't stereotypical nobles, concerned only with reputation and lording over others. Maybe Ferris's parents were the only nobles like that. "Ahh, stop it, stop it! I can't go making meowself all depressed at such an important moment!"

He gave himself a slap on the cheek to bring himself back, but he made sure to do it gently so his face wouldn't turn red.

Ferris had prepared much more thoroughly than he usually did for his engagements. The maids who had attended him at Crusch's behest had done a fantastic job. It was a sign that she was expecting a lot of him, even though she couldn't be present herself. Just the thought made his heart feel as light as if it had wings.

"All right..." he said to himself. "Here goes nothing, Ferri!"

He imagined Crusch giving him a little push to get him started and stepped out of the changing room. He swept the hem of his skirt with much the same resolve as a soldier going to the battlefield, and the viscount, waiting outside, saw him off with a smile. Ferris let the nobleman's unexpected enthusiasm carry him toward the fateful room.

One of the viscount's men, standing with a nervous look just outside the closed door, gave Ferris a nod. Then Ferris stood in full view as the door opened, before striding proudly into the meeting room.

"I am His Highness Fourier's lover," he announced in a girlish tone, "and I will not allow this meeting to proceed!"

If Crusch couldn't be here to undermine this meeting, he would have to do it himself.

4

Ferris's unexpected entrance threw the meeting into confusion. Apparently he had barged in just at the moment when the two young prospects had been left alone together. It was two against one, and the numbers favored Fourier's side.

But from the point of view of sheer quantity, it was very much the other way around.

"The... The young lady looks very strong, doesn't she?" Ferris muttered, sizing up the other party to the meeting, who sat across from them. As things stood, the three of them were in a meeting room with a small table between their side and hers as they faced one another. Ferris seated himself next to Fourier, while the prince's prospective match was seated across from them. She had presence enough to overcome the disadvantage in numbers.

"Oh, there's no need to dance around it," she said with an elegant shake of her head. "I know I'm a bit bigger than most." She looked down, embarrassed. The quality of each gesture, however, communicated the refinement of her upbringing.

—Unfortunately, her body was so large that the phrase *exceptional carriage* was simply inadequate.

The girl was seated in front of Fourier, but she took up so much room that it would have been fair to say she was seated in front of Ferris, too. They felt more like they were faced with a boulder than a person.

"A-and so you see, Miss Tiriena..."

But she had a lovely name. It sounded like a spell that could be used to summon snow sprites, but she herself looked like a mountain in a blizzard. Ferris had heard that, in Gusteko, with its continual snowfall, girls prized skin as white as new fallen snow, and this figure was no exception. Up close, her skin was peerless; from a distance, it evoked the image of a peerless cliff.

Even the normally charismatic Fourier seemed cowed by this woman, his words uncharacteristically inarticulate. Still, he managed to throw an arm around Ferris's shoulder, pulling his slender body close.

"I—I'm so sorry you had to come all this way, but I already have someone I've set my heart upon. I'm afraid I just won't be able to accept your proposal."

"It's true. Oh, I just can't imagine being betrothed to anyone but His Highness. I beg you, don't tear the two of us apart...!"

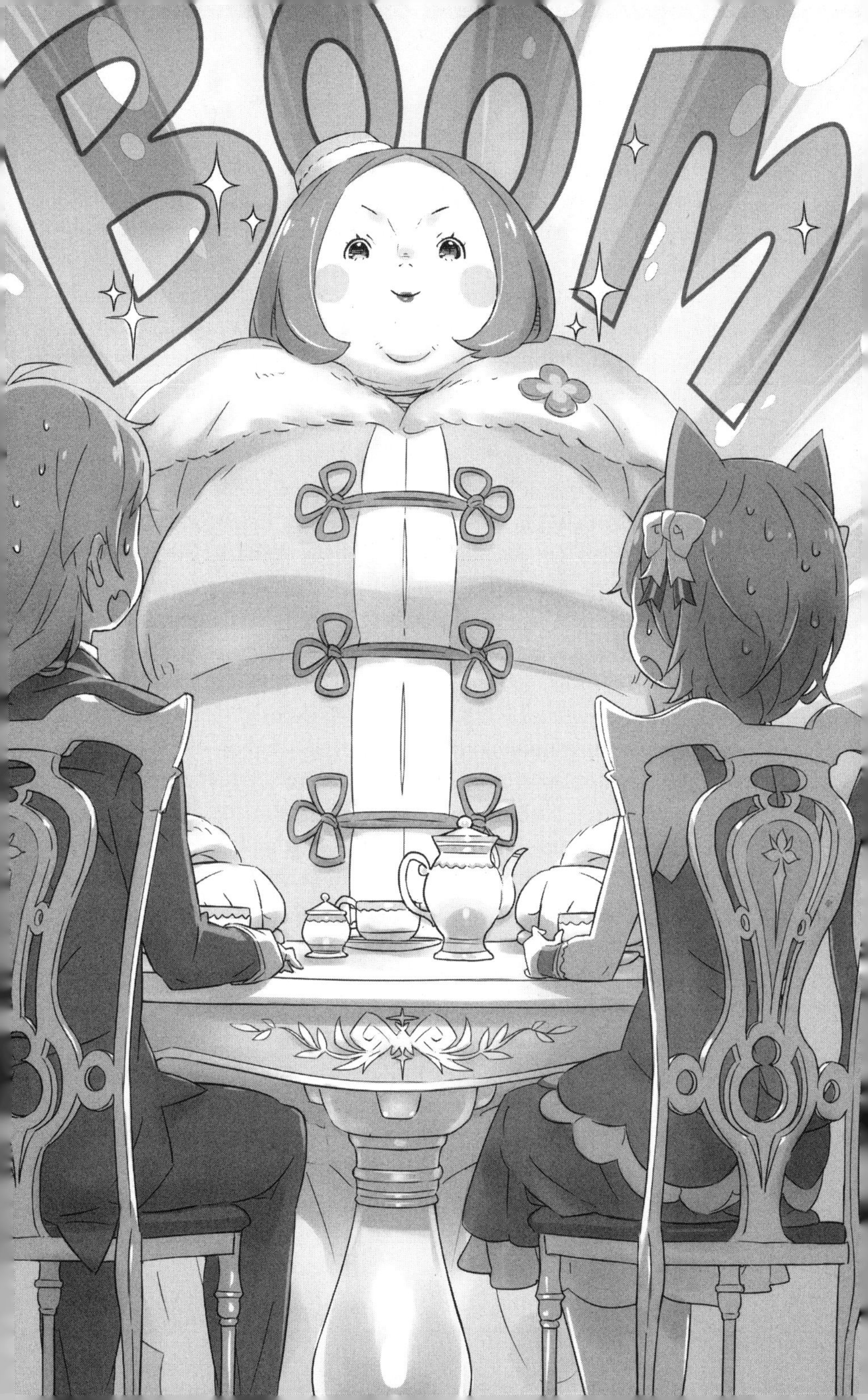
BOOM

In contrast to Fourier's near inability to speak, Ferris was an accomplished actor, augmenting his pleas with a tear in the corner of his eye. Perhaps he had tugged on Tiriena's heartstrings, because she lowered her eyes with an expression of pity on her sculpted features.

"There's no need for either of you to apologize. I can see all too well the love you share. It's enough to make me ashamed..." Tiriena, wearing one of the uniquely unrevealing dresses common in the northern country, pressed a hand to her chest gently, then regarded Fourier and Ferris with clear eyes. "Even we in the Holy Kingdom know of the civil war from decades ago. I had heard resentment still remained from those days, but...I see it hasn't stopped the two of you from cherishing each other. What a beautiful love you share."

Ferris realized Tiriena was looking at his cat ears. The civil war she spoke of was a lengthy conflict Lugunica had waged against the demi-humans. The ears were simply something Ferris had inherited from his ancestors, but they played no small role in the trouble he had experienced as a child. He couldn't keep his face from stiffening at Tiriena's words. His pale shoulders, exposed by the cut of his dress, began to tremble, and he reflexively tried to make himself smaller. But the arm around his shoulders drew tighter.

"Just so, Lady Tiriena." Fourier was gazing directly at her now as he attempted to hold Ferris steady with his arm. The bewilderment he had shown a moment before had vanished, replaced with a commanding presence and strength of spirit. "In friendship and in love I pay no mind to birth or species. One loves whom one loves. Others may say what they please—but I cannot do anything about the yearnings of my own heart. I love this woman beside me, right to her very ears. I even adore her feline fickleness."

Fourier smiled proudly. Ferris felt his cheeks grow hot, their faces close. For as long as they had known each other, Fourier had only brought up Ferris's ears once or twice. And it was true that he had demonstrated his magnanimity by never belittling them. But saying he loved them? That he had never done before, and it brought a flush to Ferris's face.

"Goodness, I envy the idea that one can be so dearly loved." Tiriena smiled like a contented bear.

Her look made Ferris realize that Tiriena agreed that the meeting had to end. She was empathetic and perceptive. Ferris could not let her have Fourier, but he could see that Tiriena deserved to be happy, too.

"Forgive me, Miss Tiriena," Fourier said. "You are intelligent and, above all, kind, and if I were not already so in love, I could do much worse than be betrothed to you."

"Please, you don't need to try to spare the feelings of a woman you have no interest in. It would be so much worse to know I was with someone whose heart belonged to another. I myself have been thoughtless, anyway. I'd heard the rumors that His Highness Fourier Lugunica was in love with a manly, martial young woman—and I have to admit, I wondered..."

Ferris barely suppressed a squeak at Tiriena's comments as she rose from her seat. It meant that this meeting had come to pass because of a misunderstanding of Fourier's feelings for Crusch. In other words, the reason they were even having this meeting was the same reason they were trying to break it up: Fourier's loutishness.

"Your Highness," Ferris said, "I hope you have a good, long think about your behavior today..."

"What do you mean?! I think I was very manly today, if I may say so myself!"

5

As Viscount Misère reentered the room with Tiriena's escort, he was merciless.

"It looks like there's no need to ask how things went."

It was simply his personality, but it was still wrong to say something that might be hurtful to their guest. Tiriena, however, had a tremendously gentle smile on her face.

"You're as cruel as ever, Viscount. Have you no words of comfort for a brokenhearted young maiden?"

"I thought we held this meeting in hopes that you would find someone to offer you that comfort. If it didn't go well, that's your problem. Complain all you like; there's nothing I can do about it."

It was a rather upsetting conversation to hear, but neither of the participants seemed to be quite bothered. Ferris gave one of Tiriena's attendants a tap on the shoulder as if it were the most natural thing in the world.

"Um, excuse meow for asking," Ferris said, "but have those two met each other?"

"Ah? Oh, yes. Viscount Misère came to the Holy Kingdom several times in his youth, on which occasions he met Lady Tiriena. They've known each other for nearly a decade now…"

The middle-aged guard's explanation cast the conversation in a very different light. In fact, the entire sequence of events started to look different. Why, for example, the viscount had seemed so aggressive in his desire to undermine the meeting. And why, with that goal accomplished, he seemed more than a little pleased.

"Could it be that the viscount has feelings for Lady Tiriena?"

"Wha?!" At Ferris's blunt question, the viscount started to turn red before their eyes. In a near panic, he turned to Tiriena and said, "It's not—it's not true! That fool's sick in the head! I don't care a whit about—"

"I know; you don't have to get so frantic. But I can't believe you would use a word like *fool* for such a refined young lady. Apologize to her!"

In his vehement effort to defend himself, Misère accidentally let the cat out of the bag.

"A fool he is and a fool I'll call him! Dress or no dress, that's a man!"

"Huh?"

Tiriena, shocked, looked at Ferris, trying to decide whether this was true. It might have been possible to go on deceiving her, of course, but if she set her mind to it, it wouldn't take too long for her to find out the truth.

"—It's true. I'm a man, just like he said."

No point in denying it. Ferris pulled down the front of his dress to reveal his perfectly flat chest. Tiriena still looked as if she could barely believe it. With no choice remaining, Ferris lifted up his skirt. Tiriena was deeply shocked.

"But—yes, I'm a man, but the part about His Highness and me being in love is true! We are in love! Aren't we, Your Highness?"

Ferris had proven his sex but continued to insist that the love itself was no lie. He clung to Fourier's arm, snuggling up against him.

"I love you, Your Highness." He looked with adoring eyes at Fourier, who stood speechless, then planted a kiss on his cheek.

The soft sensation of his lips seemed to finally rouse Fourier. The young prince gave a shake of his head and looked Ferris full in the face before declaring:

"I…I don't care if you're a man! As long as you're *you!*"

It was, in a way, the manliest, least loutish thing he had ever done.

6

"I heard how things went. Word is, the young lady Your Highness met will become Viscount Misère's wife," Crusch said, unable to repress a smile. It was unlike the ever-rational girl to fight back a grin. It was evidence of how close to home these events had hit for her.

Ferris, on the other hand, didn't appear to be enjoying himself. "I guess it's good that we managed to avoid that match. But now things are kind of awkward with His Highness. It makes Ferri lonely."

"To think that's how His Highness would find out about your true sex…but surely you didn't think you could hide it from him your entire life?"

"Nah, I don't think even His Highness is that dense." That he still had never said anything was testament to Fourier's fearsome obliviousness.

But Viscount Misère had finally been able to reveal his long and patient love, and it seemed Tiriena would find her happiness. A happy ending for all, if only Ferris could find a way to repair his relationship with Fourier.

"Incidentally," Crusch said, "perhaps it's just the way the story was told to me, but the rumor is that His Highness prefers men. When that gets out, offers of marriage may stop coming. As soon as the word started circulating, though—well, I felt like I got quite a few sympathetic looks in the castle. I wonder what that was all about."

"Oh, uhh, you know, there are all kinds of people and all kinds of opinions…"

"Mm, it's a question with no easy answer. I see. I shall consider it further." Crusch, as serious as she was, would no doubt end up deducting some reasoning she could accept. Although being as ignorant in matters of the heart as she was, she might never arrive at the correct answer.

Meanwhile, Ferris found himself under a cloud, even though it represented an uncharacteristic moment of disloyalty to his master. But even Ferris was surprised by how hurt he felt when faced with this newfound distance from Fourier.

The two of them had parted ways after they had left the viscount and the young lady in the meeting room together, and Fourier had gotten into his dragon carriage. His last, trembling words to Ferris had been, "I command you to leave me alone." He had never "commanded" Ferris to do anything before, and it was a sign of how deeply shaken he was.

Truth be told, Ferris had pictured this situation more than once. It was his own weakness that had kept him from telling Fourier the truth when they first met and led him to instead deceive the prince. And in all the times he had imagined this moment, he had never been able to work out an apt way to handle it when the truth came out.

"—Ferris." Crusch drew close to him, cutting through his anxious self-reflection. In a quiet voice, she said, "Trust His Highness. He is the man you think he is."

She had no proof for these words and offered none, but Ferris found them more comforting than any lecture on Fourier's virtues. The bond and the trust between Crusch and Ferris were just that strong. And he wanted to believe he shared something similar with Fourier.

That was why...

"This is terrible! The greatest crisis of my life! Where are you two?!"

He was surprised when Fourier flew in with his usual commotion, looking at Ferris and Crusch just as he always did, every bit as panicked as he always was. He skidded to a halt in front of a wide-eyed Ferris and crossed his arms, looking cornered.

"My elder brother and my father got ahold of me the other day. They asked if it was true that I only love men. I wondered what they could possibly be talking about—and apparently it's some rumor everyone in the city is spreading! This is grave indeed!"

Ferris just about lost it when he realized Fourier was upset about exactly the thing they had just been discussing. But...

"Ahhh-ha-ha-ha-ha-ha-ha!"

Before he could burst out laughing, Crusch beat him to the punch. It shocked him: Crusch virtually paralyzed with hilarity was a very unusual sight.

Finally, Ferris could restrain himself no longer and started laughing, too. "Ha-ha...ha! Ohh, Your Highness! You are too—ha-ha-ha!"

He pounded Fourier's shoulder in his merriment, nearly hard enough to injure the young prince.

"Ow! That hurts! Anyway, what do you two find so amusing? The sky is practically falling! We have to do something about this misunderstanding!"

"Aww, why not just leave it? Ferri sure doesn't mind being treated like Your Highness's lover. Didn't mew tell me yourself how much you loved me?"

"That's a completely different subject! It's true that gender doesn't stand in the way of my love for you, but you're a special case! I wouldn't feel this way about just any—wait, what are you making me say?"

Fourier put his head in his hands, thoroughly confused by his own pronouncement. Ferris hugged him from behind, throwing himself against the prince's broad back. The cat-boy shot Crusch a happy grin. The smile was still on her face, and she nodded as if to say she understood how Ferris felt.

All his anxiety from earlier melted away; he felt as if his heart had wings again. At that moment, he felt as if he could float right up to the sky and let the wind take him anywhere he wanted to go.

<END>

THE VALKYRIE OF DUKE KARSTEN'S LANDS

1

The first order of business in the morning was to address the reflection in the mirror.

"Cute! I am cute. A girlish young woman, a wonderful and cute girl."

For quite a long time now, this had been the mantra, the words repeated like magic. No, not like magic. They were magic, for all intents and purposes. A magic spell was simply words that contained the power to change things, to affect the way the world worked. A vow to one's self that brought about change could be called nothing less.

After this incantation, it was time to run a brush through distinctive shoulder-length flaxen hair. Ensuring it was full and neat before biting back a yawn and changing out of pajamas.

While moving over to the closet, cold air hit pale, slender—and at the moment—naked, trembling skin. It was important to pick a shirt that wasn't too loud and a skirt with a hem short enough to perhaps raise some eyebrows, then check how it all looked in the mirror. Then came the culottes and knee-high socks, along with white ribbons to be tied into the hair. And just as the earlier magical incantation had affirmed, the picture of the ideal young woman was now complete.

Striking a pose in front of the mirror, then checking once more to be sure nothing was out of place. No detail could be overlooked; there could be no mistakes. This girlishness was borrowed, though it ought to have belonged to this person to begin with, so it was important to treat it carefully.

"Okay! Looking good today—again!"

Everything was wrapped up with a satisfied nod and a wink. *Perfect, no mistake about it.*

Truth be told, a point had long ago come where the regular affirmations were no longer necessary. These words were a part of the person who spoke them now. After all, it had been six years already.

"It won't do to look meowlancholy." A pat for each cheek. "Now, let's attack the day!" And with a tiny yawn, it was time for them to leave the room.

The hallway of the mansion was silent in the early morning, a chill noticeable in the air. This was the hour when one could sense the cold season arriving. Even though this person was used to saving money wherever possible, mornings like this made them consider adding another layer.

In the hallway, morning greetings and easy smiles were exchanged with the servants who had already begun the day's work. Everyone remarked on the sudden cooldown, and there was even a gentle warning not to catch a cold.

"What are you talking about? You mean that old saying, 'Illness spares not even doctors'?"

After smiling and waving, they went their separate ways, while a certain person continued to the mansion's main entry hall. An elderly steward opened the door. Walking through it while unconsciously bracing against the cold wind that came blowing through, a single figure hunched over.

"—You're here." Another had arrived at the entrance earlier and now tossed the brief remark over her shoulder. She was beautiful. The woman tugged on the reins of the white land dragon that was her faithful steed, holding her long green hair against the rising wind. Feeling her upturned, amber eyes watching made the newcomer unconsciously attempt to straighten up from their previous stooped position. It wasn't an attempt to look good for the woman; her eyes simply had the power to provoke that reaction.

"You didn't wait long for me, did you, Lady Crusch?"

"No, you're right on time. I just woke up a little early. My father finally decided to permit me to take longer rides again. I've been dying to go for one."

The dragon put its face close to hers, and she stroked its head, her expression relaxing into a smile. She looked very collected, and yet it spoke of something childish within her. Her name was Crusch Karsten.

She smiled even wider as she noticed her companion looking her way. "Go get yourself a land dragon from the stables. Our destination will be the same as always, all right, Ferris?"

"Yes, ma'am." Ferris responded with a perfect curtsy, appearing every inch the perfect lady.

This was how Ferris—the young man Felix Argyle—began every day.

2

Ferris, now sixteen, was a firm believer in the power of a person's will and faith. If you kept believing, surprising things could happen.

For example, he should have developed secondary sexual characteristics long ago, but as if in response to his daily wishes and prayers, he showed no sign of becoming more masculine. His voice grew no deeper and his body didn't thicken. He was quietly thankful to his ancestors that he didn't grow a beard.

But the things for which he was grateful to his bloodline didn't stop at his body.

"Have I bored you, Ferris?" A calm voice brought him out of his reverie. He was taking a break, sitting in the grass and leaning against a large tree. Crusch had knelt directly in front of him and was looking intently into his eyes.

"...Sorry, *meow*. Kinda drifted off."

"Oh? That's unusual for you. Are you tired? Did I work you too hard?"

"No, I just let my mind wander a bit... Are you going to punish me? Lady Crusch, are you going to punish Ferri? My heart's pounding!"

"Punish you? I would hate to be so coldhearted." Crusch shook her head, oblivious to the significance of Ferris's reddening cheeks. The cat-boy sighed. Crusch, still peering down at him, continued: "And there's no need to stand on ceremony here. Let your mind wander if you wish. No matter what happens, I'm here."

"Aww, Lady Crusch, you always know just what to say...even if you never seem to realize it. Ferri might just be in love..."

"—? Your face is red. It's chilly today—don't tell me you've caught a cold?"

"No, not at all! That's not it at all! Oooh, Lady Crusch, you are just too cruel! I can't stand it!"

Ferris's mistress was completely oblivious to any feelings of affection deeper than close friendship and took his words completely at face value. "I see," she said. "I'm sorry." She looked properly embarrassed. Her very innocence itself was endearing—and completely unfair.

"—"

Satisfied by Ferris's declaration of good health, Crusch returned to her original position, almost as if she were being pulled over. This grassy field was where the two of them always came when they wanted a longer ride. It was about an hour away from the mansion, a place of pure mana and full of wind. It seemed to border on holy. Ferris was always overjoyed to spend time with just the two of them, in a place where no one could interrupt.

"—Yah!"

The lithe Crusch went through a series of movements with her sword as Ferris watched from his spot beside a tree. Her polished strikes, the aggression she exuded—even Ferris, who was an amateur when it came to swords, could tell how accomplished she was with the weapon.

Crusch was completely taken with the beauty of steel; she had begun learning the sword even before she met Ferris. But still, the fact that her swordsmanship had reached this level was thanks to him. And that knowledge made him prouder and happier than anything.

That was why he would never grow bored of watching Crusch work with her blade. Seeing talent that he had helped cultivate captured his heart like the shimmer of a jewel.

"You're even more into it than usual this morning, Lady Crusch."

"True enough. It's what comes of waiting so long for the sword and an extended ride. Without you to keep me from getting cabin fever, I'm sure I would've made some ridiculous complaint to my father out of sheer boredom."

It was hard to tell from the side, but he almost thought Crusch was smiling pleasantly as she swung her blade.

Her eyes had been shining like a child's during the ride to this place. For more than a month she had been denied the two things that made her feel most alive, and it must have been killing her.

"But it was just like you, milady, not to try to sneak out and do it on the sly."

"Of course not. My father was right to reprimand me. I was the one who caused the trouble. If I saw fit to break the rules after that, people would surely say I had no shame."

What made Crusch wonderful was the way she embodied words like *honesty* and *uprightness*. Because she believed it was natural to uphold the rules, she was wont to protest her innocence when it was clear she had done nothing wrong. This had certainly been one of those moments.

"You know, Ferri is not very happy with Lord Meckart's decision. It was exactly because mew were there that things didn't get any worse!"

"It's only natural that my father asked me to act appropriately as the daughter of a duke. Although I do wish he'd accept me one of these days... So which of us is more stubborn—me or my father?"

Ferris puffed out his cheeks, but Crusch just gave a rueful smile.

The event that roused Ferris's ire had occurred about a month before. On a day much like this one, Crusch and Ferris had taken one of their long rides through the Karsten domain. Along the way, they'd run across a group of pirates, the source of some local unrest, attacking a dragon carriage, and Crusch had gallantly driven them off.

Crusch had never been in any real danger, although she faced nearly ten brigands. But her father—Meckart Karsten, current head of the ducal House of Karsten—had been extremely distraught when the story reached his ears.

Crusch had known he would be and so had left the grateful carriage owner without giving her name, but she was far too famous for that to work. Her penchant for swordsmanship was common knowledge in the Karsten lands. And since the crest with the lion baring its teeth had been perfectly visible on her sword, there was no room to deny anything.

A duke's daughter who eschewed dresses for men's clothes and preferred crossing blades to admiring blossoms. The rumors were all too readily substantiated, and as punishment, Crusch was forbidden to take up a sword or travel very far from the palace for one month.

Crusch seemed to accept this, but Ferris had voiced his outrage directly to Meckart more than once. But the man would not relent. A month of waiting had finally led to the current day.

"I definitely ackmeowledge how much I owe Lord Meckart, but that doesn't mean I have to accept everything he does."

"I wish you wouldn't criticize my father so much. He seems thinner every day lately. The responsibility of running a ducal household must weigh on him. I want his time with his family, at least, to be a source of good cheer for him."

"Do you mean Ferri is a part of the family?"

"—? Of course."

Ferris's cheeks flushed at being included so readily in the family. He quickly patted his skirt to distract from his cheeks.

"It's—it's fine," he said. "Lord Meckart practically seems to like it when Ferri puts him on the spot like that. He said he enjoys having people say outrageous things to him…"

"What? My father said that? I didn't know…and I think I'll see him a little differently from now on."

Crusch was completely taken in by this bit of gossip Ferris had strategically deployed to distract her from his embarrassment. Meckart's daughter wore a look of plain surprise. Ferris tried to fix the expression in his memory, as it was something he saw all too rarely. And silently, he apologized to the duke, albeit mentally sticking his tongue out while he did. He didn't try to correct Crusch's misunderstanding, though. Maybe that was a sign of just how displeased he still was.

3

"Felix, may I have a moment?"

"Yes, sir?" Ferris turned at the voice, offering his most girlish look in a fit of pique. The other man seemed dismayed at the openly flirtatious glance. Ferris enjoyed the moment. "Ooh, it's just too easy to get a rise out of you, Lord Meowckart. It's too much fun to tease you! You bring out Ferri's inner trickster!"

"What? And you blame me for this? Er—I mean, I'm sorry."

All you have to do is look a little bit put out, and he'll apologize. What a pushover.

Standing before Ferris was a man in his fifties. He had grown a mustache, ostensibly for the gravitas it provided him, but the strange shape of his eyebrows and his gentle face robbed him of any benefit from it. The only thing he shared with Crusch, his blood daughter, was the color of his eyes.

It was all the more surprising, then, that this was Duke Karsten, head of one of the most famous noble houses in Lugunica. And he was also Crusch's father—Meckart Karsten.

A doleful smile came over Meckart's friendly face. He tugged at his rather incongruous mustache as he said, "I believe you were off on a ride with Crusch this morning. How is she doing?"

"If you're concerned about her, sir, please let me humbly suggest that you ask her yourself. This is you we're talking about, of course, but even so, do you think Lady Crusch would lie to you, Lord Meckart?"

"I'm not quite sure I like the way you put that. But no, I'm not worried that she would lie to me. It's just... Well, I was the one who imposed that prohibition. I thought it might be hard for her to say how she was really feeling... Um, or rather...hard for me to ask."

His good heart won out over his desire to deceive himself, and he voiced his true problem. Father and daughter were also alike in their inability to tell a blatant lie.

"I see... Well, put your mind at ease. Lady Crusch isn't mad at you or anything. She even seems to understand why you did what you did."

"You say that as if I were the villain... But, ahem, thank you."

"For the record, though, Ferri is still mad. Nasty, nasty Lord Meckart!"

"What? Um, I mean, I'm sorry... Even I think I went a bit overboard."

Meckart, looking weak, rubbed his upper abdomen. Thanks to the stresses of his position, combined with his anxious personality, he and stomach pain were close personal friends.

"Shall I use healing magic on you? It might take the edge off."

"Right. Now that we've chatted, perhaps you could heal me. Would you mind coming to my room?"

"Nuh-uh! I've no idea what mew might do to me in there, sir...!"

"Nothing! I won't do anything to you!"

Even though he gave the duke a hard time about it, Ferris eventually followed Meckart to his room. The place was simple: a desk for

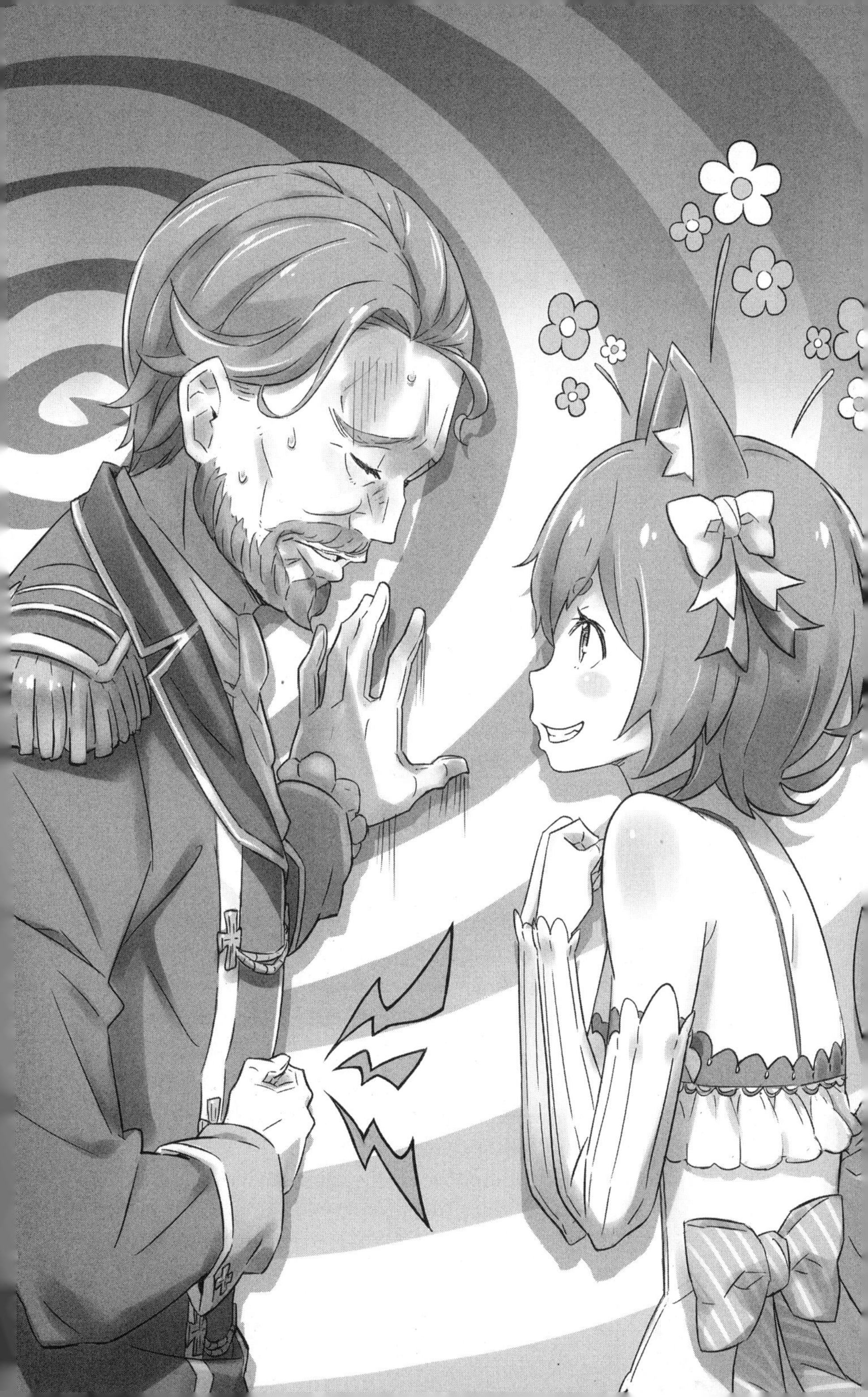

a secretary, along with a low table and leather couch for receiving visitors.

Ferris and Meckart sat facing each other on the sofa, and a servant brought tea as readily as if this had all been planned. After setting out the steaming cups, the attendant departed with a dignified bow.

With the servant gone and the door closed, Meckart put his cup to his lips and sipped at it carefully. "...Crusch will have her seventeenth birthday soon."

Ferris knew that, of course. The joyous day was just two weeks hence; indeed, it would not have been an overstatement to say Ferris was more grateful for this day than for any other day on the calendar.

"I'm thankful for the stars and the sky and the earth...and for Crusch, definitely. I'm so glad she was born."

Meckart cut into Ferris's reverie. "Excuse me, Felix, but would you mind letting me make my point? There's...something I'd like you to ask that girl about her birthday. Something I find...difficult to express." From his awkward tone and his evasive attitude, Ferris had a fairly good idea what Meckart had in mind. After all, it came up almost every year.

"...You want Lady Crusch to wear a dress, don't you?"

"Yes, Felix, exactly. It's her birthday. And this year I have something more extravagant than usual in mind. So I really wish she would wear something appropriate..."

"If it's at all possible, sir, I really think you should speak to her yourself. You don't have to go through me..."

"That girl won't so much as nod her head if you don't, isn't that right?" Meckart asked in a low voice. Ferris's cat ears immediately detected a change in the air. The flaxen animal ears he had inherited from his demi-human ancestors were exceptionally sensitive to subtle shifts in the atmosphere and environment.

"I know about the promise between you and Crusch," Meckart went on. "And I'm sure you've spoken to her in light of it before."

"You know how I know you two are related? Neither of you ever gives up."

"Perhaps she does get her obstinacy from me... But we can't simply run parallel to each other forever. I'm desperate to find some compromise."

"Compromise, sir?" It was not a term to be used lightly, especially with Crusch, for whom that word might have been the least congenial thing imaginable.

"It doesn't matter if it's only in public, only for show," Meckart said. "Of course, deep down, I've always wished she would comport herself as expected of a duke's daughter, but my requests on that front have been rebuffed often enough that I know better by now. My hope is that my suggestion this time will allow us to meet in the middle."

"—"

"I know her promise with you is the reason Crusch continues to play with her swords and dress like a man. Therefore, if I wish to mitigate it at all, it makes sense to go through you. Will you not speak to her?"

"—I understand what you're trying to say, Lord Meckart. But I..."

Meckart cut him off sharply. "I don't believe you do understand, Felix."

Ferris caught his breath. The duke looked grimmer and lonelier than he had ever seen him.

"Crusch is my only child. She has turned out so well as to be wasted on me. I haven't been a reliable father by any stretch. But the more pathetic I am, the more admirable she becomes... I do want her to follow her own dreams. I pray she grows up to be exactly who she truly is." Meckart lowered his eyes, affection for his daughter overcoming him. "But I am a duke as well as a father. And she is the daughter of a duke as well as my child. So long as she lives in this house, supported by the people of this domain, she will have certain duties she must perform. And when she is performing them, people will expect dress and decorum befitting her position. Well, Felix? Am I wrong?"

"...No."

"In fact, I *am* wrong. I am trying to force my daughter to do something she doesn't want to do. Doing the right thing can be a mistake, and a mistake can be the right thing to do. Such are the difficulties of this place where I and my daughter must live."

As the duke laid out his argument, Ferris began to feel ashamed of himself. He had been so superficial. Until this moment, he had simply assumed Meckart was just an oaf. It had never occurred to him that behind the stubborn exterior was a father deeply concerned about his relationship with his daughter. Ferris found himself choking up as he realized he had been saved from this thoughtlessness by Meckart's compassion, his willingness to try to talk things out instead of simply imposing his will through his ample authority.

"His Highness Fourier will be in attendance at the birthday celebration. I'm sure he's looking forward to seeing what dress Crusch will wear."

"...Yes, I suppose he would be."

"Indeed! So not just for my sake, but for His Highness's—will you please talk to Crusch?"

The invocation of the young prince's name relaxed the tone of the conversation. Perhaps that, too, was Meckart's considerate touch. Ferris put the cup of tea, cold by now, to his lips while attempting to ignore his own meanness of heart.

He recalled a promise he had made, back when he was still young enough to take youth as an excuse. Unconsciously, he touched the white ribbon Crusch had given him that day.

"You know, I've always thought that promise wasn't right."

"...Mm, perhaps not. You and my daughter are both good children."

"But I've been so happy to do what I promised... It's made me happier than anything else in my life. And maybe I take her side too much because of that."

His hand was still at his ribbon. Meckart nodded quietly.

In his own way, the words were Ferris's answer to Meckart's request.

4

His little tea party with Meckart over, Ferris furrowed his brow anxiously. There was no room for argument after that conversation. And he had no intention of reneging on their promise.

"But how in the world am I supposed to bring it up now?" he wondered aloud. It would be difficult to find the right timing and a natural opening to talk about it.

Today was especially bad. The month-long prohibition on Crusch wielding a sword or riding a dragon had only just been lifted. Of all the times this could have happened, this was the least opportune time he could choose to appear and ask her to wear a dress.

"Oh, but! But! The birthday celebration is just two weeks away. It might be even worse to put off talking about it…"

The subject could hardly wait until the last moment. This was a birthday celebration for a duke's daughter. The longer there was to prepare, the better. Even two weeks barely seemed like enough time. Meckart himself had no doubt been hesitating to talk to Ferris.

"Arrgh! Meow will I ever manage this?!"

"What's going on, Ferris? You'll scare the rest of the household, standing in the hallway looking so grim."

"Mrrrrow!" Ferris just about jumped out of his skin when Crusch herself called out to him while he stood there, dancing from one foot to the other with worry. He flew back against the wall. Crusch crossed her arms and stared at him.

"I still think you look tired. If you're feeling worn down, I could give you some time off…"

"What? No! I'm totally fine! Never better! Hooray for Lady Crusch!"

"—? Ha-ha, you're a strange one."

She smiled slightly as he stood there with his arms raised in a cheer. It was obvious he hadn't really thrown her off the trail, and he hadn't quite calmed down, either.

"By the way," Crusch said, "you spoke with my father, didn't you? What did he want?"

"Oh, uh, I mean, you know, *meow*..."

He couldn't have asked for better timing to broach the subject. The only problem was that, mentally, he felt completely unprepared. Then again, the moment was so fortuitous that it seemed like a sign from the heavens. Now was the time to talk.

"Well, um," he began, "Ferri does, uh, want to talk to you about something, Lady Crusch..."

"I thought so. Your wind is difficult to read, but that was the impression I got. You know you and I don't have to hold back from each other. Talk to me about anything."

"I love you, Lady Crusch."

"And I you."

He had confessed his feelings in an excess of happiness, but the serious reply quickly doused his enthusiasm. Hadn't he been reflecting on how moved he was by Meckart's kindness just moments ago? To immediately return to letting Crusch's kindness spoil him instead would not say much for his personal growth.

"I love you, Lady Crusch."

"—? And I you."

He was repeating himself, but it calmed him down and made him feel better. He was about to embark on a very difficult conversation.

"Well, uh, this is just Lord Meckart's opinion, and Ferri wouldn't want mew to meowstake this for agreement, but..."

"This is an awfully roundabout way to start a conversation. Fine, I understand. And what is my father's opinion?"

"Yes, well, it will be your birthday soon, milady..."

He had laid all the groundwork and was about to come to his point when—

"—Crusch, are you there?! I am in dire distress! Crusch, show your face!"

"—?!"

Ferris stiffened with surprise at the bellow that rang through the hallway. In front of him, Crusch was looking up and cocking her head at the voice.

"I hesitate to believe it, but was that His Highness Fourier just now?"

"I—I don't care if he is a prince," Ferris fumed. "How could he spoil my perfect moment...?"

"Crusch! Aren't you there? I said this is a crisis! Come quickly, or I shall wither for loneliness!"

"That's him, all right," Crusch said.

The initial shock had passed, and the second exclamation was more than enough to verify the voice's owner. Ferris and Crusch exchanged a glance and then trotted to the entryway. At the door, the servants, including a steward, had formed a receiving line, and right in the midst of them was the man himself.

"Ah! Crusch and Ferris!" he said when he spotted them. "Are you both in good health? I'm doing quite well, myself." Then he smiled with genuine mirth. He was a young man whose eyes appeared guileless despite his years. He had long golden hair and unblemished scarlet eyes, and his canines stuck out ever so slightly. He gave a very likable impression.

Sloughing off his rich fur coat, Fourier Lugunica appeared as energetic as ever.

The fourth prince of the royal family ought not to drop by so casually, but Crusch and Ferris were both used to it, and neither showed any surprise. Crusch made a modest bow to Fourier, who stood imposingly.

"Your Highness," she said, "it is an honor to see you. But what prompts such a sudden visit? Is something wrong? I haven't heard anything from my father..."

"What are you talking about? Was it not precisely the two of you who invited me here? For Crusch's birthday celebrations? I even brought my invitation. Look!" With many a huff and sigh, Fourier went over to Crusch, who had greeted him so respectfully, and held out a letter. She took it, scanned it, and then nodded slowly.

"This is indeed an invitation from our house…but, my lord, you seem to have mistaken the most crucial part—the date. I'm happy you took the trouble to come all the way here, but my birthday is still two weeks away. Your Highness has been a tad too eager."

"What?! You mean…I am the first person to congratulate you on your birthday! Perfect! Ferris always beats me to it, but for once I've got a leg up on him!"

"—"

"You did well to be born, Crusch! I am overjoyed! What a wondrous day!" Fourier laughed suddenly, apparently ignoring his own mistake. Crusch found herself speechless at this audacity, but a gentle smile was soon on her face.

"Thank you very much, Your Highness. Your well wishes mean a great deal to me."

"Good, very good. But does this mean there are two weeks yet till your birthday celebration? Well, that is a problem. What shall I do until then?"

Fourier tended to act without thinking of the future, rush in without thinking of the future, speak without thinking of the future, and just in general not think about the future at all, but he had enough charm to excuse all of it. As he stood there struggling to figure out his plans, even Ferris couldn't help a smile. The prince hadn't changed a bit since they had first met.

"Hmm?" Fourier said. "What is it, Ferris? Why the grin?"

"I just find you amusing, Your Highness."

"Me?! Ah, yes… I am no ordinary leader. I bring smiles to the faces of my servants without even meaning to. Do you not think so, Crusch?"

"I can only admire what a grand personage you are, Your Highness. Ferris, punishment later."

"Awww!"

Leave it to Crusch to ensure that he didn't go without paying the penalty for his lapse in etiquette. But at the same time, the three were so close that such irreverence could go without genuine reprisal. For Ferris, who had so few things he considered precious, this bond was something he cherished. When he thought about what was important to him, he thought of Crusch, Meckart, and Fourier. And the servants in the Karsten household. Not to mention the patients and colleagues he had encountered thanks to his work as a spell caster. It turned out there were quite a few people he valued.

Compared to when he had been shut up in his family's house, with nothing ever given to him, he was so much happier now.

"...Ferris," Fourier was saying, "I am aware of my dashing appearance, but please try not to stare too much. All this attention from you might just lead me astray—even knowing your true gender."

"I was even your fiancé once, and I still couldn't get my paws on you, Your Highness!"

"That was just...! Ahem, that's enough. I'm a boy, too, you know! I shan't make excuses! Aren't I quite manly, Crusch?"

"Yes, my lord. Although if I may say so, you have yet to defeat me in a sword duel."

"Lady Crusch! Milady, His Highness is on his knees already, so perhaps we should go easy on him..."

Fourier had slumped to the carpet. Crusch gave him a quizzical look, entirely devoid of malice. With her friends, Crusch tended to state the facts a bit too bluntly. But she delivered even the most stinging remarks with a friendly expression, making it hard to consider this a truly bad habit.

Fourier, for his part, was quick to bounce back from such disappointments.

"—Ngh, well then! In that case, Crusch, bring me a wooden sword! I have some time to kill for the first time in a while, so let today be the day when I outdo you in swordsmanship and prove to you what a man I am!"

Crusch met this bold proclamation with a "yes, my lord," as though she knew full well what was going on.

Crusch and Fourier's duels with wooden training swords had been going on for six years, since about the same time Ferris began wearing women's clothing. It had become a sort of tradition.

Fourier would find any excuse to visit Crusch. His love for her was not at all difficult to see, except for Crusch herself. As for Fourier, he was outgoing in everything except matters of his own heart, so the relationship had never gone beyond that of dear friends. Fourier saw this duel as a simple way to provoke a change in their relationship.

"If you win, I shall force you to dress in women's clothes! You've become evermore obstinate about your manly attire... Not that it doesn't look good on you! But I wish to see you in a skirt!"

"You'll have to settle for Ferris, my lord. I assure you, his legs are no less dainty than mine."

"I am proud of these legs. Have a look, Your Highness!"

"Arrgh! Don't confuse me, you two!" Fourier turned red and stomped his feet in frustration as Ferris lifted his skirt teasingly. With one hand he pointed at Crusch; with the other, he displayed the birthday invitation, which she had given back to him. "It's almost your birthday! And I will not permit the birthday girl to dress like a soldier as she did last year! This year I shall see you in a dress! In one of my choosing, at that!"

"Ah..."

Fourier was so fond of these proclamations. And this one just happened to line up perfectly with what Ferris wanted. He caught his breath in surprise, and a certain tender feeling for Fourier welled up within him.

This silly prince...

"He's the only one besides Lady Crusch who can get at Ferri's weak point..."

"—"

Ferris's cheeks flushed, his breath hot with a combination of affection and envy.

Crusch, the only one standing close enough to overhear his

murmured words, shot a look at him. But Ferris didn't notice, and before Crusch could speak...

"All right! To the garden, then! Ready, everyone! This is the day I become a man!" Fourier exclaimed with what appeared to be entirely unwarranted confidence, and Ferris and Crusch had to rush after him as he headed outside.

5

It was six years ago, but he remembered it as if it were yesterday: the day the duels between Crusch and Fourier had started. The day Felix became Ferris.

"I hardly see how Your Highness can interfere with how I choose to live."

"Hmm...but you say you'll throw away your femininity so it won't stand in the way of either your noble family or your swordsmanship? No! I won't allow it! I simply can't allow that to happen!"

"In that case, my lord, what do you intend to do?"

"The sword! Use the blade to prove your resolve to me! And I shall show you the error of your ways!"

"A sword fight? Between you and me, Your Highness?"

"Yes, exactly. In the off chance you win, you may take whatever path you choose in life. But if I win, you'll have to reconsider. I will make a woman of you!"

Such was the promise they made with each other. Fourier had all the enthusiasm, but Crusch had the resolve. And then the duels began...

"You are truly without mercy, Crusch! I'm a prince! A member of the royal family!"

"All right, Your Highness, all right," Ferris said. "There's no need to mewl. Here, look! I'll get rid of that boo-boo for you."

It crossed his mind that he had healed Fourier just like this on that day six years ago.

Nearly weeping and covered in dust, Fourier clung to Ferris. The cat-boy used his healing magic. A wave of comfort washed over the bruises inflicted by Crusch's wooden sword. Fourier slowly stood up.

"Ha-ha-ha! Did you see that? How I pretended to snivel and cry in order to win my opponent's sympathy and buy myself enough time for Ferris to heal me? Just another of my fearsomely clever calculations...!"

"Your knees don't agree, Your Highness," Ferris pointed out. Despite the smile Fourier had carefully arranged on his face, his knees were shaking. It only served to highlight how refined and gallant Crusch looked in comparison. She had taken off her jacket, revealing her slender frame. She held her weapon at the ready and stood so straight she could have been mistaken for a sword herself.

"Now, compare that to His Highness..."

"I can hear you, Ferris! Save your praises of me until the battle is over!"

"You know what I love about you, Your Highness? Your irrepressible optimism."

Fourier turned his back on Ferris's gentle jibe, closing the distance to Crusch in a rush. In that moment, he seemed to forget that his opponent was also the woman he loved. But she turned aside his blow, and his own momentum sent him tumbling through the grass once again. Pain followed a moment later, causing him to cough violently as he tried to stand up.

There was a tremendous difference in their abilities, but it wasn't Fourier's fault. Ferris was somewhat biased in his evaluation, but Fourier was far more skilled then the average noble dilettante of his age. His desire to defeat Crusch, combined with many years of these duels, had turned him from a coddled princeling into a man who could hold his own with a blade. That he still couldn't best Crusch spoke to her talent and how hard she had worked.

"Do you wish to continue, my lord? I fear my father's heart might break if I beat you any harder."

"Of course I shall continue! You take me too lightly, Crusch! And I don't think Meckart's heart is as fragile as you suggest, either. Come at me with all you've got!"

True to form, his declaration was asking a little much.

This battle was taking place out in the center garden, and servants with nothing else to do were spectating. There was someone else there as well, someone looking rather ill at the sight of the entire spectacle: Meckart himself. He came out every time this happened, even though the stress of it was enough to make his cheeks sunken. *Well, he doesn't have to watch.*

"Oh, why are they so much more serious than usual?" Meckart fretted. "But if His Highness were to win..."

Meckart grimaced from the pain in his stomach, torn between what he hoped for as a father and what he wished as a duke. At that moment, Ferris knew all too well what Meckart was feeling.

I don't even know if I want Crusch to win or lose right now!

"Yaaah! Crusch, wear a dreeeesssss!" It might be too generous to call this a battle cry, but with those words Fourier rushed in again, and again he was beaten. When she saw Fourier rise again after being folded double, Crusch narrowed her eyes.

"Your Highness seems less inclined than usual to concede. What is driving you?"

"You, of course! You make me this way... No, at the heart of the matter, *I* make me this way! I have foisted this on you, so now I must play my part!"

"...Your Highness?"

Fourier, his handsome face smeared with dirt and sweat, shook his head. "I shall not forget how foolish I was those five years ago, how little I knew my place. Not knowing my strength, I bound you to an impulsive promise. I made you swear that so long as I failed to best you with the sword, you would wear no women's clothes but dress as a man—I know now what a cruel act that was."

Making this confession seemed to pain him greatly, but of course he was wrong about the five years. It was six. But Fourier's words referred to the promise they had made on that day Ferris remembered so well...

"Do you remember your fifteenth birthday, two years ago?" Fourier asked. "You had grown up so beautifully. In full regalia that night, I know you would have been more stunning than any flower. Yet you kept your promise. I shall never forget the sight of a young maiden walking under the moonlight in military dress. You were impossibly handsome...but that was a feeling inspired by the sword at your side. It is not a feeling I want to receive from a young woman who should outdo the blossoms in beauty!"

Crusch was silent.

"That night, I realized what my thoughtlessness had wrought. It was I, and I alone, who stole the joy of being resplendently dressed from a young woman and forced her to hide herself during what should have been her most glorious moment! I must take responsibility for that!"

In all the time they had known each other, Ferris had never seen Fourier like this. The immense emotion that burned in his scarlet eyes touched something in Ferris's chest, made his throat tight. The audience, too, from Meckart to the servants, was at a loss for words. They knew now why Fourier fought these battles and heard him express what he'd never been able to express before.

But he was wrong. Mistaken. His resolve was tremendous, but it was misplaced.

The promise he and Crusch had made was real enough. When, six years before, Crusch had declared that she would wear only men's clothing for the rest of her life, Fourier had responded that he would allow her to do so just until he defeated her in a sword duel. The pretext that she was keeping her promise to the prince was the reason Meckart had not been able to object more strongly.

Fourier had been nursing regret about it all this time. Somewhere along the line, he had begun to believe that Crusch didn't want to wear men's clothes but was doing so because of the promise they had made. And, with a combination of honesty and foolishness, he felt responsible.

"I'm a fool..."

Watching Fourier from behind as he raised his sword, Ferris unconsciously put a hand to his mouth. He had always taken Fourier's improvement in combat to be a result of repeated duels and simple tenacity. But there was more. All this time, he had been motivated by regret for his own outburst.

He's been fighting to let the woman he loves, the woman he bound with a promise, be a woman.

"Crusch! Love flowers! Appreciate poetry! Put on makeup, wear dresses and jewelry, and let me see that innocent smile! You don't have to repress yourself anymore! I permit it! Here, today, I will make right my foolishness and allow you to be a true woman!"

"Y-Your Highness...?"

It may have been a misunderstanding, but Fourier was ready to make good on it. He charged at Crusch.

The hard sound echoed through the garden, and Crusch was clearly shaken by the impact.

"Your Highness!"

"Prince Fourier!"

"Your Highness, help our lady!"

These were cries from the servants, many of them red-eyed and with a tremble in their voices. They had known Crusch since she was young, and they wanted to encourage the prince in his resolve. Fourier pressed his attack, and Crusch looked more shaken still.

His sword rose and fell in an arc; Crusch was completely occupied with defending. For a battle against her to be so one-sided was unprecedented. That was simply how impassioned Fourier's blows were. His attack was, in its way, his suit to Crusch's heart. His clear dedication may have sprung from a misunderstanding, but it touched many people present.

"—I shall entrust this to His Highness," Meckart murmured. When had he come up beside Ferris?

The cat-boy looked up at him, and Meckart nodded. Ferris knew

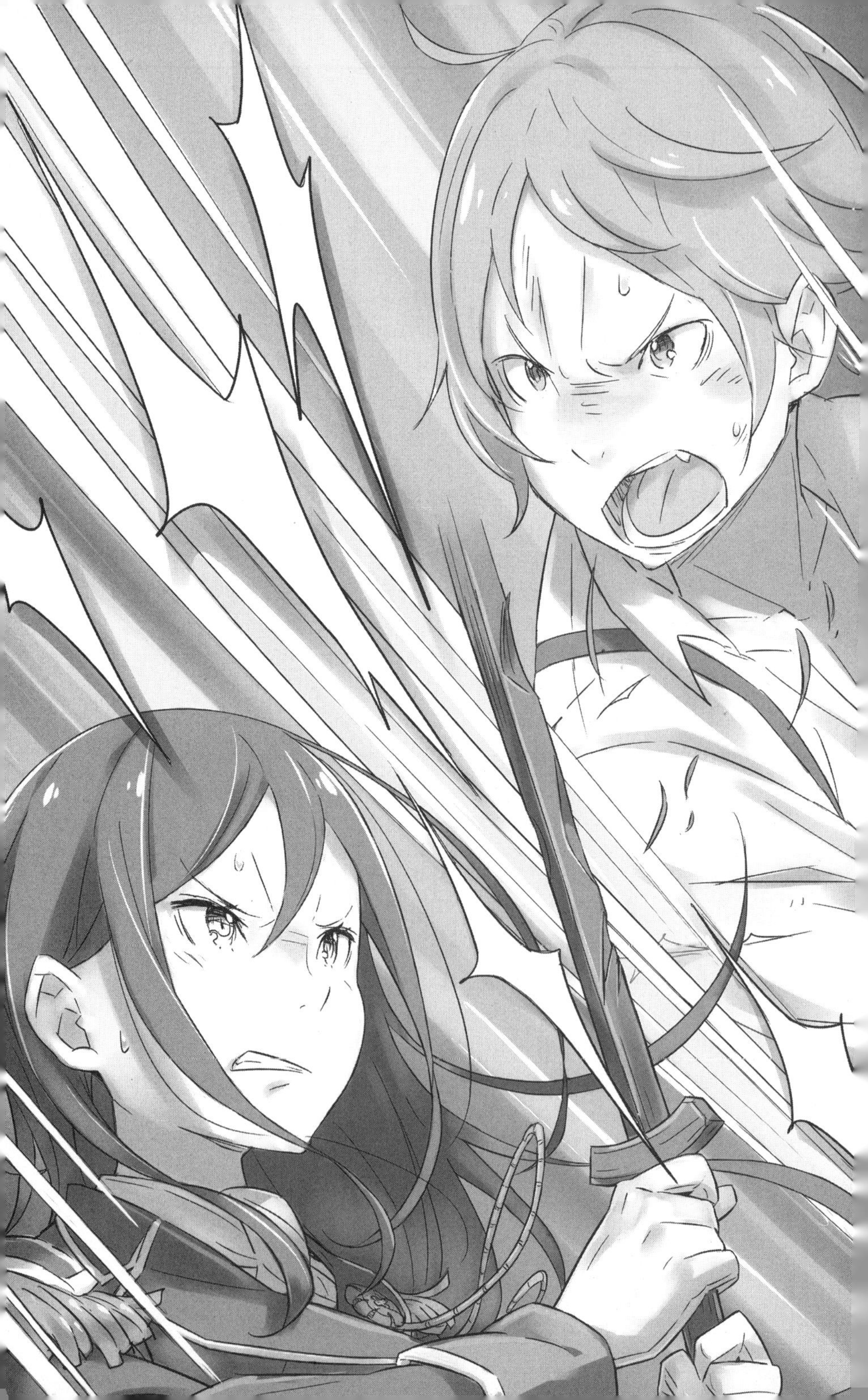

immediately what it meant. He joined his hands in front of his chest as if in prayer and waited to see how the battle would turn out.
"A dress! Makeup! And jewelry! Flowers and cooking!"
"—ngh."
"Crusch! Kneel before meeeee!" The wooden swords groaned with the force of his blow, splinters flying from the blades. Both weapons were at their limits. But the fight would be decided by which of the participants gave out first.
Fourier bellowed as he pushed Crusch back step by step, blow by blow. His lovely face was red. What did Crusch see when she looked at his gallant form bearing down on her? Perhaps she saw herself in his scarlet eyes, a woman being pressed to do her utmost.
"...Ah."
As she found herself pushed up against a wall, Crusch cast her amber eyes on Ferris. They looked at each other, and it seemed to him like she was asking for something, but he didn't know what.
"Lady...Crusch..." Fat tears rolled from his round eyes and down his cheeks.
The next moment, there was a crack as the wooden sword finally gave way, and part of the broken blade skittered across the ground. The one blade that remained more or less intact was pointed at the chest of the loser.
"...All that, and still I cannot outdo you."
Fourier spoke with strained breath, still holding what was left of the hilt of his sword. He looked at the ground, his shoulders trembling. He might have been crying.
A sigh. Disappointed, but not despairing. But everyone's shoulders slumped as they realized he had not prevailed.
But then—
"No, Your Highness. I've lost."
Crusch shook her head gently. The sword in her hand was broken down the middle as well. She tossed the useless blade to the ground.
"You still hold your blade, Your Highness, while I have cast mine

aside. The victor should be clear...indeed, has been clear since your battle cry shook my spirit—I have lost this contest."

"—"

Fourier was absolutely silent. Crusch knelt down, ignoring the dirt that got on her, and placed her hands on the ground. The gesture was that of offering a sword—it was one of utmost respect and loyalty.

"You have indeed fulfilled your former promise. I, Crusch Karsten, have met Your Highness Fourier Lugunica in combat with the sword and have been bested. I shall put on women's clothing, then."

"Er...ahem. Will you, now? I...I see." Fourier's response to Crusch's solemn words was halting and unsteady. He nodded once, and then his tall frame began to lean backward, until finally he fell spread-eagle on the ground.

"Your Highness?! Oh no! Felix, tend to His Highness!"

Ferris was rushing over to Fourier long before the astonished Meckart ordered him to do so. He slid his knees under the head of the collapsed young man, supporting the prince's body weight as he used his healing magic.

"Your Highness, Your Highness! Stay with me—! Your Highness!"

"Heh-heh! Did you see it, Ferris? Did you see my...great... victory...?"

Healing magic would cure his wounds, but it wouldn't restore the strength he had lost. Fourier had spent every ounce of his endurance, and now the familiar easygoing smile came over his face just before he slipped into a deep sleep. Ferris was amazed to hear the calm, even rhythm of Fourier's breathing.

"Ferris."

"Oh, uh, yes, Lady Crusch. Um, Ferri, I mean— What can Ferri say...?"

"I'm sorry for being so selfish." Crusch smiled gently as she watched Ferris tend to the unconscious prince. As her words sunk in, the tears started streaming down Ferris's cheeks again. He looked up, wiping furiously at his eyes.

"I...I'm the one who hasn't been fair to you...! Lady Crusch, you... You and Prince Fourier are always rescuing me..."

"Are we? Then you've amply returned the favor. Your presence is a constant salvation for me. And I am only just now realizing that the prince saved me as well. I suppose it goes to show how ill-bred I really am."

"Ill-bred...? Lady Crusch, no...! You're wonderful...!"

"All the more reason I must strive to live up to your and His Highness's estimation of me."

Ferris continued sniffling, not quite able to speak. Crusch patted his head lovingly as she stood. Then she went over to Meckart, who watched agape.

What she said to him, Ferris didn't know. He couldn't hear over Fourier's snores and his own weeping.

6

"I did all the work to make this possible—and yet I don't get to see Crusch in her dress until the party? Most unorthodox!"

"Well, you know. Lady Crusch has a lot to deal with. She has to get ready mentally and physically. Plus, it's not easy to find the exact perfect dress for Lady Crusch!"

"I know you'll do everything you can for her, Ferris. Very heartening!"

Ferris gave a dark smile. Across from him, Fourier laughed easily. They were in Ferris's personal chambers at the Karsten mansion. His Highness had shown up there as though it were the most natural thing in the world. Ferris had personally made tea and was now entertaining the prince. Perhaps he ought to have been a touch more intimidated—but neither Ferris nor the prince seemed to be holding back. They were old friends, if it was not too audacious to consider oneself as an old friend to royalty.

"The two weeks since that battle have been truly vexing. By the time I woke up, I was already in a dragon carriage on the way home. Being sent away before I even got to speak to Crusch? I have never before been subjected to such a ploy."

"You simply wouldn't wake up, Your Highness, you were so tired. And besides, you could hardly stay at our meownsion for ten whole days until the party. I know your station isn't very demanding, but surely even mew have some duties to attend to?"

"Indeed, I am in great demand! But one thing worries me. I recall subduing Crusch with my sword, and then comforting her as she wept, but..."

"...Guess we'll see where this goes..."

Events seemed to have become rather more dramatic in Fourier's imagination, but Ferris was not going to correct him. After all, it had probably been Ferris's own weeping that had inspired this flight of fancy.

"Though thrilled to have accomplished my goal, I collapsed from fatigue, and what happened after that, I know not. What became of Crusch? Did she say anything about me?"

"She lay in bed, her pillow soaked with tears of regret over her loss to you. She might have said something about murdering you in your sleep..."

"Ha-ha-ha! An amusing diversion. But I know you're joking. Crusch would never say such a thing. She would certainly challenge me face-to-face. A simple matter, to see through your little japes... You are joking, aren't you?"

"If you're going to act that confident, at least stay confident until you're finished. It was a joke, though." He could never deceive someone who had known Crusch even longer than he had. With a small sigh, Ferris winked at Fourier, who wouldn't stop glancing at him for confirmation.

"Relax, Your Highness," he said. "Lady Crusch knows she was beaten. I think she sees you in a new light, the way you overcame her through sheer determination. Although she hasn't spoken of you once since then."

"She's angry—I knew it! What do you think?! Tell me what you think, Ferris!" He leaned over and shook the cat-boy emphatically.

"Eek, don't pull on me, you'll stretch my clothes out! I know it's just the two of us, but—!" Ferris shoved the prince away and hugged himself, his eyes swimming. A shaken Fourier sat back, and an awkward silence descended on the room.

"I'm called here, and what do I find? Ferris, you must not tease His Highness so cruelly." The door opened, and Crusch peeked in.

"Eeeewhooa!" Fourier let out an unusual cry and spun around. Ferris, who found this rather gratifying, waved at Crusch.

"Right on time, Lady Crusch. We were waiting for you!"

"You told me to come in without announcing myself. Was this your goal? Your Highness, I see Ferris has been most disrespectful to you. But are you so astonished to see my face?"

"No! It has nothing to do with your face! Which is beautiful as always! A picture! You should be more confident; I give you my royal guarantee, you look wonderful!"

"You are too kind, Your Highness. Though I am a touch embarrassed."

Crusch wore a wry smile; Fourier had red cheeks. Despite their sword fight, despite the two weeks of separation, now things went on as if they had never been apart.

"Looks like Ferri's done it again… My skill as a strategist is almost scary…"

"What are you muttering about over there, Ferris? And you, Crusch!" Fourier stood and pointed at his friend, who stood just inside the door. "Why do you still wear men's clothes even now? Where's your skirt?! Your dress?! What about our promise that you would adorn your hair with precious gems, surround yourself with flowers?"

"Your Highness, Your Highness, that promise is taking on a life of its own!" Ferris protested.

"My apologies, Your Highness. It is very true that the events of two weeks past remain firmly in my heart. But I have spent so long in men's outfits. I hope you will give me some time to ready myself. And of course, for my birthday celebration tomorrow—I do promise."

"Hmm… I have your word on that?"

"That depends on whether you believe I'm one to betray my promises to Your Highness."

Fourier was left with no choice but to back down. Crusch sat easily next to Ferris, across from Fourier, who was adjusting his position on the sofa.

"You've very much put your heart into this, haven't you, Your Highness?" she said. "I don't just mean our battle. You're staying overnight here."

"I was just terrified I might oversleep if I stayed at the castle, so instead I couldn't get to sleep at all! Here at the mansion, I'll have plenty of time no matter how late I sleep. How's that for a bit of princely wisdom?"

"Seems like overkill. Like planning to meet up with someone and then camping out there the day before," Ferris said lightly, earning a smirk from Crusch. The bond among the three of them was such that not even a turning point like the sword battle would keep them from getting along.

"On that note, what do you plan to do for the birthday celebration, Ferris?" Fourier asked. "Going to wear a dress?"

"Oh my, Your Highness, is Lady Crusch not enough for you? Got your eye on Ferri, too? Anyway, sorry. You can look forward to finding out *tomorrow*."

"A dress, yes... A dress... Say, Ferris, my father seemed more than happy with the dress you picked out, but I worry it won't quite be appropriate for me..."

"Lady Crusch, we need you to have the best dress, and the best jewelry, and just all-around look the best you can! And believe me, it'll be great!"

"Yes! Crusch! I'll be savoring the anticipation!"

The combined enthusiasm of the cat-boy and the prince finally overcame Crusch's objection. Her amber eyes turned to look out the window, presenting her face in a somehow transient-looking profile. Ferris naturally followed her gaze, and looked up at the night sky.

The pale, cold half-moon floated against a field of stars. The next day would be Crusch's birthday. The moonlight shimmered weirdly, as if presaging a great many changes to come.

7

The next day, Crusch Karsten's seventeenth birthday was blessed with clear skies.

"Mm! What beautiful weather!" Ferris laughed as he pulled back the shades and opened the window. The breeze caught his shoulder-length hair. He was up earlier than usual, and the morning sky was clear and cool. The night before had been spent talking late into the wee hours with Crusch and Fourier, but he was so excited for today that he barely felt tired. He was completely awake and ready to go, more than he'd been on any other morning.

"Perfect for a birthday party!" he said merrily. "Looks like the weather gods are working overtime." Quickly, he took off his pajamas and pulled on his feminine clothes, just as always. The white ribbons in his hair made his outfit complete. He gave himself a once-over in the mirror, then veritably danced out into the hallway, where he found the servants already at their work.

"Gooood morning to you!" he chirped.

"Ah, Master Ferris, good morning. You're up early today."

"Well, it's a very important day. Need to put my best foot forward, you know? And you're still all up even earlier."

"It is our job, sir. And you aren't the only one looking forward to today. We want to make sure everything is perfect." The elderly steward smiled. Ferris had known him for quite a while, and the normally reticent man looked about as happy as Ferris had ever seen him.

The other servants around were the same; although they were at work, not one of them looked unhappy. That was just how much the object of today's festivities was beloved by all.

"But! But I love Lady Crusch just as much as anyone here! I'll do anything I can to help—just tell me what needs doing!"

"How enthusiastic. I'm sure there are plenty of little chores you could do…"

No one was so insensitive as to suggest that Ferris should avoid menial labor just because he was a close personal attendant of Crusch's. They saw how excited he was and were kind enough to let him help. Ferris resolved to repay them by working as hard as he could.

The birthday party was scheduled to start that evening. Guests were expected to arrive in the hours before that, so all the preparations for the party had to be completed before noon. Of course, most of the work had been done in the days prior, but there were some final details to be settled, including the serving order of the food, along with who would do what when.

"I can't wait to see Lady Crusch's dress tonight," one of the servants said.

"I couldn't agree more. I had begun to doubt I would live to see her in such an outfit."

The long-standing servants and the old steward laughed together, but Ferris found himself feeling self-reproachful. When he and Crusch had made that promise as children, he had never thought about how many people might quietly be hurt by it.

They weren't intentionally being critical of him, of course. They were simply overjoyed to see Crusch, whom they had cared for since she was a little girl, in women's clothing.

"I'm so sorry, everyone."

It was a very modest form of atonement: Ferris spoke his apology only under his breath and only out of his own feelings of guilt. But it inspired him to redouble his efforts, and when the servants saw him, they knew they couldn't let themselves be outdone. So they all threw themselves more and more into their own tasks, and the preparations were finished well ahead of schedule. All that remained was to wait for the guests, and nightfall.

Or anyway, so it should have been, if nothing had happened.

Just as Ferris entered the front hall, he heard a voice:

"I must speak to Duke Karsten! I have a message of utmost importance!"

As Ferris went to ask what chore he should tackle next, he found a group of servants circled around someone. He went over to get a better look and saw a young man, out of breath and sweating profusely. He appeared to have come running at breakneck speed from his carriage, and every inch of him screamed trouble was afoot. He wasn't hurt, but was clearly exhausted, heavily burdened both emotionally and physically.

"I must tell him what brings me here…!"

"Tell us, then. What is going on?"

As the young man fell to his knees, he happened to look up at Ferris. The cat-boy gulped when he saw the ghastly appearance of his face.

Shuddering and fearful, the young man said, "Demon beasts have appeared on Foutour Plain—massive bunnies!"

8

"Giant Rabbits have appeared, have they?" Meckart sighed as he received the news. "What a stroke of bad luck…"

About ten people were squeezed into the duke's office, looking worriedly at each other. All of them were Meckart's trusted subordinates, people who had arrived at the mansion early in anticipation of Crusch's birthday celebration. But no one could have known that the happy meeting would turn into an emergency council.

"Bad luck indeed, but the silver lining is that we were all here already. The first moments of a demon beast attack are the most crucial. We will be able to respond as quickly as possible."

"As ever, I am saved by a retainer who knows how to look on the bright side," Meckart said. "To begin with, I want to know how things stand. Any damage or injuries? Can you tell me?"

"Y-yes, sir." The young man was absolutely petrified to be standing before not only the pillars of the ducal house but also Duke Karsten himself. But he wanted to fulfill his duty, and Meckart and the others nodded along as he explained.

Centuries before, a witch had created a variety of demonic monsters—and Giant Rabbits were reputed to be among the three most powerful of them. The very name portended destruction.

The White Whale. The Black Serpent. The Giant Rabbits. They were sometimes treated like natural disasters, and they were so overwhelmingly destructive that entire nations had dispatched forces to defeat them to no avail. That these creatures had survived such determined efforts to exterminate them hinted at just how dangerous they were.

Today, Giant Rabbits had appeared on Foutour Plain, a wild area on the edge of the Karsten domain.

"The first people to notice the rabbits were a group of trappers in a nearby forest. They were trying to get pelts from an animal that can be found there called the ubzus when the rabbits ambushed them."

"Poetic justice, one might say. What happened to them?"

"The herd ate most of them, including their leader. The only survivor was a young man who had stayed with the dragon carriage. He worked his way back to the nearest village, and that was when we first heard what had happened."

Meckart's face darkened at the young man's report. "He went to a village...? And what became of that village?"

"Forgive us for not consulting you, my lord, but we packed all the villagers into the local dragon carriages and evacuated them. Including the young survivor, sir. My father, the village chief, sent me here to inform you."

Meckart nodded at the terrified young man. "I see. A wise decision. I shall remember your father, and you." Then he turned to his advisers. "I believe the first order of business should be to contain the damage the rabbits are causing. Hopefully only the one village at most will be destroyed. Gentlemen, what do you think?"

One of the men, middle-aged and with a thoughtful look on his face, raised his hand. "This young man's village made an excellent choice. Perhaps the best move would be to expand the scale of the evacuation to other nearby villages and keep the Giant Rabbits under observation. If the rumors about the ways of demon beasts can be relied on, we need not provoke them and deliberately let them know where there is prey to be found."

So the first suggestion was to avoid combat. A grim-faced man offered a counterargument. "That would only work if the rabbits remain satisfied with their current situation, which is an awfully optimistic assumption. What if they destroy the woods and the villages and still aren't sated? What then? If the herd scatters, we'll never be able to deal with it."

"What do you propose we do, then?"

"We must take the initiative. I request the Karsten domain muster a unit to exterminate the creatures. We must not cede any part of our lands to some beast, not even the untamed wilderness. Not to mention that if we stay shut up in the heartland while the people are terrorized, it will undermine ducal authority."

"We have nothing to gain by defeating these creatures."

"We have nothing to gain, but we do have something to lose. The people's trust, and our own pride."

Those for battle and those against it clashed, and neither opinion was wrong, exactly. Both had merit. That was why a decision had to be made.

"—"

Meckart remained silent. His own thoughts were as much in conflict as his advisers'. And at that moment, a hand went up that seemed out of place. It was none other than the person who had brought the young man to the office and then quietly stayed to listen to the proceedings—Ferris.

"Um, Lord Meckart? Sorry. I know it's not really my place, but..."

"...Ah, Felix. Yes, thank you. What is it? What do you want to ask?"

"It's about Lady Crusch's birthday party. I know we have to cancel it, but the guests will be arriving soon. What should we tell them?"

"That... That's a good question. Another problem to resolve. Terribly unlucky, all of this." Meckart chewed on his lip. But then he suddenly looked up. "Speaking of Crusch, where is she? You haven't spoken to her about this, have you?"

"Don't worry, sir. I brought the messenger straight here... I suspect Lady Crusch is busy entertaining Prince Fourier right now. At least we can thank His Highness for that."

"I see, that's good. That gives me all the more esteem for His Highness."

A palpable relief shot through the room. Meckart was not the only one to relax; everyone there who knew Crusch shared the feeling. If the young woman, with her sense of pride in her noble house and her devotion to chivalry, found out that the people were threatened by demon beasts, it would be hard to stop her from flying out the door to save them. All those who were familiar with her passionate nature could tell it only made sense to ensure she got no wind of this situation.

"—Now then, time is short. We don't have long to spend fretting and arguing," Meckart said.

His momentary smile of relief had become a frown again, and he adjusted his position in his chair. This caused everyone else to straighten up as well. They attended silently to his words.

"First, evacuate all towns and villages near Foutour Plain. Send our own dragon carriages to help, as well as those from any other villages who can spare them. Evacuate all the people and as many of their possessions as is feasible. When the rabbits come through, nothing will be left. You must ensure there is absolutely no looting. Bardok, you're in charge of the evacuation effort."

"Yes, sir!"

"Further, set up a combat perimeter around the Foutour forest. We can't have the rabbits destroying an area we haven't even cultivated yet. However, our objective is not extermination. It is simply damage control. So don't put too many hot-blooded young soldiers on the front line, hmm?"

"Understood, sir. Who will be in command?"

"The old coward who's charged with looking after this domain," Meckart said with a shrug. "Ahh, no rest for the weary, is there?" His advisers smiled at one another. And then, as the room grew increasingly tense, Meckart turned to Ferris. "I have an order for you, too,

Felix. Do not let Crusch find out about the rabbits. And make sure her birthday party comes off flawlessly."

"You're not going to cancel it, sir?!"

"Whatever happens on Foutour Plain, it's not likely to affect the mansion. And our guests have gone to all the trouble of coming here."

"But! But! Without you here, Lord Meckart, it'll be awfully hard to hide that something's going on..."

"I'm not telling you to keep the secret with your life. If you can just keep it quiet for this evening, that will be enough. I assume Crusch will find out by tomorrow. I would appreciate if you would be so kind as to bear her wrath for me this time."

Meckart spoke lightly, but Ferris could see further argument would be futile. He pursed his lips and made his displeasure obvious, glaring at Meckart.

"You'd better promise to bear it with me, sir. Otherwise, I'll be awfully upset."

"Gracious, you're most intimidating, Felix. But in the event I can't keep that promise..."

"...then it had better be because you underestimated the demon beasts too much and died fighting one or something."

"My boy, you do say the most inauspicious things!"

As they bantered back and forth, Ferris found himself resigned. In stubbornness if nothing else, father really was like daughter.

"All right, sir. I, Ferris, will stake my very life on making this party a success. I'll be praying for your good fortune in battle, Lord Meckart." He offered a curtsy along with his wish for Meckart's good fortune in battle.

The duke nodded at him, then began to discuss the next steps with his advisers. Ferris slipped quietly out of the office, and hurried to rejoin the deeply disturbed servants. They would have to move quickly now.

—For they were about to try to pull off the biggest lie of their lives.

9

Several hours after Meckart had left the estate, Ferris, outfitted in a resplendent dress, was in the party hall with the biggest smile he could muster.

"Welcome, thank you so much for coming."

It was evening, and well-appointed dragon carriages arrived at the Karsten mansion one after another. Their riders—nobles and VIPs of every kind—looked every bit as impressive as their carriages. They were the lucky few to be invited to the birthday party of the duke's daughter, and as such, they displayed a sophistication that would have left the average person breathless. Luckily for Ferris, he lived at the estate of the very duke hosting the party and was close friends with an actual member of the royal family.

Having said that, the woman he knew spent her time looking very grave and generally not being sociable, so whether that experience would help him today was questionable. Regardless, Ferris greeted each of the guests and showed them to their places with exactly the right amount of deference and respect, never obsequious or impudent. As he stood ready to receive visitors in his blue dress, even those who didn't know him stopped when they saw him, some looking as if they might fall head over heels in love.

At the moment, he was gently rebuffing the advances of some well-heeled young man.

"To think I overlooked one as beautiful as you... I can only castigate myself for this lapse in judgment!"

"Oh, you're sweet. But you mustn't be so lavish. The young woman with you is giving me the most terrible glare..." As the young man walked away, Ferris gave the couple a wink. No trouble. It was all so easy. The least he could do was keep a smile on his face for the night.

"Excuse me," someone was saying to the nattily dressed maid beside him, his fellow receptionist. "Might I inquire as to the whereabouts of Duke Karsten? I should like to ask him to say a few words of introduction before we announce the woman of the hour, Miss Crusch."

"I'm terribly sorry," the maid replied, "but Lord Meckart is indisposed at the moment... I think he'll be about shortly, but I must ask you to wait until then."

"What a shame, and on such an important day. I understand. Please forgive my impertinent request."

Since the moment guests started arriving, there had been no end of people asking after Duke Meckart. It was only natural. Only a handful of people had been chosen to attend the party. Not counting the members of the household, most of the people at the estate were probably there to check in on Meckart or otherwise ingratiate themselves to him. They would of course be disappointed to find him absent.

"Well, if mew ask them, they'll say they're not upset, though..."

"Master Ferris, be careful. You're frowning."

"Oops! I'll have to be meow careful." Ferris's muttering to himself had drawn the maid's attention. She must have felt the same way he did, because she didn't chastise him for what he actually said. As much as they were used to it, it still hurt those who simply wished the best for the household.

Still, emotions of every kind could be observed among the guests. It was just as well. When the star of the party showed up in her most beautiful dress, they would all feel nothing but admiration.

"Heh-heh... Heh-heh-heh!"

"Master Ferris, I don't like the look in your eye..."

"Oops! Have to be meow careful." He stuck out his tongue in embarrassment, having now been called out twice, albeit for different offenses.

The party was only just starting, and the guests were still arriving. The introduction of the evening's star, Crusch, would be the main event. Until then, she would have to remain in her rooms. She would no doubt be bored, but Ferris couldn't help a feeling of relief.

Thanks to her special blessing, it was hard to keep secrets from Crusch for long. Her blessing of wind reading allowed her to interpret the wind—not just the actual breeze but the air in a room or surrounding a person, the aura that communicated their emotions. She was quite good at it, and it made her very difficult to deceive.

Although, with Crusch being as upright as she was, she sometimes let herself be misled about minor daily matters.

"You can't treat Lady Crusch like an ordinary person...although I guess that's part of why I love her so much..."

"Master Ferris, there's drool dangling from your mouth..."

"Oops! Have to be meow careful."

That was three strikes, and the maid was not looking very pleased. Ferris knew it was silly to be so anxious over a little bit of banter, but it also looked likely to be a long night.

Okay. Time to put the smile back on his face and throw himself into receiving guests again...

"Ferris! Ferris, are you here?!"

As if in response to his thoughts, just as he was trying to turn himself into a smiling machine, a voice in the distance called his name. There was no doubt who it was—this particular manner of calling for attention could belong to only one person.

Even as Ferris registered who the owner of the voice must be, the crowd parted. There, raising his hand and calling in that familiar, carrying voice, was Fourier.

He was dressed in lustrous clothing, his golden hair and scarlet eyes both sparkling. As people realized the fourth prince of the nation was standing among them, heads began to bow.

"Hm? Oh, stop that, you're all much too formal. I am a magnanimous and friendly young man. And I am not the center of attention on this night. Go over to the young lady's dais and enjoy the party." Fourier threatened to distract from the point of the evening by provoking the surprise show of reverence. Then again, since he was in fact a prince, the display of respect for him should not have been surprising—but his everyday attitude made it easy to forget that.

"His Highness... Now there's someone else you can't handle like an ordinary person..."

"What are you muttering about, Ferris? Um..." Fourier walked through the now-parted crowd, straight up to the maid and the boy. He looked Ferris and his dress up and down, then gave a deep and genuinely appreciative nod. "As beautiful in a dress as always! Be it a birthday party or a matchmaking meeting, I never get tired of seeing you like this! You have my enthusiastic praise!"

"Ha-ha-ha, thank you very much. You look quite dashing yourself, Your Highness."

"Don't I, though? I wracked my brain deciding what to wear tonight. I needed something appropriate for Crusch's birthday party, something in which I could hold my head up high beside her. What do you think, Ferris?"

"An excellent job, my lord. You practically look a man."

"Heh-heh! Yes, I think so, too." He put his hands on his hips, puffed out his chest, and generally looked terribly pleased with himself. It was very much like him not to notice the jibe in Ferris's words; this was part of his charm.

Fourier's arrival had diffused some of the building anticipation for the star of the party, and Ferris patted himself on the chest, glad for the breather.

"But what have you been doing all this time, Your Highness? I certainly haven't been able to entertain you. Were you in Lady Crusch's rooms or something?"

"Ah, if only I could have been. But I could hardly spend all day in the chambers of the most important woman of the evening. Let me be clear, I did not withdraw because of the overpowering stares of the maids who were trying to help the young lady change! Nor did I wander the mansion at loose ends afterward, either!"

"Of course not, Your Highness. I'm glad you were able to find me."

"Yes, a great relief. Frankly, I was getting rather lonely."

The honest, almost naïve remark warmed Ferris, and he was surprised to find a genuine smile on his face. It was the first real expression of happiness he had made since the party started. The smiling and greeting had gone on so long, he had begun to think he would never be able to make a real smile again.

Not that he disliked smiling, but it was so much easier when he was calm inside. He just wished he could share his burden with somebody there, even if telling the star herself was out of the question…

"Oh well. That's why they trusted me to watch things here—because we can't."

Despite his best efforts, he found this little bit of self-pity slipping out, and he used a rueful grin to cover it. When he thought of what Meckart was doing—why the duke couldn't be there to greet the guests—he knew he could hardly feel sorry for himself. And anyway, this was the job he had been entrusted with. The important task the duke had entrusted to Felix Argyle.

"That's all very well. But is Crusch not to be introduced yet?"

"We're saving the best for last. Your Highness, you look as excited as a child."

"Well, what do you want? I am excited! Aren't you?"

"I accompanied her to the fitting, so I already got to see. Ah! Lady Crusch was so beautiful in her dress, *meow*! A goddess among us!"

"Grr! That's not fair, Ferris! In fact, it's downright cruel! Remember who did all the work so that we could see Crusch in her dress."

Fourier crossed his arms and gave an angry snort. Ferris desperately held in his laughter.

"It was all thanks to you, of course, Your Highness. Lord Meckart knows that, and all the servants, and of course I do, too. We're all grateful to you. Thank you very much! Heh-heh."

"Hm, are you, now? Well, that's good. A man must be generous of heart. I forgive you! Is my magnanimity not as vast as the sky? What do you think?"

"Oh, it certainly is. Your magnanimity is like a vast blue sky." This wasn't flattery; Ferris really did feel that way. In fact, he thought of Fourier as the sun in that sky. And that would make Crusch the wind, the invisible breeze that blew past that sun and through the sky. What did that make him, then? He could wish to be at least a cloud carried through the sky by that wind.

"Your Highness?"

As Ferris stood, lost in these thoughts, he suddenly found a hand in front of his face. It belonged to Fourier. The prince looked into Ferris's subtly darkened face, then gave his usual bright smile.

"This is no time to be looking unlike yourself, Ferris. This is all because you've been forcing yourself to smile, going this way and that like a puppet on a string. Take my hand—we're going to dance."

"...I'm no good at smiling, huh?"

"Oh, I wouldn't say that. I just thought you looked different from usual. How long have we known each other? Five years already? It's only natural that I should know my friend's smile inside and out."

"Do you consider me a friend, Your Highness?" Ferris replied, raising an eyebrow at the unexpected word. That caused the prince's handsome face to take on a serious cast. He gave Ferris a questioning look.

"It's been five years, we don't hesitate to converse with each other, we even share our little secrets... If this is not friendship, then I have no friends. What have you considered me all this time, Ferris?"

"Well, I... It's just, I would hate to be presumptuous..."

"Hah! I am giving you permission here and now. There is no presumption. Ferris, you are my friend. Stand proudly beside me and share my joy in all things. Yes? Is it a promise?"

It was classic Fourier: forceful and without much consideration for either the other person's situation or his own station. But the words were like salvation for Ferris, and he was deeply moved. He looked at the ground, suddenly finding himself on the verge of tears. He took several deep breaths. Only after he had calmed the wave of emotion did he look up. There was a teasing smile on his face.

"Then, Your Highness, perhaps I could ask you for one song before our beloved Lady Crusch arrives?"

"Seeing as how I already asked you—yes, of course. You can dance the woman's part, can't you? I certainly don't know how."

"Relax. Actually, the woman's part is the only part I know."

"Well and good, then—because I only know the man's part!" Fourier puffed out his chest, and this time Ferris really couldn't resist a burst of laughter. Then he looked at the maid beside him; she gave him a forceful wink as if to say, *Let me handle the guests.* He nodded, grateful for her thoughtfulness.

"Let us dance, then! Follow me!"

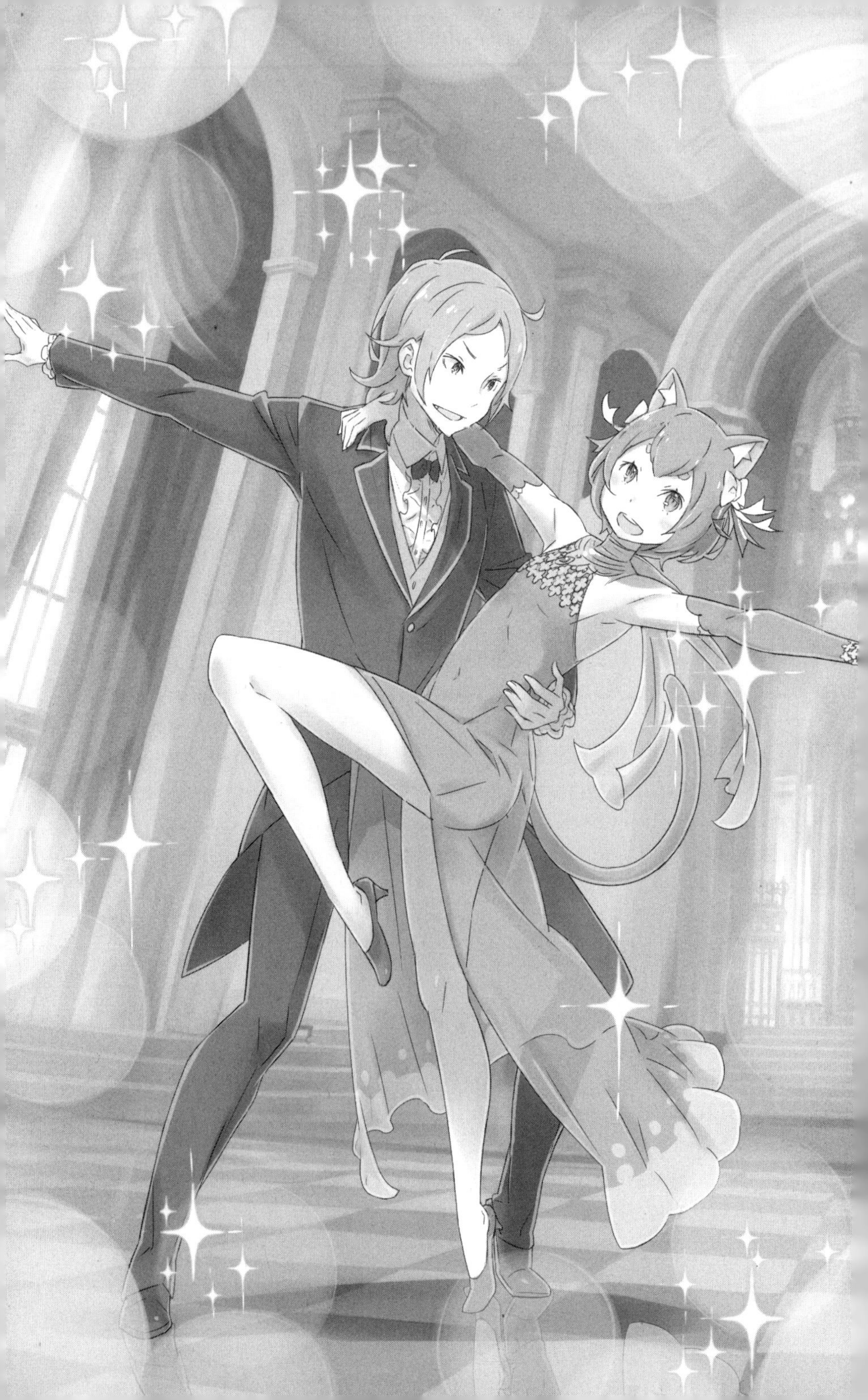

"Of course, my lord."

Fourier was full of enthusiasm, yet when he held out his hand, the gesture was gentle. He escorted Ferris to the dance floor, looking tall and brave. At the sight of him, Ferris put a hand to his chest, his heart just a little bit lighter.

"By the way, Your Highness, you're wrong about how long we've known each other. It hasn't been five years. It's been six."

"Hmm? Is that right? Hmm. Well, it matters not. In light of how long we will know each other, it is but a small thing. Don't you think so?"

"Gosh… Well, if Your Highness says so."

At the middle of the dance floor, they faced each other and joined hands. Ferris suppressed a smile, but the edges of it tugged at his lips. Fourier saw it and smiled, too, and then the music began.

They started dancing, tracing the steps in the dazzling orange light of the sinking sun.

Night was falling, and they waited anxiously for the person they were all here to celebrate. The birthday party was just beginning.

10

"Your Highness, I never knew you were so well built. I can feel my pulse racing."

"Can't you, though? It's because I am such a fine young man. But, um, stop blushing and snuggling up to me like that. It gives me a very strange feeling!"

"Aww… Weren't you telling the truth when you said we were friends, Your Highness?"

"Of course I was! B-but I'm concerned that if things go any further we're not going to be just friends anymore! Stop teasing me! Who do you take me for?!"

They had finished their dance and left the floor to thunderous applause. They were walking through a corridor of the mansion, heading for Crusch's rooms, Ferris teasing Fourier along the way.

He had nearly forgotten his assignment, caught up in the dance as he was, but he was supposed to be making sure that the party went smoothly. He was surprised by how much he felt he had been able to contribute to that goal. The next objective was to make sure Crusch was properly dressed. She would soon need to be ready to be presented to the party.

"As a man, Your Highness, you can't come in the room," Ferris told Fourier. "You'll see her dress when everyone else does. Come on, shoo!"

"What? And to think, you were treating me so very kindly up until this moment. Anyway, I had no intention of trying to force my way into Crusch's rooms. I only thought she might be nervous and wanted to be here to comfort her."

It sounded like an excuse, but Ferris gave in to the nobility of it and permitted the prince to accompany him. Anyway, it was certainly true that Crusch might be a bit anxious about appearing in front of a crowd in a dress. It was possible that having Fourier along would not be a complete waste.

With this in mind, the two of them arrived at Crusch's rooms. Ferris knocked on the door.

"Lady Cruuuusch! It's Ferris. Can I come in?"

"—Ferris. I've been waiting for you. Enter."

The same masculine voice as always greeted him and invited him to come in. He and Fourier entered the room—and then went completely stiff.

"I see you have His Highness with you. That is unexpected."

Crusch was not in a dress, but in the military uniform they were so used to. No problem. She just needed to take off the men's clothing and change into her dress. The issue was what was at her feet.

A butler was sitting there, bound and gagged.

"L-Lady Crusch?! What's going on here?!"

"I understand your surprise, but stay calm. Maloney is unharmed. I only tied him up because I couldn't have him getting in my way. I'm sure the next maid to come by will set him loose."

"You tied him up. Why did you tie him up?"

"You know I'm bad at beating around the bush, so let me be direct. Where has my father gone?"

"—"

As Crusch's amber eyes bored into him, Ferris's throat constricted with terror. His reaction only made Crusch more certain. She put a hand on the window of her room. They were only on the first floor; she could climb out easily. And she was obviously about to.

"W-wait, milady! Where are you going? And how will you know to go there?"

"My destination is Foutour Plain. My father is headed there because of a disaster... Demon beasts. He left the mansion with Bardok and some other confidantes, intending to arrive there tonight. Am I wrong?"

Terror piled together for Ferris; he could only tremble. He couldn't imagine anyone had let the secret slip to Crusch. But she had such a clear grasp of the circumstances that a leak seemed the only possibility. How had it happened?

"I knew it would be impossible to get everything from one person. So I went one by one, piecing together the fragments of what each person knew. And you just gave me my proof, Ferris."

"Oops..."

"I will stand by my father's side. Perhaps I will not be any help. Perhaps they will mock me, saying I hadn't needed to come. But I must go. When our most loyal retainers gather to the lion crest, shall I be lolling about in a gown, waiting to hear what becomes of them? I shall not stand for it."

Of course she would say that. They had known that was how she would react the moment she heard of it, and that was why everyone in the household had worked so hard to keep it from her. But the young woman's singular genius and exceptional sharpness had undone all their efforts.

"Wait a moment, Crusch! Who said you could do such a thing?" Fourier called out from beside Ferris, who had been cowed into silence.

Of course, Crusch was not able to ignore him. "Your Highness..."

she said, her tone more subdued than before. "Please, forgive me. I must do this in order to be who I am. I swear I will make up for being so rude to all my guests. But I am a member of the ducal family. You must let me go."

"Don't try to rush the discussion. It isn't a question of going or not going at the moment. First and foremost—I don't have the slightest idea what's going on! Isn't Meckart in bed with a fever? That's what I heard. Although, looking at Ferris, I don't suppose it's true." He glanced at the cat-boy, whose shoulders were trembling, out of the corner of his eye. "Well, regardless." He shook his head. "I don't know exactly what Ferris and Meckart are planning, but it is you I have trouble forgiving, Crusch. What has led you so astray?"

"Astray, Your Highness…?"

"If you truly have pride in the blood of the servant of the Lion King that flows through you, it is your duty not to make a waste of today's festivities. It isn't yours to decide which is more important, the battlefield or the birthday party. Nor is it you who will ultimately determine your reputation—I won't let you forget your vow to see this through."

"—"

Crusch's face tensed slightly at Fourier's stern words. Ferris, looking on, didn't fully understand whatever it was that most seemed to strike home with her. A most important thing seemed to have been communicated privately between Fourier and Crusch alone.

"Forget…? No, it is as Your Highness says. But I… I must…"

"Lady Crusch…"

Ferris knew all too well the pain, the wave of emotion that swelled in Crusch's heart and threatened to swallow her. Her pride as a member of the ducal household now warred with the layers of her identity that she had built up. Both were indispensable parts of her; without either one of them, Crusch could not be Crusch.

"Your Highness, are you telling me to stay here, put a fake smile on my face, and…?"

"—? No, I'm saying no such thing. I think you're still misunderstanding something."

"What?"

Fourier's perplexed expression evoked sounds of surprise from both Crusch and Ferris. Fourier's eyes sparkled at the unusual reaction of both attendant and mistress, and then he gave one of his toothy smiles.

"Listen. What I am trying to say is not that you must protect your position as a member of the duke's family. It is that you must protect who and what you are as Crusch Karsten, the duke's daughter."

"What do you mean by that, Your Highness?"

"You wish to support your father, and you must go through with this birthday celebration. Both duties are equally demanded of Crusch Karsten, the duke's daughter. And she must not fail in either but see them both through, just like the you that I know."

"—?!"

Fourier spoke with all the confidence of someone who was saying something very simple. And while he seemed to think he had given a fine bit of advice, the young woman listening to him looked troubled by this paradoxical opinion.

"Of course it would be ideal to do both," Crusch said. "But realistically...with my strength, I couldn't..."

"Wrong again. You have me. You have Ferris. You aren't alone."

"Your Highness..."

"Who hasn't been at a party where things didn't quite go according to schedule? What with all the celebrating and the drink... If the star of the show is a little late, the master of ceremonies will find some way to buy her time. Perhaps I could do a sword dance," Fourier said, striking a pose as if dancing with an invisible blade. This caused Crusch, who until that moment had been standing dumbfounded, to blink. Then a soft smile came over her face.

It was natural and beautiful enough to ensnare the hearts of both Ferris and Fourier.

"Your Highness's concern for me is a greater gift than any other.

Let my person and my heart be given utterly in loyalty to you. Thank you very, very much."

"Oh, stop, stop! I feel most awkward when you speak to me that way. You and I are friends. We mustn't let the little things worry us. More importantly—Ferris!"

"Er—yes, sir!" He straightened up as the prince abruptly called his name. Fourier gave him a pat on the shoulder.

"Crusch is going to do something foolish. And you are going to protect her. You are her knight, after all."

"I'm…Lady Crusch's knight?"

"A true knight must always be at his mistress's side and constantly act to keep her safe. I can think of no other knight for Crusch but you."

A thousand emotions overflowed within Ferris at those words.

His physical weakness had long ago caused him to give up hope of wielding the sword to protect Crusch. He had exchanged that dream for a promise with his lady, but today he had looked set to lose that promise. On this day, when it had seemed he had nowhere to turn and no one to look to, he would receive a new vow instead.

"But I can barely hold a sword… Some knight I'd be."

"It is His Highness's will. As for the sword, let me wield it. I want you to be by my side, doing what only you can do. That is the only thing I ask of my knight."

Crusch's declaration sent a single hot tear rolling down Ferris's cheek. It felt as though it would sear him, and he quickly wiped it away. Then he turned to Fourier. He knew the prince so well, but now he looked at him with an even greater respect.

"Felix Argyle, acknowledging orders, Your Highness. I will protect Lady Crusch, without fail."

He made the most elaborate bow possible. Fourier nodded at him, then suddenly handed something to Crusch. He had specifically brought the object with him when he had heard that they were heading for Crusch's rooms.

"What is this, Your Highness?"

"You said my consideration is gift enough for you—but it isn't for me. Therefore, I have prepared a gift for you as well. I think it will suit you better than anything else."

It was a long, thin, but remarkably heavy package. Crusch's eyes went wide as she unwrapped it. She held a sword in her hands—one that was obviously masterwork quality.

"This is the best of all the blades in the royal armory. I asked Bordeaux to verify as much, so I'm sure it's true. It is my gift to you."

"Your Highness...I thought you were against my wielding the sword."

"What else could I do? All my life I have seen you with the sword in your hand. That is the you that I like best. I'm sure you'll be stunning in your dress...but in my mind, you will always be the girl who grips the sword." Fourier had begun to flush red from speaking his mind so directly. "If you won't give up the blade, then I hope I can at least choose the one you hold. Otherwise, you might never replace that dagger. And I might never get you back from the Lion King."

"My Lion King has always been... No," Crusch said, cutting herself off. She shook her head. Then she held the sword aloft and said, "I am grateful for this happiness. I promise I will do deeds with it worthy of your precious consideration for me."

"Good! ...Well, I admit that wasn't exactly how I expected you to accept it, but just the same!"

Fourier had, in his own way, done his utmost to communicate his feelings, but thanks to Crusch's obliviousness, they had gone straight over her head. Ferris felt bad about that, but his respect for Fourier grew even more.

Then Crusch said, "Well, let us go, Ferris. We shall help my father and return immediately to the party!"

"Yikes, sounds like a lot of work! And here Ferri's already been so busy all night..."

But Crusch was already out the window. Ferris hitched up his dress and followed her. He stepped out onto the grass where the night air enveloped him, and heaved a sigh, wondering what they were getting themselves into.

But the desperate feeling of isolation he had felt while trying to deceive his mistress was no more.

After he had seen the two of them safely away, the first thing Fourier did was close the window.

"I'm glad to have seen them off safely…but I never did figure out exactly what was going on. I wonder what it could be? Hmm…"

As he spoke, he knelt down so he was eye to eye with the butler, whom they had simply left there. First he took the gag out of the gratetul man's mouth.

"I need you to explain a few things to me. Then you and I will have to figure out how to get through these rather dire straits. As Crusch's representatives, we have a grave responsibility!"

And then he laughed merrily, as if this were just another perfectly normal night.

11

—The attendees of the party at the Karsten mansion were slowly growing disgruntled.

It was only natural. The celebration had started hours ago, it was already well into the night, and the mood was quite expectant. Now they were all waiting for the main event, the introduction of Crusch, the duke's daughter. And yet the crucial person utterly failed to appear. What was more, Meckart Karsten, the host of the party, was also nowhere to be seen, claiming illness. How could the invitees not feel a little put out?

"Inviting us to a party where neither the host nor the celebrant shows up—are they mocking us?" Although no one spoke too loudly, many made such remarks under their breath.

Despite the extreme difficulty of their position, the butlers and servants did their utmost to fulfill their duties for the sake of their master and mistress. This was loyalty of the highest order.

"Erk... Even with me at the helm, it could be difficult to draw things out much longer..."

Fourier alone among the guests knew what was really going on. He used his position and a few well-placed rumors to soothe the rising discontent of the guests, but it was getting more difficult. He could divert them with amateur sword dances and decent lyurilay performances only so many times.

This left him with only one choice, a secret art passed down in the royal line. Fourier would set aside his pride as a member of the royal family and perform the trick—but just as he was about to do so, a commotion ran through the hall. It appeared to originate with the guests near the door. Suddenly the vast portal opened, and someone entered. Her long green hair danced, and she looked startling and refreshing in her military uniform.

"It's Lady Crusch Karsten," someone said, proclaiming the beauty's name.

Crusch turned her amber eyes to the source of the voice. The person who had spoken stiffened, but she placed a hand over her chest and gave a single, elegant bow.

"Esteemed guests. I thank you from the bottom of my heart for coming all this way. And for the inconveniences we have imposed on you, let me apologize in place of the master of this house, Meckart."

The hint of surprise that ran through the room might have been due to the powerful resolve that was almost tangible in her gorgeous voice. This girl had only just turned seventeen, but her forthright attitude silenced even those who had been muttering before; they listened closely to her clear, resonant voice.

"If I could beg your further indulgence," Crusch went on, "I would ask that you be patient just a short while longer. I wish to make my official greeting to you all in clothing more suited to the occasion."

She stood straight and raised her head, taking in all those in the hall. Her gaze, as sharp as any blade, left the guests no choice but to accede in silence.

"My thanks—Ferris, come."

"Yes, ma'am."

A figure in a blue dress had appeared behind Crusch. This person, too, was quite beautiful. The figure's hair and the hem of the dress were both in rather bad shape, but neither attendant nor mistress seemed to notice. The two of them began to walk, and as if by some silent agreement, everyone made way for them.

Crusch advanced, dressed in her military clothes; all those she passed found themselves unconsciously straightening up. The jeweled sword at her waist seemed to express her very being.

The maids began following her as she went, and then they, Crusch, and her knight exited the party hall. No sooner had they done so than the hint of anxiousness vanished from the air, and everyone breathed a collective sigh of relief. All the guests looked at one another.

"I'd heard rumors about Lady Crusch, but…"

"They said she was mad for the sword, that she was a noblewoman who could outdo any man… So that's what they meant, ha-ha."

Small and trembling voices tried to make light of Crusch. But it was only a front, a way of pretending they had not just been overawed by a young woman—and those who spoke realized this best of all.

Those who had heard her voice and seen her walk by them were of one mind: the derisive talk of a girl obsessed with swords, of Meckart's prodigal daughter, was sheer nonsense. She fully deserved the seal of her family as she was every bit the lion. Crusch Karsten was a true heir to the ways of her house.

"—"

Many of the guests, properly astonished, felt that the party had been quite eventful enough. It was safe to say none of them were expecting a further shock. But they got one, when Crusch returned after changing her clothes.

"She's beautiful…" someone breathed.

No one knew who had spoken, not even the person who had whispered the words, so enraptured was everyone by the sight. Crusch entered the moonlit hall wearing a black dress. She had tied up her long green hair, and precious stones glittered here and there against her white skin. In her military outfit, she had seemed as sharp as her sword, but in an instant she had come to shine as bright as a gem in her dress. It seemed rude even to breathe in the presence of such a polished jewel.

The sound of her high-heeled shoes echoed as she walked, and the first place she went was to Fourier.

"Your Highness Fourier, my apologies for all the trouble I've caused you."

His arms crossed, the fourth prince drank in the sight of Crusch in her dress, then he nodded in satisfaction.

"I knew my judgment was correct. Crusch, you are truly stunning."

"Your Highness is too kind."

"I promise, it is no flattery. If I could, I would love to keep you all to myself right now. But I mustn't—best you show yourself to all those who have been waiting so anxiously for you."

With a hint of red in his cheeks, Fourier nodded at Crusch. Crusch nodded back and then turned, the hem of her dress flowing behind her. With every eye in the hall on her, she made a refined curtsy.

"Please be so kind as to forgive my rudeness earlier. And for the extra moment of time you granted me, I am most grateful. I offer you all my profound thanks."

"—"

"Thank you, each of you, for coming here today for me. I am seventeen now, too old to be seeking the indulgence of my father or any of you. Both today and in my life to this moment, I have been supported by a great many people in a great many things. So today, I would like to make a vow." She looked straight ahead, her voice unabashed, carrying to everyone in the room. "From this day I, Crusch Karsten, shall live as a noble, in a way that shall gratify the expectations of both my family name and all of you here today. You all are my witnesses. Watch me in the future, see if I break this promise or not."

"—"

"Forgive me once more for bothering you all with this. Please,

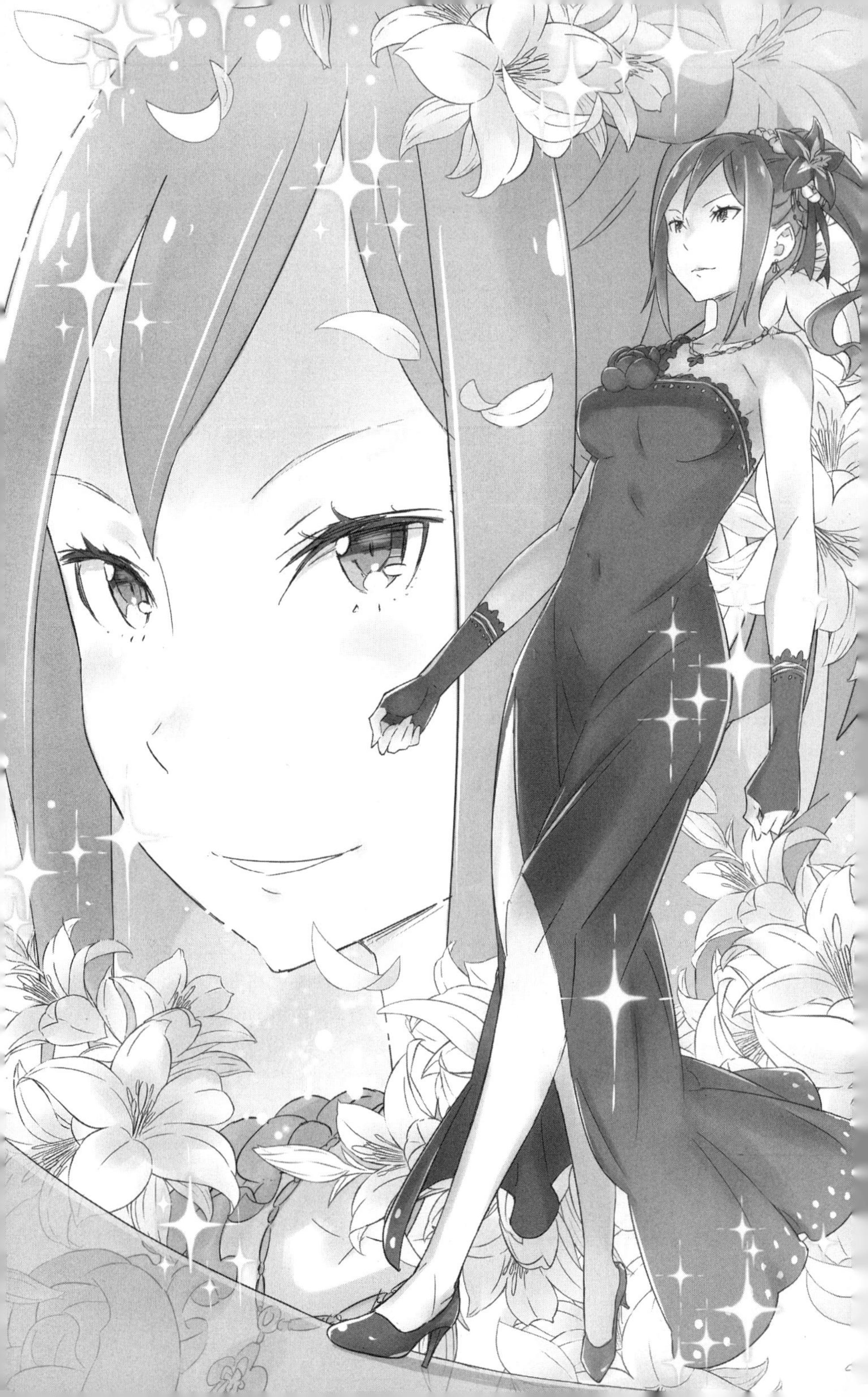

enjoy chatting with one another. I extend to you again my profound gratitude for joining me here today."

So her address ended, but there was no applause. Partly this was because people were overwhelmed. But partly, it was because Crusch's words and attitude had sought no acclamation.

Despite the mood, Crusch made her way back to Fourier and extended her hand. "Your Highness, may I have this dance?"

"Um..."

Fourier, every bit as taken with Crusch as everyone else around them, took a moment to respond. But soon his usual expression had returned, his eyes sparkling.

"Yes, certainly. But of course. As it was I who made you a woman, it is only fair that I should have the first dance."

"—?!"

He meant his words to be lighthearted, but they quickly produced misunderstanding and shock among those who heard them. Crusch only smiled gently and didn't try to rectify the misapprehensions as she and Fourier headed for the dance floor, hand in hand.

"Incidentally, I'll ask you what I asked Ferris—can you dance the woman's part? I'm afraid you can't expect me to do so."

"No worries, Your Highness. I know both the male and female parts. I would certainly be happy to let Your Highness dance the woman's steps, if you'd prefer...?"

"That might be interesting in its own way, but I don't think it would look right for you to be supporting me in your dress." Fourier offered a wry smile.

"In that case," Crusch replied, "I shall be the woman." Then she signaled the orchestra with a look, and they began to play.

A man and a woman dance under the moonlight, the party just as it should be.

—The guests will remember the steps the pair takes as their measured, elegant movements draw the tumultuous day to a gentle close.

12

"Still, I wasn't sure how things were going to turn out for a while there!" Ferris said.

It was the day after the party, and the main players had all gathered together. Crusch was seated next to Ferris, and he clung to her arm as she patted him on the head.

"I must have made you very anxious, Ferris," she said. "I'm sorry for that. Without you, who would have treated my father's battlefield wounds? You've done very well as my knight."

"Aww, you don't have to thank me. Just keep petting me..."

"Look at you two," Fourier grumbled. "One night away together and I can't pry you apart."

Ferris pursed his lips. "How long do you plan to stay here, anyway, Your Highness? The party's over. You don't have any reason to stick around. What about your job?"

"Try to chase me out, will you? Grr, when did my friends get like this?"

"Maybe exactly *because* you said I was your friend, Your Highness. Meowch!"

"Ferris, that will be enough. Don't disrespect His Highness," Crusch said with a firm tug on one of his ears. She nodded at Fourier. He crossed his arms at all this, but soon raised an eyebrow in Crusch's direction.

"There's something I want to say to you, too! First of all, why are you back in that outfit? What happened to your women's clothes? This isn't what you agreed."

"Your Highness, my promise to my father was that I would dress appropriately when we were in public and when it was otherwise necessary. He has allowed me to dress this way at home, and so I shall."

Crusch was back to her all-too-familiar military uniform. It in no way reduced her beauty, but those who had seen her the night before could not help longing for her to wear a dress again.

"Yes, and I'd like to talk to Meckart, too. I heard everything from your butler, Maloney, after you left, and I thought I would die of fright. Giant Rabbits! Were you able to drive them off in the end?"

"We sure were! Lady Crusch charged right in and gave those bunnies what they had coming! When Ferri got there, Lord Meckart was out of action with a battle wound, so I don't know what would have happened without her..."

"You overstate the matter, Ferris. Even without me, Bardok and the others would have taken care of things. If there is anything to be proud of, it's that my blade was of some small use, as was your healing." Crusch attempted to brush off his praise, but Ferris was still very proud of what she had done.

In reality, Meckart had discovered his own powerlessness the hard way. All the demon and non-demon beasts that normally lived on Foutour Plain had lost their homes to the Giant Rabbits and were running rampant. That was when he had received his wound. They had later made contact with Crusch, and her support and careful judgment had been crucial in pulling victory from the jaws of defeat.

Above all, everyone who had been part of that battle would speak of Crusch's sword technique—the skill that would later be called "One Blow, One Hundred Felled."

By the time the party had ended the night before, Ferris had already begun to hear the appellation "the Valkyrie of the Karsten Lands" applied to her. He thought it was a very appropriate nickname.

"All the same, it remains that I defied orders. My father shouted at me until his throat was raw. And I'm once again forbidden my sword and my land dragon."

"Even though Lord Meckart broke his promise, too... Well, that's a dad for you!" Ferris commented.

"There are a few things I myself would like to say to him once he's recovered," Crusch agreed. "Until then, I will get a little taste of my father's work."

Meckart had decided to vacate the mansion for a few days while his wounds healed. During that time, it fell to Crusch to administer the ducal domain. Her eyes suggested she rather looked forward to it.

"I like the expression on your face," Fourier said.

Crusch's eyes went wide with surprise, then she smiled. "Yes, perhaps it is a good look. Last night I had some experiences that would normally be difficult to gain in a number of ways. I suppose Father wouldn't be happy to hear me say this, but I feel as though yesterday's offense finally allowed me to become myself." Her face was as clear as a fine day as she described her feelings. Her smile was perfect, and Fourier was utterly captivated. As the prince worked his mouth, trying to speak, Ferris got a mischievous gleam in his eye and gave Crusch's arm an especially tight squeeze.

"And! And, you said wearing a dress wasn't so bad, didn't you?!"

"I was somewhat anxious before I put it on, but when I tried it, I found it could have been worse. From now on... Well, I suppose I could use such a thing to sleep in."

"I think that's perfect! Ferri is happy to dance with you in your usual clothes, but if we could both be in dresses, that would be ameowzing!"

"That's something that bothered me! Should a woman in a dress really know both parts? Or...wait, do I have that backward? Should a man in a dress know... Hm? What...? What am I even asking?!"

Fourier had managed to confuse himself with his own outburst. Crusch and Ferris looked at him and sighed in unison, but this only caused him to laugh once more.

"There's a good deal to be done yet before we can say all's well that ends well, but the better part of this affair has been settled. And that will do for now!"

"I love how Your Highness is always looking on the bright side. Ferri might fall for you yet!"

"Ha-ha-ha! That is one of my good points. Um, but don't cuddle up too close. Stop that! Don't confuse me! Stop making those adorable faces at me!"

As Ferris snuggled up to the prince, Fourier struggled to muster his self-control. Crusch watched them both fondly, then let out a small breath. "I really am blessed beyond measure—I wonder if I'll ever be able to repay this happiness," she murmured. She sounded profoundly moved, as if she feared that she had been given too much.

—It was a mere six months after these events that Crusch Karsten took over the position of duke from her father, Meckart.

She became immensely busy, and the three of them had less and less time to sit and laugh together.

Crusch would find herself returning to this day over and over again.

But at that moment, all of this was still in the future.

<END>

FELIX ARGYLE'S CURSE

1

The royal guard were the idols of every knight in the kingdom, the cream of their crop. Only the most elite of the two thousand knights of the realm were permitted to join, and the members of the royal guard were sworn to protect the king and the royal family—essentially, they were the sword and shield that safeguarded the heart of the kingdom. It was said that in former times, family status and personal backing had played a major role in who joined the guard, but today that was not the case. They represented the strongest spirits among the kingdom's knights.

"Don't mew think it's a bit much, asking Ferri to join such a remeowned group?"

Ferris stretched out across the table, pouting.

It was noon, and the mess hall at the knights' garrison was crowded. Most of them were, in fact, knights, which made the place quite a spectacle.

Those who served the kingdom, rather than working independently, were distinguished by the color of their capes. There were four armies, which wore red, blue, green, and black, respectively.

Clusters of the same color moved together, mostly; there seemed to be great camaraderie among men belonging to the same army.

There also seemed to be an unspoken understanding about the seating in the mess hall, with the first army sitting closest to the entrance and the fourth sitting farthest away. Generally speaking, the seats farthest from the doorway were yielded to the knights of the highest stature. And, also according to custom, the farthest seats of all were given to those who had been permitted to prepare to don the white mantle of the royal guard—in other words, Ferris and his companions.

Someone suddenly spoke up from in front of Ferris as he looked disinterestedly around the mess hall. "It won't serve you to look quite so bored, my friend."

"Hmm?"

The speaker sat down across from him, studying Ferris through squinted, almond-shaped eyes. His hair was a light purple, and his face bespoke careful cultivation of refinement and masculinity. It couldn't compare to the face Ferris loved most in the world, but it was certainly handsome.

"Julius Juukulius…right?"

"I'm honored that you know me. And I've heard of you, too, Felix Argyle. Your…unorthodox promotion has fueled many a rumor."

"Huh…?"

The hint of a smile floated on the young Julius's face. He was looking at the cat ears on Ferris's head. Ferris didn't let his emotions reach his yellow eyes; he was used to being gawked at.

Prejudice against demi-humans was common in the Kingdom of Lugunica, so the promotion of a conspicuous demi-human to the royal guard, the elite of the elite, was bound to set the malcontents whispering, even if they were mistaken about his background.

Perhaps Ferris's feelings had crept into his gaze, because Julius furrowed his brow, coughed, and then gave him a polite nod.

"My apologies. I didn't mean to stare. I'd heard the talk, but I couldn't quite believe it without seeing it for myself."

"Maybe I'll forgive mew if mew tell me what kind of talk you've heard. Let me guess. A monster with bulging muscles and fur all over? It'd be very disappointing if people were spreading rumors like that about cute lil' Ferri!"

"The captain told me they were a reflection of the demi-human blood of your ancestors. And they are fine ears. I can see why you might try to take a bite out of anyone over them."

"...Are you trying to pick a fight with Ferri?"

It was a rare person who spoke of Ferris's ears with anything other than open disdain. And Julius had evidently even heard the details of Ferris's background from his commander. Perhaps this was his baptism into the ways of the privileged class—Ferris had left his status as the heir to a noble family too early to learn them.

Unlike Ferris, Julius was a knight who was obviously accomplished in swordsmanship. If this went on and things really did come to blows, the cat-boy had no hope of winning.

"But don't think you'll get off without a scratch! Ferri is cute, but not *that* cute!"

"I hate to interrupt you when you're doing such a fine job of working yourself up, but I think we may have a misunderstanding on our hands. Perhaps we could talk about it?"

"Meowhat?"

Julius didn't pick up the gauntlet, and his reaction was so unexpected that Ferris could only blink in surprise. At that moment, someone pulled out the chair immediately beside him.

"Didn't I tell you, Julius? Let me start the conversation, I said. You're too prone to miscommunications, I said. Especially with people you've just met."

"And I appreciate your concern. But I don't believe my judgment was wrong. I don't think we could have avoided a certain amount of confusion no matter who spoke first. Look at him now."

The young man who had spoken so easily to Julius turned his gaze to Ferris. He had blue eyes, and hair so red it might have been a burning flame. Ferris unconsciously stiffened.

"Might you be...Reinhard van Astrea?"

His appearance was too distinctive for it to be anyone else. At

Ferris's question, the red-haired young man gave an affable smile and said, "Ah, I see I needn't introduce myself. That is indeed my name. To elaborate, I, like you, am a member of the royal guard. As is Julius there."

"Since you are new, it's natural to have some reservations about what you hear from your fellow knights," Julius said. "But we have our captain's word to go on. I'm willing to accept his evaluation as is."

"Um, I'm afraid I'm not sure what mew mean."

Reinhard and Julius appeared to be friends, and there was an unfettered intimacy to their conversation. Even so, Julius seemed to be holding something back. Not that Ferris, totally left out, cared in the least.

More important to him was the question of why these two were paying any attention to him at all. Especially the Sword Saint, Reinhard. From what he had heard of Reinhard's personality, Ferris wanted to believe he was not the type to drive out a newcomer.

"What do you want with Ferri that would make you go out of your way to come here? You're not here to…to bully me, are you?"

"Oh, hardly. Could we wear the white of the royal guard while taking part in such nefarious activities? We're just carrying out our captain's orders."

"You mean Captain Marcus?" Julius's roundabout words made Ferris think of the captain, a man with a face like a boulder. What could the two of them have come to do to him on that man's orders?

"Well, to be brief," Reinhard said, "we want to be sure that what you were afraid of doesn't happen to you. Julius and I are about your age, and we thought you might be able to turn to us for advice, since we've been in the royal guard for quite a while."

"Oh, I see," Ferris said, resting his chin on his hands. The captain had charged the two knights with looking after him. The boy had a volatile mixture of factors in his background: his cat ears, his less-than-stellar ability with the sword, and the fact that he had entered

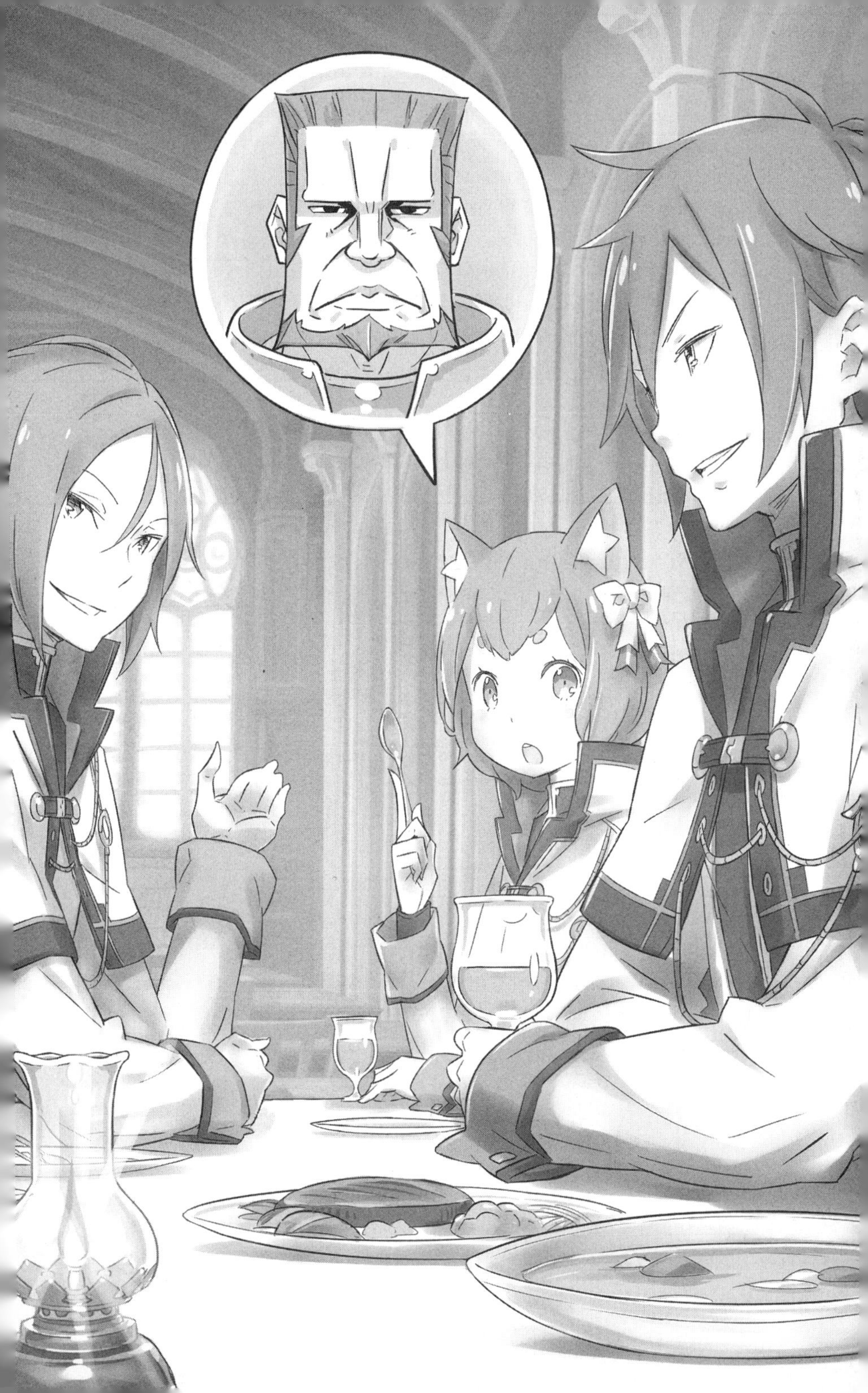

the guard through his connections. No doubt it had weighed on the captain to be entrusted with such a knight.

He would only be there for a year, and there was a probationary period attached—but all the same, it was a tremendous burden.

"Judging by your reaction, it looks like you understand the position you're in," Julius said.

"If it were happening to someone else it would all seem like a joke, but it's a lot more trouble when it's happening to me," Ferris said. "By the way, what exactly did the captain tell you two about Ferri?"

This caused Reinhard and Julius to go wide-eyed, then they looked at each other and lapsed into thought for a moment.

"That you're a favorite of the fourth prince," Julius said, "and that you got into the guard because he forced the issue."

"I also heard that you got a very strong recommendation from the healers at the royal castle, as well as the royal academy of healing," Reinhard added. "I simply hope your abilities haven't been exaggerated to justify the captain's accepting your unusual promotion."

Their answers told Ferris, to his disappointment, that the reputation that had preceded him was more or less as he had expected.

At the same time, he was sure he could feel more eyes than before fixed on their little group from all around the mess hall. He didn't seem to be the only reason people were looking their way. Even the Sword Saint Reinhard didn't account for all the looks. There must have been something about Julius as well.

"Surely the captain isn't just trying to keep all his biggest problems in one place…?" Ferris muttered. But he couldn't shake a bad feeling as his thoughts turned to the probationary period with the royal guard that was about to begin.

2

There was, of course, a complicated story behind how Ferris had come to join the royal guard, and with an evaluation period attached, no less.

Ferris was now eighteen, and he would have been more than happy to live out his life under his mistress, Crusch. She herself had indicated her approval of this, and the two of them were so close that they often shared nearly the same thoughts. The real problem, however, was one of their other customs.

Ferris—his real name was Felix Argyle—typically wore women's clothing, but he was biologically male. As such, if he was going to serve Crusch, it would be more socially appropriate for him to do so as a knight than as a servant or aide.

It so happened that, due to a particular series of events, Ferris had been appointed Crusch's knight, and she had accepted him as such. All he really lacked was practical experience of knighthood.

Of course, if his mistress recognized Ferris as her knight and performed the ceremony of investiture, there was no formal problem. But Crusch, Duchess of Karsten and head of the family, was of too high a station to take on a knight with no history. Crusch was a woman, and a woman whose behavior in the past had led many to look down on her. If, on top of that, she were to accept a knight with no proven skills or actual ability and based solely on the length of their acquaintance, even more unfavorable rumors were bound to circulate.

In order to avoid that, Ferris would need to establish himself as a knight whose résumé would not be an embarrassment to his mistress. The fourth prince of the nation, Fourier Lugunica, gave them some help in resolving this problem.

"Your becoming Crusch's knight is important to me as well. I should hardly even need to exert myself to get you in with the knights. I'll just... Ahem! Perhaps I can simply speak to Marcus or someone. You just relax and wait!"

Fourier had graced Ferris with a heartfelt laugh and then rushed out of the room before anyone could stop him. Shortly thereafter, Ferris's appointment to the royal guard had been decided, and he embarked on the year of service that would allow him to gild his legend.

Which was not to say everything had gone entirely smoothly.

Around the time of Ferris's entry into the unit, Captain Marcus had addressed him with a stern look and said, "You are here at the urging of His Highness Fourier, as well as a number of other strong recommendations. The Duchess of Karsten has also recommended you to me. In light of all this, I'm willing to grant you entry to the royal guard...but not without conditions."

As they spoke there in his office at the garrison, the captain proposed the probationary period—in effect, a time during which Ferris could experience the life of the royal guard, but then throw in the towel and run back home if he wanted to.

"If, during that time, I decide you won't be of any use to me, then you're not staying in my unit. However, if you get kicked out during the probationary period, I'll ensure that it's done in a way that doesn't leave a blot on your record. I can't speak for the feelings of the prince or your other backers, but it would be better than having to spend the whole time being publicly regarded as a stain on the guard. I trust you accept my proposal?"

Marcus had been blunt and did not try to hide the fact that he had been put in a rather delicate position. Ferris liked him immediately. It was a tremendous relief to see the truth in someone's eyes and not have to worry about politely beating around the bush.

"May I ask just one thing?"

"What?"

"Once the probationary period is over, it'll be considered part of my twelve months of service, won't it? To be honest, I can't stand to be away from Lady Crusch even a month longer than I have to be."

"—"

Marcus was left dumbfounded by Ferris's declaration, if only for a moment. There was an instant when he looked tired, but then his face was once again that of a ferocious soldier.

"I like your nerve. You've got a lot of guts for such a small boy—you might surprise us yet," he had said roughly.

* * *

"So I was kind of scared at first...but being a knight has turned out to be sort of more boring than I expected."

"You've only been here a few days. It's a little early to think you've seen everything knighthood has to offer," Julius said. "It's true the royal guard doesn't take the field as often as some of the other units, but we must devote ourselves fully to whatever we're given to do. We have to be ready at all times."

"Yeah, yeah, you're tough, I know."

Ferris waved a hand, trying to soothe Julius. He had only brought up the topic to pass the time, but when they were on the job, Julius always and only thought about the task at hand. It had been about ten days since Julius had started keeping an eye on him, but even what Ferris had seen to that point suggested how difficult things could be.

Although...

"Nobody would be upset if mew relaxed just a little more," Ferris said.

"When I hold the sword I am naturally relaxed," Julius said. "But when I set it aside, then I must be a knight. You could do with a bit more of that yourself, Ferris."

"Bleh! Mew're so uptight!"

Ferris made a face, and Julius sighed. But soon they were both smiling again. They were already close enough to exchange banter like this. Julius could be rather unbending while he was performing his professional duties, but when he wasn't working he could be quite interesting to talk to. His somewhat overwrought fixation on his position as a knight felt like a manifestation of a certain unbecoming childishness. But all this was why Ferris liked him. He had much more trouble with...

"Ah, there you both are. I'm glad I didn't miss you."

"Meowhat?"

Reinhard squeezed in where Ferris and Julius were chatting at their usual place in the mess hall. He gave Ferris a pat on the shoulder with an easy motion and smiled at Julius. Ferris's ears went flat against his head.

"Grr, ambushed again. Reinhard, you really just come out of nowhere. Ferri's senses aren't used to being tricked so easily. Are you sure you're human? It's kind of scary..."

Ferris's demi-human ancestors had given him more than his looks; he also had exceptional sensory organs. His cat ears in particular could detect tiny changes in his surroundings, so much so that he could practically tell when someone had turned to look at him. Yet Reinhard was the exception to end all exceptions. Ferris had never once heard him coming.

"It's the way I was born, my dear Ferris. I'm afraid we'll both just have to live with it. More importantly, you have a summons. His Highness Fourier is asking for you. Since you seem to have some time to kill, you should go see him. Show him how well you do your duty as one of the Knights of the Royal Guard."

"...Were you listening?"

"Certainly not intentionally."

Reinhard at least had the good grace to look embarrassed. Ferris felt a touch of annoyance. The mess hall was a little emptier now than on some days, but there was still plenty of chatter. Ferris and Julius were seated at the far end; not even Ferris's ears could have picked up a conversation at that distance.

"If His Highness has asked for you personally, it would be best to hurry," Julius said. "You don't mind if I accompany you, do you, Ferris?"

"...Oh, sure. Umm...what about you, Reinhard?"

"I'm delighted by your invitation, but I have other plans," Reinhard said apologetically. "I'll be taking a little trip to our border with the Empire. I've been asked to have a look."

"Wow. It's not often they send mew out, Reinhard." Ferris gave the other boy a perplexed look. Julius, rising from his seat, gave Reinhard a knowing nod.

"Don't worry, I can keep an eye on Ferris by myself. You see to your own mission."

"*Mission* makes it sound awfully serious…"

"He simply means I should approach it with that mind-set. All right. I'll leave everything to you." Reinhard nodded at Julius, who waved as the Sword Saint left the mess hall.

A summons from Fourier meant they would be headed to the prince's rooms at the royal residence. They strode boldly along the road that went straight to the castle, as was the well-known privilege of the royal guard.

"His Highness asks for you often. You two must be pretty close."

"Well, we've known each other a long time. It's going on…eight years meow? It gives Ferri a lot of power, you know…" He gave Julius a nasty smirk as they walked the road between the garrison and the castle. But Julius only smiled ruefully.

"You don't have to pretend. I don't sense anything calculating in your relationship with His Highness. We've known each other for a brief time, and even I can tell that. Both you and the prince seem to value each other greatly."

"…It's kind of embarrassing to hear someone say it. Anyway, mew say there's nothing calculating, but I got into the royal guard because of His Highness, didn't I? You don't think that's taking advantage of his position?"

"I apologize for saying such a rude thing to you at our first meeting. But within a week after you joined…I don't think there were any of us left who doubted you were capable enough to be part of the guard."

Julius bowed his head in apology, to which Ferris responded by giving him a karate chop. Gently, of course. As Julius looked up again, Ferris smiled. "Well, I'm glad you guys think so. If Ferri had screwed up, it wouldn't just be embarrassing for Ferri, *meow*. All the people who backed me would look bad, too…"

"I think you've done more than enough to justify your recommendations by now. Happily, you even had a chance to show off what you're really good at—I guess none of us are a match for the captain yet."

"Guess not," Ferris said lightly, but inside he was nodding furiously.

Lacking skill with the sword, the only way Ferris could prove himself to the other guardsmen was to show that he had some talent in something else. In his case, that would certainly be healing magic, and luckily for him, he'd had plenty of opportunities to show what he could do that week. That was because at the practice field, Captain Marcus had decided to personally train his subordinates. As he healed each of the carefully calculated injuries, Ferris was grateful for the captain's rather unorthodox way of showing kindness. As a result, everyone recognized Ferris's abilities, and while it wasn't possible to silence what people said behind closed doors, public objections to his entry into the guard ceased.

"That made my life a lot easier. Meowbe I should thank the captain."

"Of course, he'd just dodge you if you said anything."

"Yeah, he's evasive that way. For such a hard worker, he sure has odd quirks. What a pain."

He could just picture the artless Captain Marcus pretending not to understand what he was being thanked for. It was a disappointing scene. Beside Ferris, Julius was nodding as though he understood exactly what was going through the cat-boy's mind.

"Even so," Julius said, "to go back to our original subject, you said you've been friends with His Highness for eight years now. I'm very curious what the two of you were like as children. Would you mind my asking?"

"No, but I don't think the stories are meowy interesting. Eight years ago, Ferri was just cute lil' Ferri, and His Highness was His Highness... We were exactly the same, really." Ferris put a hand to his mouth and laughed. He was remembering bits and pieces from the whole span of their friendship. Fourier had grown into a strapping young man, but deep down, he was the same as he'd ever been. "Y'know, I think I respect that about His Highness."

"If Prince Fourier's virtues haven't changed, that's what counts. Eight years... Once childhood ends, not everyone is able to remain the same." In contrast to Ferris's suppressed laughter, Julius looked somehow melancholy. Ferris noticed this and gave him a questioning look.

"Come to think of it, I haven't heard much about you, Julius."

"That's because, unfortunately, my life has not been rich enough to warrant any stories. It has been perfectly ordinary, boring as a bedtime tale."

"Bleh. If you really don't want to talk about it, I won't ask… Have you known Reinhard a long time, though? You seem closer to him than most of us." At the Sword Saint's name, all the sadness vanished from Julius's face.

"Reinhard? He and I have a long history, much like you and your prince." He brushed his bangs aside and looked into the distance as if thinking back. "It's almost ten years since we first met. But it was only after we both became knights that we grew to be friends. We aren't blessed with quite as many good memories as you and His Highness."

"You mean you just knew each other in passing, as fellow nobles?"

"Maybe, maybe not. I knew who he was, but I'm not sure he knew who I was. Because he was so special to me, I was particularly happy to be able to become friends with him."

"Special, huh…?"

There was nothing deeper in the friendship between Julius and Reinhard. And yet, neither was it quite possible to declare it mere friendship. But Ferris was not yet close enough to Julius to ask about such things. Ferris was very eager to avoid accidentally alienating him by saying the wrong thing—that was how much he valued Julius Juukulius.

The two of them found they had chatted all the way to the castle. They greeted the guards and the officials on duty, and then they came to the staircase that led to the castle's upper levels, where Fourier and the other members of the royal family lived. They told the men guarding the staircase who they were and where they were going and were quickly allowed in.

They ascended the stairs that led to the royal chambers and

proceeded down a carpeted hallway. Ferris found the room they wanted and used the door knocker.

"Your Highness!" he said in a singsong tone. "Just as you asked, your dear Ferri has arrived!"

The greeting caused Julius to put his palm to his forehead.

"Ferris, however close you may be, that's… Well, I suppose it's too late now."

He shrugged, and at the same instant, the door opened.

"Are you going to let him off that easy? That means trouble for me! If that's all you're going to do, why even have you keeping an eye on him?"

Bounding out of the room came a young man with golden hair and clear scarlet eyes: Fourier Lugunica, fourth prince of the kingdom. He looked from Ferris to Julius, then laughed, showing his teeth.

"Ahh, never mind! Welcome, both of you. Are you both in good health?"

"I have been most well, my lord. Your consideration humbles me."

"…says Julius," Ferris remarked. "But we just saw you two days ago, didn't we? We've hardly had long enough to get sick!"

"I see, maybe so. But if you're well, that's all that matters. Anyway, there's much to talk about, but let's not do it out here. Come in, both of you." Fourier gestured them into his room. He was equally generous with both the deferential Julius and the happily impertinent Ferris.

Fourier's room was so sparse it was hard to believe it belonged to a member of royalty. Not that Ferris had been in a lot of other royal chambers for reference—but Fourier's quarters were almost as simple as Crusch's. Perhaps her distaste for excess had affected him.

"You seem kind of antsy, Your Highness," Ferris said, sitting on the sofa in the reception area. "What's going on?"

"You get straight to it! And on what basis do you say I seem antsy?"

"You can't trick Ferri's ears. There's a tremble in your voice, your pulse is faster than usual, and you've swallowed several times trying to calm them both down."

"Goodness! Your ears can even hear my heartbeat?"

"Nuh-uh. Just bluffing," Ferris said innocently. Fourier slumped into a chair. His reaction was proof enough that he was keeping something from them. Julius shot Ferris a stern look for being disrespectful to such an august person as Fourier, but Ferris simply ignored him.

"All right, I know you're doing everything you can to hold out on us, but really, what's going on? The way mew've chased out all the maids and servants so you and Ferri and Julius can talk alone gives me a meowy bad feeling."

"Yes, well noticed. I should have expected as much of you, Ferris. Before that, though, there's one thing I want to be sure of. You, Julius." Fourier's gaze settled on the knight. For a moment, Julius raised an eyebrow in surprise, but the respectful deference soon came back into his face. He answered with a nod.

"Yes, Your Highness. Ask me anything you wish."

"A good answer— Can you look me in the eye and tell me that you are Ferris's friend? If so, you may stay for this discussion, but if not... Well, I will need to ask you to leave the room."

"Your Highness is quite direct..."

Fourier was incapable of trickery or artifice. It could be irritating at times, but it was unquestionably one of his good traits. Julius responded to the question by placing a hand to his chest, assuming a formal expression.

"I have known Ferris for but a few days, and our fellowship is not deep enough for me to unabashedly call him a friend. However, I sincerely hope that as time goes on, we will only become closer. Does this answer please Your Highness?"

"Yikes," Ferris said, "talk about direct..."

Julius had perhaps not been as frank as the prince, but it was clear that he spoke from his heart. That meant he was deliberately entering into a potentially risky situation—pretty overbearing for a brand-new friend. He was overbearing, likely to go against the tide—but Ferris liked that just fine.

Fourier seemed to feel the same way, because he nodded repeatedly and then gave Ferris a happy smile. "Looks like you've found a good companion, Ferris! I see it was worth my while to recommend you for the royal guard. You mustn't turn up your nose at Julius's friendship!"

"Your Highneeess, it sounds like I just joined the guards to make friends when you put it that way and it's not very flattering…"

"Yes, yes, dear," Fourier said with a smile at Ferris's rapid attempt to hide his embarrassment. But then his expression tightened. "—Now, to business."

Ferris's ears picked up an immediate change in the air. The source of it was none other than Fourier.

"Your Highness…?" He let the words slip out in an attempt to make sure this was still Fourier, that the young man who sat before him looking impossibly grim was still the friend he knew.

Fourier didn't respond to Ferris's prompting but slowly began to speak in a quiet voice.

"First of all, I am telling you both about this on my own prerogative. Crusch told me not to speak of it, so I really shouldn't be telling anyone…"

"Lady Crusch told you…?" When his mistress's name came up, Ferris grew even more uncomfortable. For her to tell Fourier not to speak of something didn't bode well, especially if she couldn't even confide it to Ferris.

"Ill rumors have been circulating about a particular place in the Karsten domain. Private investigations have been ongoing, but I've received word that Crusch has gone to inspect the place herself."

"…Is that it?" Ferris had been so worried by Fourier's opening that when he heard what was actually going on, he was almost disappointed. Crusch knew how to handle herself. There was no need to worry about her, even if she ran into a little trouble on her tour.

"And if they were already investigating it," Ferris went on, "then I don't think Lady Crusch could be caught off guard. She's more than a match for any ordinary opponent. Your Highness should know that better than anyone."

"Mm...I can't imagine her losing to anyone but me, and yet..." This was apparently the best answer Fourier could muster.

To judge by what had been said so far, Ferris could not understand the source of Fourier's concern. But even when the things the prince said seemed baseless, they often turned out to be much more than idle speculation. Perhaps this was another one of his unpleasant premonitions...

"Your Highness, if I may?" As the two of them sat there silently, Julius broke in.

"Mm. Go ahead."

"I haven't met the Duchess of Karsten personally, so I can offer no judgment there, but...since you've called Ferris here, may I presume you have something in mind?"

"Julius, you should know that His Highness often does things for no real reason..."

"No, not this time. This time I have a basis for my actions. For my...worries," Fourier said, not quite able to look up.

This caught Ferris by surprise. But, to be fair, he had not been paying full attention. Perhaps because he hadn't wanted to believe that Crusch could be in danger. And if Fourier's last words had been a surprise, his next words were an absolute shock.

"The place all these rumors are about? It's your home, Ferris. House of Argyle."

3

—There were dark things afoot at the House of Argyle.

Word had first reached Crusch at the beginning of that year, almost two months earlier. The first thing she thought of when she heard the name *Argyle* was none other than Ferris. Her meeting with her beloved servant could never have come about without the House of Argyle, where he had been born.

But that did not mean Crusch was grateful to the Argyles. She was thankful they had brought the person named Felix Argyle into the world, but what they had then done to him during his youth was difficult to forgive.

As a result, ever since she had rescued Ferris from his family and taken him under her wing, Crusch had endeavored to have as little contact as possible with the Argyle family. Ferris didn't raise the issue, either; they were effectively on the same page on this matter. So when she received a report about the House of Argyle for the first time in nearly a decade, Crusch found herself uncharacteristically troubled.

"Something untoward is happening at the House of Argyle...?"

"For the time being, milady, we're trying to keep Ferris from hearing about it, but...what shall we do?"

They were in her office. Crusch's arms were crossed. The official reporting to her had a pained look on his face. He was one of the phalanx of retainers she had inherited from her father, Meckart, along with the duchy. He had known Crusch since she was a baby, and Ferris since he had come to the House of Karsten. Someone who had been so close to them and the family for so long naturally shared Crusch's concerns.

"You're right, I'd rather Ferris not find out," Crusch said. "But it depends on what exactly is going on. There may be a natural need to tell him."

"That's true, milady. According to the report, Bean Argyle—Ferris's father—has been inviting a suspicious character into his home over these past several months. He may be a slaver."

"A slaver...?"

Crusch's brow furrowed slightly at the word. Officially, the Kingdom of Lugunica didn't have slaves. Anyone who worked was to be compensated; the relationship between nobles and their servants was one of employer and employee. Perhaps some people were treated no better than slaves—but on paper, slavery did not exist under the laws of the kingdom.

By the same token, then, the slave trade could not be allowed to go on within Lugunica's borders, either.

"And yet there is no end of people who want to sully their hands with that kind of business... Is the claim that the House of Argyle is working with the slaver to sell off the people of our domain to other kingdoms? That would mean..."

That would mean they were traitors. And responsibility for the problem fell to Crusch, who ruled this area. An immediate investigation would bring the facts to light. If the charges were true, the head of the household would be punished, and the House of Argyle itself would most likely cease to exist. If that happened, it would be difficult for Ferris to avoid repercussions.

"'What the parents sow, the children reap.' This is no joke. What are the Argyles thinking?" In her mind, Crusch found herself reliving the day she had first met Ferris.

He had been nothing but skin and bones, nearly black with dirt and grime, a boy so weak he could barely talk. Was it not enough for the Argyles that they had squandered the first half of Ferris's life? Crusch found herself filled with such roiling anger that she bit her lip to hold it back, a most unusual gesture from her.

But the official met her rage by saying, "Please wait, milady. There is more to the report. Don't make your decision until you've heard the whole thing."

"...I'm sorry. I got a bit agitated."

"Completely understandable. You and I are both affected by anything that concerns Ferris. Regardless, as far as the House of Argyle goes, it appears to be more than simple slave trading."

"More?"

"Yes. The details aren't certain yet, but it appears that rather than selling slaves to the trader, the Argyles are buying every slave they can get their hands on."

"Buying them?"

She gave the man a look of incomprehension. Because slavery didn't officially exist in Lugunica, people engaging in the slave trade in the kingdom could not, in principle, have any other objective but selling slaves to other nations. To buy slaves as laborers would hardly appear different from hiring them normally and wouldn't arouse any ugly rumors.

"The question is whether the House of Argyle is up to anything that would move them to purchase slaves," the official said, voicing the same question Crusch had been entertaining.

The decline of the House of Argyle had begun nine years ago, when the House of Karsten had become aware of Ferris, and had subsequently meted out its wrath upon his family for their transgressions. Bean Argyle was a noble without court rank, the overseer of a collection of towns and villages within the Karsten domain, and he was valued for his work. But that changed after the incident with Ferris, and ultimately the House of Argyle lost any and all trust.

Bean had made a number of attempts to recover after that, but all ended in failure, and now the only assets the family had left were their house and a parcel of uncultivated land. They had had to let all their servants go, and the last anyone had heard of them, Ferris's mother and father were living at best a modest existence.

"In that state, what could the House of Argyle be doing that would require slaves...?"

It would have been much easier to believe that they were selling people to the brigands. Of course, had they been doing so, there would have been no consideration of extenuating circumstances in handing down their punishment, but at least she could have understood their motivation.

"Whatever the case, the moment they entered into the slave trade, the House of Argyle violated the laws of our kingdom. And a slaver operating boldly in my lands is no better. We will have to arrest both parties and deal with them."

"In that case, milady, will you be moving to apprehend them immediately?"

"Yes, I... No, wait." It would be easy enough to send her soldiers to capture Bean Argyle. But such a decision would be too hasty. They needed to get more than Bean. "If we move too precipitously, the slaver himself might escape."

"A real possibility. These past months, the frequency of his visits to the House of Argyle has been once every month or two."

"When did this report come in?"

"Two days ago. That would mean leaving them a window of two months..." The official seemed to guess what Crusch had in mind. She considered for a long moment and then shook her head, seeing that she had no other choice.

"Make sure the House of Argyle is watched at all times. The next time the slave trader comes to their door, we grab them both at once. Any objections?"

"Just one— You aren't doing this for Ferris, are you?"

"Hardly. Of course I bear him in mind, but my responsibility as duchess is more important than my personal feelings. And Ferris wouldn't want me to put him ahead of my duty."

The official nodded in satisfaction. "Then, as you command, milady."

He withdrew, leaving Crusch alone in her rooms. She slumped into her chair. She leaned into her seat, looking out the window at the sky. Wisps of white clouds drifted through clear blue, an unmistakable sign that the wind that day was strong.

I don't believe I gave Ferris undue consideration simply because this matter involves his family.

However, during the ensuing two months, during which nothing changed at the Argyle household, the appointed time came for Ferris to join the royal guard. And it was true that, secretly, she was glad.

4

"Foul things afoot at the House of Argyle. Hmm, I see..."

Fourier nodded. Crusch had called him to share tea and speak face-to-face. They were in the parlor of the Karsten manor, and the guest list for this tea party included only the two of them. Fourier's custom of visiting the household had continued even after Crusch became duchess, although with less frequency than before.

"I just happened to have business in the area, you understand!" he would say. "I thought I might drop in to see if you were in good health." It was strange that Fourier "just happened" to show up primarily on days when Crusch would not be too busy to see him.

These odd coincidences had gone on for the better part of ten years now, but Crusch had chosen not to question them.

"Just happened, you understand! Sheer chance! Don't go getting the wrong idea!"

"Certainly not, Your Highness."

"Yes, a fine answer! A fine answer indeed, but...you could afford to get just slightly the wrong idea..."

Crusch Karsten possessed a divine blessing, the ability to see the wind. This blessing of wind reading allowed her to see the invisible and read its flow. With it, she could even tell the true state of people's hearts. It was a minor point of pride for her that she was rarely deceived.

For all this blessing and power, though, there were two people who could lie to her and get away with it. One was Ferris, who knew Crusch's heart better than any other and therefore knew how to keep things from her. The other was Fourier, whose bald-faced lies Crusch had no desire to call out.

"And although it's chance that I came by, it seems it was a good one, yes?"

A wind of untruth blew every time Fourier spoke the word *chance*. It was not chance but certainty; Fourier had come deliberately to visit. Crusch was honestly very happy that he felt such friendship toward her and Ferris. That was why she felt no need to reveal his lie. And now, she had been letting him hide his true intentions for ten years.

"At any rate, Crusch, I know all about it, of course. Of course I know. But just to be sure we're on the same page, let me ask you—where *is* the House of Argyle, exactly?"

Crusch had put a great deal of thought into this, but the first thing Fourier said turned the conversation on its head. He tried to find out what was going on while simultaneously pretending to already know. Crusch made a half smile at this very Fourier-esque attitude, and said, "Pardon me." She bowed her head. "Sometimes the magnitude of my friendship with you causes me to forget myself. My apologies."

"Not at all, there's no need for you to say you're sorry! I assure you, I remember everything in great detail. I simply…want to make sure we remember the same thing! Don't hesitate to speak."

"Yes, Your Highness. The House of Argyle is Ferris's family. His real name, as you'll recall, is Felix Argyle, and he was the family's eldest son."

"Ahh, Ferris's family, are they? And you say he used to be called Felix Argyle? What an interesting fact—that, uh, I of course knew already!"

The wind of untruth gusted again, but Crusch said nothing. From Fourier's flustered reaction, however, it appeared that he had been totally ignorant of the connection between Ferris and the Argyles. She'd expected Ferris might have shared his personal history with the prince, but apparently not. If Ferris wanted to keep this quiet, then it wasn't for Crusch to talk about, and yet…

"You look unhappy, Crusch. Whatever you wanted to talk about, is it really such awful business as to darken your face so? And on Ferris's behalf, no less."

"Your Highness…"

"You're wondering how I know? Surely you needn't ask. I've seen your face all these years, just as I promised I would in the flower garden. Clarity and calmness suit you best. This anxiousness is most unusual in you. Tell me what's happened."

When Fourier spoke like this, it shook Crusch to her very heart. She thought back to their first meeting. Ever since then, even to this very moment, Fourier had sometimes appeared to see more clearly than Crusch, who supposedly had the gift of wind reading. And Crusch knew from experience how the words he spoke could have the power to break an impasse.

"If he finds out that I told you, Ferris will be angry at me."

"Oh, just tell him I forced it out of you. I held you down, said I would never forgive you if you didn't tell me. Yes! That's what you should say."

"You jest. You could never hold me down, Your Highness… Your Highness? Are you all right? You fell to your knees very suddenly…"

"Y-yes, I'm fine... I'm perfectly fine. Please, continue."

Fourier had these moments sometimes, some kind of attack or reaction. Crusch frowned, but she told the prince about Ferris's history and the dark dealings going on at the House of Argyle.

—Crusch and Ferris had met nine years earlier. The reason for that meeting had been the same as for this one: Crusch had accompanied her father, Meckart, who was investigating rumors of inharmonious goings-on at the House of Argyle.

Ferris's parents had both been perfectly human, yet he had been born with cat ears. He and his ears might raise suspicions that the House of Argyle carried impure blood, so for nearly ten years after he was born, Ferris was locked in the basement of the house day and night. Later, the House of Karsten took him in under the pretense of adoption, and that was how Ferris and Crusch met. Thus, they had spent their days as attendant and mistress.

"—"

As Crusch related all this to Fourier, she left out the unnecessary parts, deliberately made her telling ambiguous where she could, but ultimately told him most of the facts. Fourier listened to everything with an almost unsettling quiet and focus.

"...Unforgivable."

The word slipped out, carrying with it an anger that could not be concealed. Fourier had closed his eyes, but now he opened them, their scarlet color shining like a flame.

"Such behavior is unforgivable! To think that my own friend Ferris was so inhumanly treated by his mother and father! And still they scheme and plot! I shall certainly show them no mercy. Even without Ferris's knowledge, I swear I will—hrk! *Cough! C-cough!*"

The rush of anger sent Fourier into a coughing fit.

"Your Highness, don't get so agitated. Here, drink some tea." She held out a cup to him, and Fourier downed its contents in a single gulp and slammed it back onto the table.

"—not forhib hem!" The hot tea turned his face red and mangled the words he tried to speak. But the emotion they contained, the feelings of friendship for Ferris, were unmistakable. "Crusch, you must apprehend these scoundrels, and you must do it immediately. Luckily, Ferris is at the capital for his training at the moment. We may not be able to keep everything from him, but at least we can shield him from having to see the ugliest parts of it."

"I understand, my lord. But we're dealing with a slave trader operating within our own borders. If we want to find out where he's coming from, we can't act too impulsively. I beg your understanding on this matter."

"Hrr... Grr... In that case, why did you tell me about this? If you're not going to act right away, then things are at a standstill. And if you've thought so far ahead, what do you need from me?"

"I wish to request Your Highness's help with Ferris," Crusch said. Judging by his outburst, it seemed Fourier didn't understand what she was really driving at. His eyes went wide as Crusch placed a hand to her chest and continued: "Your Highness, Ferris will spend the next year at the royal castle, as one of the Knights of the Royal Guard. This year could all but determine his future—such is the importance of knighthood to Ferris. Therefore, I wish to see it pass without incident."

"And you're asking me to see that it does? Just so you know, Marcus, the man who oversees the royal guard, is stubborn but fair. He's not the type to dole out undue favors. I could ask him to give Ferris special treatment, but I guarantee it would fall on deaf ears. And I have no intention of giving Ferris that kind of help, anyway. It could only hurt him—he may dress like a woman, but he has the pride of a man!"

Not once in the ten years they'd known each other had Crusch ever seen Fourier take advantage of his position or otherwise make any unwarranted demands. Of course, people often deferred to him because of his rank, but he was not the kind to ask for such consideration himself.

"If you expect such things of me," he went on, "you're making a mistake. Crusch, I know how much you care for Ferris, but in this case it's led you astray. He isn't as weak as you fear, nor so soft as to want protection from you and me."

"—"

Then Fourier crossed his arms and coughed again briefly. His face was red. Crusch was silently thankful for his words. There were some who might see Ferris's abilities and value him for them. But there was no one other than Fourier who would so thoroughly trust and defend Ferris's heart.

"Your Highness, I must apologize. I seem to have given you the wrong impression. What I wish to ask from you is not that you get any breaks for Ferris in his unit."

"Oh? It isn't?" Fourier was startled to find that his passionate outburst had been misdirected. Crusch didn't press the point but assumed an attitude of imploring respect.

"Your Highness, I understand I'm asking a great deal, and I'm prepared for you to reprimand me. But if it is possible, should you see Ferris at the royal castle, I ask that you would speak with him."

"...That I speak with him? That's all?"

"Yes. You understand Ferris's position. He isn't likely to be welcomed."

Ferris's cat ears, which made people suspect him of being a demi-human, made his admission to the royal guard exceptional. His preference for women's dress and inexperience with the sword would be no more likely to win him any friends. But Ferris was apt to act perfectly according to his nature, no matter how hostile people were to him. No matter how much it hurt.

"I don't doubt his strength of spirit. But everyone has their limits. Even he may not realize how emotionally fatigued he's become. If he could have a kind word from you before that happens..."

"You think a familiar face will ease his mind...? Is that it?"

"Yes." Crusch let out a breath, glad that she had gotten her point across. Then she smiled and stretched her neck gently. "However much I may care for Ferris, I am not quite so overprotective as to rely on your rank for favors."

Ferris would not appreciate it if they were constantly holding out a hand so he would not fall, or giving him a push on the back so he would not stop, or shielding him so he would not get hurt. But a moment's respite they could offer. That was what she asked of Fourier.

Now that Fourier understood what she really wanted, he frowned and looked askance at her. "But even so, Crusch—"

"What is it, my lord?"

"I think you're quite overprotective just the same. Better you admit it to yourself."

She had by no means expected Fourier to make such an allegation, and it left her dumbfounded. Her reaction caused Fourier to burst out laughing, slapping his knees in amusement.

"Excellent! I shall let your most unusual reaction just now persuade me. Anyway, the royal guard has quite a bit of free time when they're not on duty. And the newcomer isn't likely to be assigned to accompany my father or elder brothers on one of their trips. They won't mind if I ask for Ferris's company."

Fourier seemed to be quite enjoying himself as he announced that he would accede to Crusch's request. "But," he added, winking uncharacteristically, "if that was all you were going to ask, why tell me about the goings-on at the House of Argyle?"

"It's simply that if matters with the family become public, Ferris is bound to hear of them. If that happens, I want someone close to him who knows what's going on. I couldn't rely on anyone but you, Your Highness."

"Um! Indeed! Because I am a most reliable man! I should like you to repeat yourself."

"—? I couldn't rely on anyone but you, Your Highness."

"I see, I see. At the end of your rope, are you? Then I have no choice—you can count on me! *Cough! Cough! Hrrk!*" Fourier pounded his chest—a bit too hard, resulting in another coughing fit. It just seemed to be the way things were going that day. It was enough to raise concerns about the prince's health.

"Not to worry. I've been suffering a bit of heartburn lately. My older brother has been coughing, too. Perhaps he's caught a cold."

"It's not my place to make yet another request of you, Your Highness, but I do hope you'll look after yourself. Your health matters to more people than just you. If you're feeling unwell, you needn't come all the way here…"

"Ah, but it's when I'm feeling my weakest that I most want to see y— Um, never mind! More importantly, have you any plan for how you'll deal with the Argyles?" Fourier changed the subject, blushing at Crusch's words.

"Once we confirm that the slaver really is going to the House of Argyle, I'll go and confront them myself. Then we'll find out the truth of the matter."

Fourier waited a moment before responding. Then he asked: "Do you really need to confront them yourself? I should think it would be dangerous."

"I'd like to handle things internally, without matters getting out of hand… And there's Ferris to think about."

If it were simply a matter of arresting them, she could send the army. But if the House of Argyle had committed a major crime, Ferris could be inadvertently placed in a questionable situation as well. In the worst-case scenario, the House of Karsten might be forced to formally adopt Ferris before dealing with the Argyles.

"Your Highness, I humbly ask that you keep this from Ferris. I'll make every effort to deal with this personally, as a local matter."

"While I keep an eye on him in the capital—very well. This is between you and me. I'll keep it to myself. But should the wind change and things turn sour, I can't promise I'll stay quiet about it. All right?" Fourier nodded, despite his continued misgivings about Crusch's plan.

He had deliberately used the metaphor of changing winds to the young woman blessed with the ability to read the air itself. Crusch saw herself reflected in his scarlet eyes. A slight chill passed down her spine.

"I understand, Your Highness. If that moment comes, I trust your judgment." She glanced toward the door—specifically, toward the crest of the House of Karsten emblazoned over it. For an instant, she saw Fourier's image overlap with the crest of the lion baring its fangs.

—A week later, it was determined that the slaver was indeed going to the House of Argyle.

5

Bean Argyle proved surprisingly willing to invite Crusch to his home. His eagerness made her suspect a trap at first, but when she arrived, he showed her inside, and her concern gradually eased.

The house was still; there was no sense that an armed party was hiding anywhere within. In fact, there was hardly any sign anyone else was around at all.

"I heard rumors you had to release your servants," Crusch said. "It seems they were true."

"Yes, they were. I'm simply not in a position to indulge in any kind of excess anymore. The only people here now are myself, my wife, and one maid who stayed with us out of personal affection." He led her down the hall. Bean Argyle was Ferris's father, and the man at the center of the doubts about the House of Argyle. The fact that Bean himself, and not the maid, had greeted Crusch at the door lent credibility to his claims of being shorthanded.

"I'm sorry that my wife is unable to greet you. She's sick in bed. And my maid is attending to another visitor, so I'm left to compound my rudeness by welcoming you by myself."

"I don't mind. It's my fault for showing up so suddenly. But this visit had to be abrupt, and for that, I have no intention of apologizing."

"Oh-ho..."

Bean stopped and looked back at this spontaneous remark. Crusch was tall for a woman, but he was a head taller than her. The most distinctive feature of his face was the lines that creased it, nothing like Ferris's sweetness. Perhaps the son had inherited his girlish face from his mother. Crusch only dimly recalled what Bean's wife looked like, but it seemed logical to her.

"Bean Argyle... You've grown thin. You look smaller than when I saw you last."

"When a man has as many troubles as I do..."

It was only when she went back to her memories that Crusch realized how much the man in front of her had changed. Bean had once had a fine beard and had seemed a good man, but now there was no trace of resemblance to his former bearing. His expression was dark, and patches of white hair stood out on his head and chin. The last nine years had not been kind to him.

"How is Felix? Is he well?"

"—"

Crusch was quietly taken aback to hear him bring up Ferris. Bean had considered the child as evidence of his wife's infidelity, and that had ultimately led to the downfall of the House of Argyle. He might well be expected to resent the boy for that even now.

Bean smirked at the dumbfounded Crusch.

"So even you can be caught off guard, Duchess..."

"I admit, I wasn't expecting it. I was sure you wouldn't think much of Ferris... I mean, Felix."

"What parent does not treasure his child? Or if not treasure, what parent wishes to leave his child to die somewhere? Especially when he knows the boy is his own blood."

Bean's voice was subdued, with scant inflection. It was hard to tell what he was really thinking. But Crusch wasn't listening to his voice. She was focused on the wind, and there she found unmistakable regret and grief. Bean at least seemed to be upset by the inhuman acts he had perpetrated against Ferris, whom he now acknowledged as his real son. If he had taken Ferris as his own from the start and loved him like any other father, things would have been very different. Would they have been better? It was not a question Crusch could easily answer.

"I'm sorry, I didn't mean to stop. As our receiving room is occupied, perhaps our parlor… But you have come for something else today, I presume."

Bean resumed walking just as Crusch began to think she couldn't take any more. Crusch blinked once, dispelling her own grief, and replied, "Yes. And I have business with your other visitor. I know I'm imposing myself, but things will go quickest if you simply take me to your reception room. For both of us."

"I see. This way, then, please."

Bean made no effort to resist, but led her to the reception room as though he had been expecting this. They walked through a dim hallway—it seemed the light was deliberately kept low—and up a narrow staircase to the receiving room on the second floor.

Bean knocked. A woman's voice answered, and the door opened. A woman of middle age appeared. To judge by her clothing, this was the household's last maid.

The woman's face stiffened when she saw Crusch. The duchess only gave her a silent nod.

"Master? Why is the honored duchess…?"

"Don't you remember? I told you I was going to have her join us here. Make tea for her." At Bean's clipped instruction, the maid bowed to Crusch and squeezed out through the door. Crusch, in turn, walked into the room. A voice greeted her as she came in.

"Well, well, quite a lovely young thing we have here." The owner of the voice was an unpleasant-looking man. His whole body was wrapped in a white robe; he had short gray hair and a ratlike face. Crusch was not superficial enough to judge people by their appearance, but an affinity for violence seemed to lay thick about him.

"I must ask your indulgence; her visit was quite sudden. Allow me to introduce Duchess Crusch of Karsten, the ruler of this area. Milady, if I may…?" Standing beside Crusch, Bean announced her, then attempted to move on to the subject of the other visitor. Crusch gave the slightest of nods, and Bean gestured at the ratlike man. "This is Miles. He deals in the antiques I so favor. He goes from country to country, trading in the most unusual things… Perhaps nothing quite so strange as a metia, but many interesting objects just the same."

"Miles, milady. And must I say, you're the most beautiful duchess I've encountered in all my travels. I certainly didn't expect to meet you here. What a great pleasure," the rat-faced man said, picking up smoothly from Bean. His words were perfectly polite, but there was a hint of toadying about them.

Crusch ignored most of what he said. She only murmured, "An antiques dealer...?"

"Does milady have a taste for the old and intriguing? I'll have to visit your honored residence at another time..."

"I appreciate it, but that won't be necessary. I'm still too young to feel the weight of history very keenly. There's something I want to talk to you about."

She shook her head at Miles's invitation and tried to draw Bean into the conversation. Her suspicions about him had lessened somewhat during their talk in the hallway, but since meeting Miles, she had begun to doubt again. Unfortunately, it was very hard to believe the man's claim to be an antiques dealer. There was an eight or nine out of ten chance that he was the slave trader she was looking for.

Bean gestured for her to sit on the sofa. He and Miles sat across from her. Crusch rested her hands on her knees, never letting her guard down. Because she had only come to talk, Crusch wasn't carrying a sword. However, she was quite capable of dealing with an enemy in hand-to-hand combat if it came to that. But she wouldn't do anything reckless.

"Now then, Lady Crusch, what is it you wish to talk about?"

"Ahem. Truth be told, my visit today was motivated by a report received by one of my subordinates. Word is that an unsavory character has been visiting the House of Argyle recently."

"Could you be speaking of me?" Miles said, chiming in. "If so, I must sincerely apologize for giving the duchess herself cause to come all the way out here." He had the same servile tone as before, but his eyes took Crusch in quite openly. His gaze was frankly unsettling. No one wants to be looked at like an object being appraised.

"Setting aside the question of exactly who it is, my subordinate was told that this person is a slave trader. I've come to hear Bean Argyle's side of the story."

Miles frowned at this open statement of Crusch's suspicions, but there was no change in Bean's attitude. He drummed on the table with his fingers, looking as dour as ever.

"I understand you have your concerns," Bean said. "But we have very few callers at this house anymore. The only person who comes and goes with any frequency would be Miles here."

"So you're saying the rumors of slave trade are just that?"

Bean nodded firmly. She sensed no wind indicating he was trying to deceive her. In fact, the eddies of his emotions were exceptionally weak, as if he were disengaged. Far from reassuring Crusch, this left her with an indistinct mistrust of Bean.

Her thoughts were interrupted by the maid, who returned to the room.

"—The tea is ready," she said, and placed a silver tea set on the table and quietly poured the drink. A sweet aroma rose from the warm liquid. Crusch caught a hint of anxiousness and uncertainty from the maid.

"Please, Lady Crusch," Miles said. "It will be easier to talk if you wet your lips…"

"It's all right…"

The maid had retreated, but Crusch remembered her nervousness. Combined with Miles's inquisitive eyes, Crusch hesitated to take the cup. Bean and Miles paid her no mind, sipping from their own cups.

Crusch's perceptions were sounding a noisy warning bell. Even the tea she'd been offered put her on edge.

"If you wish to dispel any suspicions, the first step will be to show me the goods Miles has allegedly brought with him. Then you will allow people in to inspect this house. If they find the rumors are baseless, then I will apologize for doubting you and offer some form of compensation. But—"

"—Compensation, you say?"

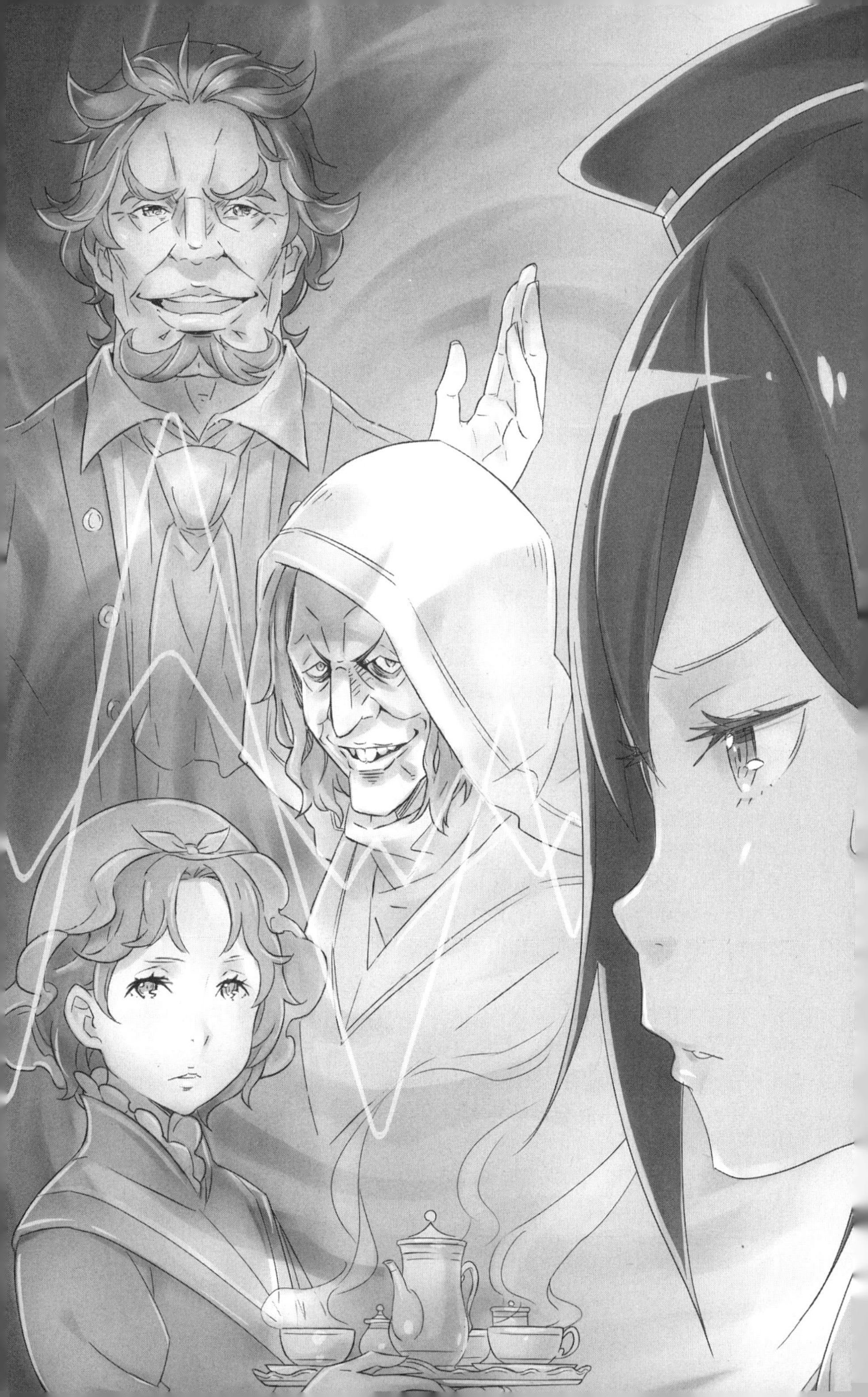

It was hard to believe the whispered voice belonged to the same man who had seemed so detached just seconds before. These few words were rife with a tumult of emotions. Dry, and yet saturated, an unfocused emotional torrent. The only thing she could understand, if anything at all, was that he was fixated on something…

"Compensation," Bean said softly. "Yes, very well. If you're prepared to do that, things will indeed go quickly between us." Now she felt something fearful rolling off him, but it was too late.

"—ngh. Whad're you talging ab…?" Crusch found her lips couldn't form the words to her reply, and then a wave of dizziness struck her. Her hand slipped off the armrest of the sofa and she fell to the floor. Her eyes spun; her consciousness wavered.

By the time she realized she had been drugged, it was too late. But she hadn't put anything in her mouth…

"Ha-ha!" Miles cackled. "The bigger they think they are, the better they fall for this trick! Don't even want a drink? You should accept your host's hospitality, *milady*. It helps wash out the bad air that gets inside…" He clapped tauntingly, and all decorum had vanished from his tone. His face contorted into a vile expression, and he ran a hand along Crusch's cheek. "Ahh, I do love to see a strong woman crawl. Ha-ha! You'll make a fine gift for me to take home."

The words certainly sounded like those of a slaver, but what he was saying was mad. Crusch was a duchess of the Kingdom of Lugunica. Anyone in their right mind would know that to take her as a slave was suicide. Which could only mean he had something besides enslavement in mind.

Bean knelt down and looked into Crusch's eyes. "I thank you for your cooperation, Duchess. Without you, I could never have achieved my goal."

"…"

His face was expressionless, like a mask, but his eyes were passionate. Anger raged in them, and a terrible pity.

"Wh…a…t… go…al…?"

"You can still talk? I'm surprised. It was supposed to put you out immediately." Bean sounded impressed. Crusch was biting her tongue, clinging desperately to consciousness.

Bean grabbed her by the hair, pulled her head up, and said, "Isn't it obvious? —I want back the child you stole from me. I *need* that boy."

6

"You let Lady Crusch go alone?! How could you ever—? How do you plan to take responsibility if anything's happened to her?"

The voice, almost a scream, echoed around the Karsten office. The owner of the shouting voice and the hand that slammed down on the black desk was Ferris. He wore the uniform of the royal guard, and he had returned to the mansion much sooner than expected. The place was in an uproar.

—Had he really given up on being a knight after just ten days?

No one dared to venture to make such a joke as Ferris stalked down the hallway with an expression of anger they had never seen before clear on his face. Everyone got out of his way until he arrived at the secretarial office, where he laid into the head official.

"H-hold on a moment, Ferris. I know you're upset. And I understand, but this was Lady Crusch's decision. There were circumstances to consider..."

"Circumstances?! You mean what might happen to me? I know what might happen! And I don't care! If it meant keeping Lady Crusch out of danger, I would gladly have given my heart and my body and my name!" His voice had risen an octave. For all his anger, his thinking was rational enough. At the castle, Fourier had explained what Crusch was up to. And while Ferris understood that she was doing it for him, Crusch putting herself in danger for his sake defeated the purpose of his service as her knight.

The House of Argyle was so steeped in villainy that the people there didn't think of other people as human beings.

"And yet none of you put Lady Crusch first...!"

"You must calm yourself, Ferris. You'll only terrify everyone around you, and then we won't be able to talk to them."

"But…!" Ferris's eyes began to fill with tears. Someone wrapped an arm around his shoulder, the same someone who had just spoken in such a powerful voice. A young man with golden hair. The official Ferris had been upbraiding caught his breath at the sight of the man.

"Your Highness Fourier! I didn't know you would be with Ferris…"

"Yes, because it was I who revealed the matter to him, even though I'd been asked not to speak of it. And Crusch did tell me beforehand that if things went badly, I was to use my judgment. I have no proof, but…I do have a bad feeling that won't go away. It swirls within me." Fourier placed a hand to his chest. If the prince had willed all this, then the official certainly couldn't be upset with Ferris for it.

"Whatever is happening, the royal castle is too far away for me to deal with it effectively. So it only makes sense that I would move closer to the center of the action. And it only makes further sense that a member of the royal guard would accompany me."

"*Does* it make sense, Your Highness? I shudder to think what the captain will say when we get back…" Fourier was happily playing out his little trick, but Julius, who had gotten caught up in the whole affair, slumped his shoulders. He didn't seem specifically upset to have been dragged along, however. "If Your Highness would be so magnanimous as to speak on our behalf…" he added.

"Since this was all my own doing, you can leave that to me! Um, well…not that I'm sure my excuses will have much sway with Marcus, but at the very least, you two will not be alone when he reprimands you. If you must get a piece of his mind, I will, too."

"Reassuring words, Your Highness— Now then, what about the Duchess of Karsten…?"

As a semblance of calm returned to the room, Julius guided them back to the question at hand. This led the official, now out of ways to distract his visitors, to slump a bit and look uncomfortably at Ferris. "It's true Lady Crusch went alone to inspect the House of Argyle," he said. "But Bardok has the area of the mansion surrounded with nearly fifty soldiers. The Argyles lack the resources to hire mercenaries at this time. Even if they armed their slaves and sent them out, it would be easy to subdue them."

"But what if they took Lady Crusch hostage…?"

"I admit they might feel so cornered as to resort to violence, but they would be facing Lady Crusch. She once cut down a Giant Rabbit with a single swipe of her sword. I doubt they could best her. And she has done all she can to prepare in advance."

The official offered all the reasons he could for peace of mind, hoping to placate Ferris. True, objectively speaking, it didn't seem there was any way Crusch could be at a disadvantage. Ferris would have trusted her diligence had the involvement of the House of Argyle not thrown his emotions into confusion. Yet an unease remained within him. Was it simply an illusion born of his own difficulties with his blood family?

"…Wait, Ferris. None of that would lay my lingering anxiety to rest."

"Your Highness?" Fourier had spoken just as Ferris was beginning to calm down and resolve to trust Crusch.

Fourier looked like a different person. Ferris, looking into his eyes, had the sense that he could see the prince's very soul. Everyone in the room caught the change in Fourier.

Fourier looked around the room, which was holding their collective breath, and put a hand on his chest before continuing. "A worry, I cannot explain what, churns within me. It isn't good for you and Crusch to continue to be apart. Indeed, we must go as soon as possible—*cough, c-cough!*"

"Your Highness?!"

Fourier's words dissolved into a spate of red-faced coughing. Ferris rushed to take his shoulders, focusing his attention on the flow of mana throughout the prince's body. The Royal Academy of Healing had recognized Ferris as its most accomplished pupil. If he wanted to, he could bring someone back from the brink of death to perfect health. So when someone complained to him of feeling poorly, he had a habit of assessing them as soon as he laid hands on them.

"What...?"

Fourier immediately moved away from Ferris's hands. Before his fingers and the mana flowing through them could do their work, the prince stood up, still sweating and breathing hard.

"Are you all right, Your Highness?!" Julius asked.

Fourier tried to act as if nothing had happened. "It's nothing major. My apologies for startling you. I'm feeling much better now, thanks to Ferris." This seemed to satisfy everyone else, but Ferris couldn't let go of his shock.

"Um, Your Highness, Ferri—I mean, I didn't..."

Worry pierced him as he watched Fourier wipe away sweat even as he tried to claim everything was fine. But Ferris's small, hesitant voice was suddenly overwhelmed by a shout from outside the office.

"It's terrible! Lady Crusch hasn't come out of the Argyle manor, and a battle's started around the mansion! The soldiers—they claim they're fighting living corpses!"

7

The first thing Crusch noticed when she came to was a terrible odor.

"Nnhn..." she groaned. Her throat was dry. She leaned up off the floor. And then the smell filled her nose, a stench so awful that it was almost physically painful. It was like animal waste mixed with something rotting; the moment she caught a whiff of it, Crusch knew she was in no place good.

She was somehow able to sit up, but her hands were manacled. So were her feet, and on top of that, she was blindfolded. It was a small blessing that her eyes had simply been covered rather than put out, but Crusch wasn't thinking of such things at that moment.

"I don't seem to have any major injuries. Is that so they have room to bargain with me...?"

She remembered the moments just before she had lost consciousness. Bean and Miles had used some kind of concoction to put her to sleep. There had been something in the tea—but it was antidote, not toxin. The drug was in the room itself, and only Crusch, who had been too suspicious to drink, had succumbed. But it bothered her that there seemed to be so many potential holes in the plan.

"If I had been careless and drunk the tea, it wouldn't have worked."

"...If you'd done that, we would've done something much more terrifying."

She hadn't been expecting an answer, but one came. The unforgettable voice belonged to none other than Bean. She'd sensed someone nearby, but she never would have guessed it was the perpetrator himself. Crusch didn't let her shock show on her face. Instead, she let out an incongruous laugh.

"You never cease to surprise me. That, at least, makes me think you're related to Felix."

"You don't know how grateful I am to hear that from someone who's closer to that boy than any other. It gives me confidence that he and I really do share a blood connection."

"You seem awfully interested in the son you gave up nearly ten years ago." She couldn't see Bean, but his tone was calm—yet this only spoke to the depth of his madness. Crusch considered it more dangerous than if he had been hysterical.

"I told you. I need him. And you are going to bring him to me."

"You're right that when Felix finds out what's happened to me, he's likely to come running. But you'll have another problem to deal with first. My subordinates know I'm here, and it won't be long before they notice I haven't returned and come down on this place like an avalanche."

The contest would be between a duchess and a subsidiary noble with no station. The difference in military strength was unquestionable. The outcome was a foregone conclusion.

Flight would be similarly futile. If they wanted to, Bean and Miles could take Crusch's head, but this would only doubly sign their death warrants.

"I won't try to convince you to surrender. But what are you

planning? I can't understand what you have to gain by putting me in this position."

"I see being blindfolded and chained hasn't made you any more meek. I guess the ducal family really is made of sterner stuff than the rest of us. Well, that only makes things easier for me."

"I take it you don't intend to answer me?"

To this question Bean did not spare any reply at all; Crusch heard his footsteps growing distant. There was the sound of some wet glop dirtying the soles of his shoes. Apparently there was something unsanitary here besides just the bad smell.

"Oh, yes," Bean called back to Crusch, as though he had just remembered something. "This is where Felix used to spend his days, those many years ago. The room that moved you to take him away from us. Perhaps you'll understand him even more intimately now."

"…Is that so? How thoughtful of you," she answered, her voice thick with sarcasm. "I'll make sure to put this experience to good use." Bean only gave an angry snort. This time the footsteps receded until she could no longer hear them, and the blindfolded Crusch was left alone.

"So this was Ferris's room…" she murmured to herself.

Crusch thought back to when she had met Ferris. If Bean was telling the truth, then she was underground. The room where the cat-boy had been confined as a child was beneath the house.

The manacles on her hands and legs were made of metal, not easily removed. Bean's attitude suggested he had a plan in mind for dealing with the guards accompanying Crusch. She saw now: She was in a desperate situation. But nothing more.

"This isn't quite what I was expecting, but it's a bit too early to just give up."

Being drugged and kidnapped had certainly not been part of her plan. But if it gave her a way to uncover the secrets of the house, then it might have been worth it. She had only one real concern…

"I guess it was asking too much to think I could finish this before Ferris or His Highness got worried."

Both of them would no doubt be tremendously anxious when they heard what had happened to her. That thought tormented her far more than any question of her own safety.

8

There was a secret spell called the Sacrament of the Immortal King.

It was one of the exceptional magics, supposedly created by a witch who held the world in thrall before the knowledge was lost. Put briefly, it allowed the user to control corpses according to their will. The witch who invented the spell had been said to be able to bring the dead back looking exactly as they had in life, but that part of the spell had not been passed down.

Most of the ritual had faded from living memory; it was impossible to replicate any of the spell's effects except animating corpses. And even that most basic manifestation was all but impossible to achieve without a caster who had a natural affinity for the spell.

It was a very rare affinity—no one had been known to possess it in more than a hundred years.

"I'm impressed we were able to come so far in replicating the effects." Miles gave a happy shrug as he watched the corpse wander around, a revolting scent drifting from it.

A dark smile came over his face. He felt no distaste for the walking body. The dead were a familiar sight to him. It was simply that those who were usually asleep had now awoken.

"Awfully intimidating name for such a useful power," he went on. "Such fine workers the dead make. I can't believe we've forgotten this ability."

"Normal people wouldn't think to put the dead to manual labor."

"Ah, master, welcome back."

From amid the dead came a man who was living, yet whose face was no different from the zombies'. A living dead man who controlled the deceased through secret magic, while Miles was the villain who worked with him. It was a place awash in a never-ending tide of sin.

"I long ago lost the good sense to be concerned about such things, anyway. And how is our little princess doing in her underground room?"

"Still defiant. The ones who are born to nobility really are a different breed."

"Fine. That makes it all the better when I finally break her. You haven't...*done* anything to her, have you?"

"I have no interest in such things. She's only bait, to bring my son here." The question hadn't really been necessary, but Bean answered it dispassionately just the same. "How do things look outside?"

"Oh, very busy. Her Ladyship's vaunted soldiers seem to be quite beside themselves at the sight of our undead fighters. I suppose it would be less human not to be scared by those rotting faces."

From the second floor of the mansion, it was possible to view the tumult outside. The soldiers Crusch had brought along with her were in a pitched battle with the crazed undead. No sooner were the zombies killed than they would rise back up, again and again. It was enough to give the bravest hero pause.

"We gave them our demands. What is their response? Have you seen my son?"

"I'm afraid I can't tell you. I don't even know what he looks like. I saw some land dragons leaving, so I assume their headquarters has been informed, but I don't see any demi-humans."

"...Don't speak of that boy as though he were some animal. That's my son, who shares my blood."

Miles had spoken the forbidden word; Bean gave him a sharp look. He seemed not entirely sane, so Miles raised his hands and scuttled backward.

The word *son* was so often on Bean's lips. He seemed fixated on it. Perhaps it only made sense, since he was hardly calling the child back out of love. Even Miles felt a certain sympathy for the boy. To have one's life wasted because of the fervent but mistaken convictions of one's father was the stuff of nightmares.

"Well, not that it means I'll hold back or show any mercy."

Bean looked down over the battlefield with glittering eyes,

awaiting his son's homecoming. Behind him, Miles sat on a sofa that hadn't been dirtied by the corpses and waited for the right moment. The house overflowed with ill intent and the fetor of rotting flesh. But he only had to wait until the time was ripe.

9

Ferris and the others arrived at the Argyle estate to find the place had become a battleground. They had run their dragon carriage as hard as possible, and it had still taken several hours. The place was hell on earth by the time they got there.

"So this is what they meant by *undead warriors*..." Ferris murmured. A man tottered forward with the point of a spear lodged in his head. What flowed from the wound was not vital red blood but yellow pus. The man collapsed on the ground. Yet, despite what was obviously a mortal wound, he flailed his body, working the spear out, and then, apparently unbothered by his shattered skull, stretched out his arms and attempted to attach himself to the next soldier he saw.

"A dark spell that makes the dead live. So this is the Sacrament of the Immortal King." Julius had been watching, too, and now he spoke in a voice heavy with fury at the awful scene. Julius was typically quiet, but given to intense emotion. He was full of righteous indignation on behalf of those whose lives had been blasphemed by this magic. His hand was on the hilt of his sword, and he looked as if he might rush in at any moment.

"—Don't do it, Julius. I shan't let you go ahead of me." The voice that held Julius back was that of Fourier, who observed the situation from inside the carriage. The prince's stern words caused the tension to go out of Julius's shoulders, as if he were embarrassed at his own impetuousness.

"My apologies. The sight is simply too terrible, and it raised my ire."

"I understand your feelings. This isn't a situation we can overlook.

But if we make the wrong choice, it could result in needless sacrifices. We must avoid that."

Next Fourier turned to Ferris, who found himself quailing slightly under the intensity of his friend's gaze. Fourier was in the grip of the sharp-edged, commanding air he had shown at the castle and the manor. It had happened before, but this was of a different magnitude. Normally Fourier didn't seem like royalty—in the best sense—but now his heritage was abundantly evident.

"According to Bardok, it will take three hours to gather enough strength to ensure we can destroy the enemy. We have to buy them time so that the worst doesn't happen before then." Fourier took in the battlefield. "Of course, we want to protect any innocents from getting hurt. Both of you understand?" Ferris and Julius nodded.

The undead warriors were ranged against Crusch's soldiers, who surrounded the Argyle house. There appeared to be at least two hundred of them, four times the friendly strength.

But while the undead had the advantage of being difficult to destroy, their ability to think and strategize was gone. The fact that the cordon hadn't been broken despite being vastly outnumbered was proof of this.

At the moment, Bardok, the ranking military official Crusch had brought with her, was trying to gather the military strength to overcome the disparity in numbers. Once they had the forces, it would be a simple matter to overpower the undead warriors.

"But that means Lady Crusch might…"

"If we don't rescue Crusch, then we could have a million men and it would mean nothing. What's more, it looks like the mastermind, Bean Argyle, is asking after a Felix Argyle."

No sooner had they finished with the urgent message about the appearance of the undead warriors than they received word that Crusch had been taken hostage at the Argyle house. A letter signed by Bean himself had demanded that they hand over Ferris in exchange for Crusch's safety.

Of course, they weren't stupid enough to fall for it.

"But we can't simply dismiss his demand, either," Fourier said. "Until we see the Duchess, we have to prioritize her safety, and that may mean going to the negotiating table."

"Yeah, a table *they* built. It's about the worst possible way to negotiate..." Ferris said, not trying to hide his frustration. He glared down at the Argyle mansion.

Normally, it might be nostalgic to see one's birthplace again, but Ferris felt nothing so pleasant for this house. He had never seen the place from outside like this. In his memory, it existed only as the darkness of that basement room.

"What are you going to do?" Fourier asked. "Bean's letter said that you and you alone would be allowed past the undead. Do you think we can trust him?"

The warriors leaped without mercy at anything nearby. They never came to attacking one another, but they didn't seem like they had the ability to do any more than distinguish between the living and the dead. But that was no reason to hesitate.

"I'll go. Lady Crusch will be in danger if I don't."

To Ferris, Crusch's life was more important than his own, worth more than the whole world. He would give anything at all to get her back. Certainly including himself.

"Ferris..."

"You can't stop me, Your Highness. You were the one who brought me here."

"I won't try to stop you. I know you would go even if I did. Because you are Crusch's knight. I have no doubt you'll protect her."

Ferris was already on his way, and Fourier answered him without hesitation.

With those words, Ferris felt as if he had a thousand armies behind him. After all, Fourier's words were part of what had fired Ferris's ambitions to knighthood, part of the reason he was who he was. The pride buoyed him up. But Fourier went on.

"But you should not do it at the cost of your life. I want you and Crusch both back safely. Because you are my life. If you're a true member of the royal guard, you'll follow my orders."

"—"

"You must come back. I won't lose a friend to something like this."

Ferris didn't even have a name for the emotion that welled up in his heart. Fourier had called Ferris his friend many times before, and each time he did, Ferris was just as shocked as the first time it had happened, just as lost for words.

"Yes, Your Highness!"

And then he set out, his friend watching him go with a familiar, audacious look on his face.

Ahead of Ferris was the awful place of his birth, the mistress he cherished, and the family he had left behind.

"You look upset, Julius."

Fourier spoke to Julius as they watched Ferris grow smaller in the distance. Julius was clenching his fists.

Apparently Bean had been telling the truth in his letter, because the undead warriors completely overlooked Ferris as he approached the house. The same could not be said for the other human soldiers, at whom the zombies threw themselves without mercy.

Julius was at least relieved to see Ferris go safely through, but he couldn't help being frustrated by his own powerlessness.

"I feel pathetic—to accompany him here and yet be unable to do anything! Why be a knight at all if I cannot help my friend in his hour of need?"

"Don't get so worked up," Fourier replied. "There will be many times to come when your strength will be needed. The vexation of this moment is not a sign of your impotence."

"Er—thank you." Julius had not expected such words from Fourier, but his surprise was overwhelmed by respect. The fourth prince, Fourier Lugunica, was not known to have a gift for flattery. Indeed, the whole royal family was quite convivial; in this way, they were unsuited to statesmanship. The administration of Lugunica was thus left to the higher nobles and the Council of Elders.

Or so everyone in the nation believed, and Julius himself could not deny that he had assumed as much until this moment. But when he saw Fourier now, he had to wonder if the prince was really just personable. He gradually found himself unable to believe the gossip that ran like wildfire through the royal castle.

"You're thinking I seem very little like what you've heard."

"—!"

"Take it easy, no need for shock. I could hardly be ignorant of the rumors about me in the royal castle. Not that I normally pay much attention to them. But I'm feeling unusually clearheaded today. At least enough to plumb the heart of a retainer sincerely concerned for our nation."

A fresh burst of awe came over Julius, who felt that Fourier had seen through his indiscretion. The sage who sighed mournfully beside him in the carriage was not a man who could be measured by rumors. Still, though that wise man's eyes saw all, he also exuded congeniality.

"Ferris is going to challenge his birth family. It is his friends' duty to support what is lacking."

"Is Ferris...? Does Your Highness consider him a friend?"

"Of course. And if you do as well, then we are in the same position." Julius found it a dizzying position to be in. Fourier looked thoughtfully toward the mansion. His scarlet eyes played over the house and the undead soldiers fighting outside.

"If Crusch is on the upper floor, then Ferris might be able to manage something... But if not, we'll have to rely on you, Julius. Take that to heart and wait for your moment." Julius respectfully accepted Fourier's words. The knight found himself painfully aware of his own pride. Lately there had been many chances for him to correct his unconscious assumptions, regarding both Ferris and other things. He had no right to take others lightly in anything, nor any reason to be taken lightly by others.

"I see I still have much to reflect on."

Julius set his hand on the hilt of his sword and waited for the moment when he would be called upon to draw it. It was he, as a Knight of the Royal Guard, who had been entrusted with Fourier. His true worth as a member of the guard would be tested on the battlefield today.

10

"Welcome home, Master Felix."

Ferris felt out of place as the maid came out to greet him. He couldn't quite tell if he remembered the middle-aged woman or not. But she seemed to recognize him. He was especially struck by the way she squinted her eyes as if she were trying to remember something.

None of this gave him any affection for a person who aligned herself with the Argyles.

"Spare me the small talk. Where's Lady Crusch?"

"—The master is waiting. If you'll follow me…"

For an instant, the maid looked as if she were holding something back before she answered. She hadn't answered his question, but when she turned and entered the house, he followed her, knowing he had no other choice.

A rotten stench drifted through the dim hallway. Undead warriors were posted inside the mansion as well; they produced a variety of scratching sounds. With no one to attack—Ferris and the maid were not their targets—they stood stupidly or slumped down against the wall, giving no real sense of being alive.

Ferris's eyes roved here and there as they moved through the house.

"Feeling nostalgic?" the maid asked him. She seemed to have misunderstood what he was looking for.

With no small irony he replied, "Not especially," and shrugged. "I don't remember this place well enough to feel nostalgic for it. And even if I did, there weren't any corpses walking around the last time I was here."

As he spoke, Ferris gave an experimental poke to the shoulder of one of the zombies that stood motionless in the hallway. He half expected it wouldn't respond no matter what he did, but when it realized he had touched it, its eyes turned toward him.

"I'm amazed you can bring yourself to touch them," the maid said.

"Dead bodies are nothing new to me. I've seen plenty of the heavily wounded, too. But I didn't come here to chat."

"—"

The maid gave no response. Ferris had replied to her because he didn't want to simply ignore the woman, but he was not in the mood to talk. He had felt a twisting in the top of his stomach from the moment he entered this house. He recognized it for the psychological phenomenon it was, a testament to how deeply he despised this place.

After Ferris pointedly broke off their conversation, the maid led him in silence to the second floor. She knocked on the door of the reception room, calling out, "Sir, I've brought him."

A man replied quietly from within. Ferris didn't remember the voice, but it sent chills down his spine. Neither his mind nor his body recognized it, but his soul did.

"—You made it back, Felix."

When Ferris entered the room, he was confronted with a large, bearded man. Ferris looked up at the man's face, and finally something flickered in his memory. The man had the same chestnut-colored hair and yellow eyes as Ferris—those were almost the only things that marked them out as parent and child, but he grew more and more sure that it was the same face that had loomed even higher above him nine years before.

"Yeah…I guess that is what he looked like," Ferris whispered as he finally managed to line up his memories with the face of his father, Bean Argyle. Emotionless words for a reunion with his own father. The maid, overhearing them, furrowed her brow, but her reaction was overshadowed by Bean's much more grandiose one.

He took Ferris by the shoulders with his large hands and said, "I'd like to ask how you've been…but first I have to ask what in the world you're wearing. You're so thin—and you're in women's clothes? I hope the Duchess of Karsten's perverse views on gender haven't rubbed off on you."

"—"

"Your complexion is good enough, but your arms and legs are so slim… What a terribly cruel sight!" Bean contorted his face in grief, raising a cry over his grown son. Ferris watched him expressionlessly, though with a tremendous chill in his eye.

This outfit is a sign of my bond with Crusch, and I'm thin because of almost ten years of abuse in this house. It's cruel, all right, but whose cruelty is it?

"But very well! Let us set this aside! You've come home. As your father, that brings me joy." Seemingly oblivious to Ferris's chilly expression, Bean broke into a smile and tried to give his son a hug. Ferris nimbly avoided his embrace, sliding to one side as Bean stumbled forward.

Ferris quickly scanned the room, but he let out a breath when he could find no sign of Crusch.

"Enough talk," he said. "Give back Lady Crusch. Then I hope you and this house just disappear."

"What a way to greet your father! Don't mistake me, Felix. I'm overjoyed that you're safe, but I'm not so generous as to indulge your impertinence. If you think you're on equal footing with me because of what happened in the past, you're wrong."

"—! As if I would think that!" He met Bean's angry outburst with one of his own. What had been done to Ferris in this household, he would never take so lightly as to use it for leverage.

Ferris had possessed his animal ears from birth, and almost immediately after he came into the world, he was locked in that basement room. His mother and father had been regular humans, so the presence of his cat ears was taken to imply infidelity on the part of his mother.

Although confined in the dark underground chamber, Ferris had been afforded a minimal education. But once out of infancy, his treatment grew worse and worse. After the age of five, he was forced into another underground room even smaller than the first, and he spent five years there doing nothing but waking and sleeping. He spent his life in darkness with no reason to be alive nor any meaning to the life he had.

It was Crusch who had brought him out from that place—Crusch, who had been gallant since childhood. She led Ferris out into the sun, and he became human.

It was thanks to Crusch that Ferris gained humanity for the first time.

"Without Lady Crusch, I wouldn't be who I am! So give her back to me—now! I don't care about mistaking you! I don't care about fathers! I'm not joking around!"

Ferris's sweet face was twisted with rage; he bared his teeth and stamped the floor. He brandished his own arms at Bean.

"Look at these skinny arms! I can't wield a sword! Can't hold a shield! I'm her knight, and these worthless arms can't even fight for her! And my legs are no better! I can't run fast or jump high... I can't do anything! All I want is to protect her, and I can't even do that!"

Once Crusch had taken him out of this house, and he had been given his role as her attendant, Ferris had done everything he could to be an asset to her. He had tried to take up the sword and be a knight. But he had been left without the body to make good on that duty.

"*You* stole it from me! You stole it from me and left me empty... Lady Crusch gave me my way of life, my way of being!"

He had been left with nothing, but Crusch had encouraged him to live the way he did now. He had been derided as a hopeless case, ridiculed for having "strange proclivities," but the only thing that meant anything to Ferris was what Crusch had asked of him. And, here of all places, would he turn away from that?

"And after all you've done, you still want to keep taking from me! Will you steal from me again, something I value more than my own life?! You won't, damn you...! Damn you!!"

If he could have, Ferris would have cut down the devil that called itself his father then and there. If he could have, he would have burned him up with magic and thrown the ashes in a river.

But Ferris couldn't do either of these things. He didn't have the power.

"___"

Bean stood silently as Ferris lambasted him. The boy's emotions washed over him, and he regarded his child with a masklike, emotionless face. His eyes weren't quite human; they didn't seem to be focused anywhere.

"...Have you said all you have to say?" he asked finally.

"H-huh?"

"If you have something to say, then let it out. I'm your father. I can overlook a childish tantrum. There must be a good deal to get off your chest after all these years apart."

"___"

Ferris was shocked into silence.

He had bared his heart and soul—and Bean considered it nothing more than a fit of temper?

But at the same time, he understood. It made all too much sense to him.

There was nothing to be gained by seeking a dialogue with this man. He should have known that from the start.

—Should have known that he had left nothing at this house.

He let out a breath. It wasn't despair or even disappointment he felt. He had simply realized how things were.

"Could you stop calling yourself my father? It's making me sick."

"I'll even forgive your defiant attitude. A father and son need not stand on ceremony at their reunion."

Ferris saw that Bean had no intention of actually listening to him. He couldn't recall ever having conversed with his father before—and it nearly made him laugh to realize this was the man Bean was. His own father was more deeply flawed than he could ever have imagined.

"Or is this rebelliousness a sign that you want to be treated as a man? I could be moved to entertain the idea. If we're both equal adults, then there's another way to handle this discussion."

"...And what's that?"

"Working out our respective views in order to get what we want."

Bean ran a hand along his beard importantly as he circled around to the far side of the sofa. He set his hands on the backrest, leaned forward, and looked at Ferris.

"I've called you here because I have business with you."

"You could have just sent a letter. Although I would've torn it up."

"I'll admit this was a roundabout way of doing things. But it was necessary. I had to test the Sacrament of the Immortal King—and your powers!" He was practically spitting by the time he finished.

"So that's it…" Ferris finally grasped why he had been summoned. Bean wasn't interested in Ferris's physical capabilities. "You needed my magic…"

"Exactly. But don't be disappointed. The aptitude for water magic that lies dormant within you—it is the greatest proof that you and I are connected by blood. A proficiency with water magic has been passed down through generations of Argyles. No illegitimate child could possess it!"

"Well. Aren't you lucky. Congratulations." Ferris gave a slow clap. Bean could prove all the familial connections he wanted. Ferris was far too alienated to care.

But Bean drew closer to Ferris, as if this were the most important thing of all. "Here's where our conversation as equal adults starts. If you want something from someone, you must be prepared to offer something of similar value in return. Yes?"

"—"

"But what do you know of that? Nothing. So I've taken the liberty of figuring out the price for you. If you give me what I want, I'll return your precious duchess to you. That's the deal."

"You don't think that's all kind of illogical?"

"The logic is flawless. There's nothing strange about it."

So Bean had gone to these ridiculous lengths just to play the tyrant. He had taken Crusch hostage not to get Ferris to listen to him but merely to bargain with him.

"It's so stupid that it breaks through the other side and becomes logical again, I guess… So, what is it you want me to do? Want me to call you *Daddy*?"

"What I want is simple. And with your abilities, it should be quite easy— You!" Bean ignored the jab with a triumphant look and shouted at the maid, who had been standing quietly in the corner.

She nodded at him. "Shall I take him? Or would you like to accompany us?"

"Hmm... Very well. Show us both there. It's been so long since Felix last took a little walk with his father. I'm sure he would like it. Wouldn't you?"

"Ha-ha-ha. You're funny." It was a fine joke. Ferris and his father had never taken a walk together.

At this point, Ferris recognized that Bean was mentally unstable. It was only natural that his conversation didn't quite seem to make sense. If Ferris pushed back, Bean would probably just destroy him. Better to play along and wait for his chance.

But he was still worried about Crusch's safety. With Bean the way he was, there were no guarantees Crusch was all right, even if he claimed she was.

"...At the very least, your friend hasn't been harmed."

"Huh?"

The whisper came like an answer to his very thoughts. The maid, who had spoken the words, made no further reply but headed out of the room to show them the way. Bean hurried her along from behind, and Ferris, the last to exit the reception room, was left puzzled.

He was sure that maid was in league with Bean. She had no reason to spare him any help or hope. But neither did she appear to be insane.

—Strangest of all, her words gave him a genuine sense of relief.

"...Weird." Ferris set the disturbing feeling aside, thinking it odd. Beside him, Bean continued in an upbeat tone. Ferris nodded and grunted but otherwise ignored everything the man said.

At last, the mismatched trio arrived at the innermost room on the third floor.

Bean stood at the door. "Do you know where we are?" Obviously, Ferris had no actual memory of the place, but this was the innermost room on the uppermost floor of a noble's mansion. He had a pretty good idea.

"The master bedroom?"

"A precocious child. You happen to be correct." Bean offered emotionless words of praise and then pushed open the door. An overwhelming stench of death rushed out. It was similar to the smell that pervaded the entire house, but here it was an order of magnitude worse. This was no fresh corpse.

The source of the smell was just inside the room.

"—My wife," Bean said. "Do you understand, Felix?"

Lying on the bed was the corpse of a woman, suffering still evident on her face. She had flaxen hair, and her face had been made up in death. For her grave clothes she wore a beautiful dress. She looked as if she had fallen asleep, never to wake.

Bean had introduced her as his wife. Meaning that to Ferris, she was…

"My…my mother…?"

He couldn't ignore the ache he felt in his heart as he realized who the corpse must be.

11

"With my magical abilities, I can only incompletely invoke the Sacrament of the Immortal King. Moving corpses are the best I can manage. But you, Felix, are different!" Ferris stood staring at the corpse of his mother as Bean pleaded. The man came up to the bed and stroked the sleeping face of his wife. "You have a special talent. Power enough to bring a girl back from the brink of death without so much as intoning a chant! With such powers, surely you can complete the sacrament! You can bring your mother back to life!"

Ferris looked at Bean's bloodshot eyes and realized what the man really wanted. He sought to bring his wife back from the dead through the Sacrament of the Immortal King. He had been gathering dead bodies to experiment and practice on them with his dark magic. He had probably been relying on the slave trader to help him collect the bodies. And the result of his work seemed to be the undead warriors who swarmed outside—how many corpses had he desecrated?

And for all that, Bean still had not achieved what he really wanted and had been forced to recognize that he lacked the power. Then he'd remembered—he'd remembered the existence of a spell caster who shared his blood and was far more powerful than he.

"You have true power! You are capable of this. You can restore my wife to me. I… I alone know! I am your father, and I grasp the brilliance of your abilities better than anyone!"

Bean scratched his own cheeks so hard that blood ran down them like tears. Immediately, a faint light emanated from the wounds, which disappeared. He had harmed himself and then healed himself. It was the most unsettling use of healing magic Ferris had ever seen.

"This is beyond me," Bean said. "But it's not beyond you. You are a genius! There is no parent who doesn't take joy in the abilities of his child! You are the best son!"

Bean was transported with joy, with wholehearted praise, and with expectation for the abilities of his boy. Ferris felt a wave of vertigo, followed by nausea.

Was this—was this how profoundly twisted his family had become?

"Look at this! This is a text describing the Sacrament of the Immortal King that has been passed down in our house. The description is incomplete, but I was able to use it. You, I'm sure, can discover what I've missed and perform the entire ritual!" Bean dug in his bag and pulled out a worn book.

The book had been read so many times that it appeared to be covered not just in fingerprints but even in blood. It had been so thoroughly used that it seemed the slightest touch might cause it to crumble to dust.

"Now, bring back my wife—bring back your mother! If you can do that, I'll give you back your mistress. This is the deal I offer you as your equal, as a man!"

Bean thrust the book into Ferris's chest. The cat-boy took hold of it unsteadily. The cover was blotted with dried blood, and it felt heavy, as though it had absorbed the souls of the dead.

The Sacrament of the Immortal King, a ritual with the power to resurrect the dead. Healer that he was, it would be untrue to say Ferris had no interest in such things. But whatever he may have felt as a healer, his sanity and basic humanity revolted against the idea.

But if he didn't look at the book and perform the spell, Crusch's life might be in danger. And the woman lying in front of him—he had no more familial feeling for her than he did for Bean, but it was still the corpse of his mother, and that was not entirely lost on him. At least, if there really was a spell that could bring her back, he wanted to do it.

"—"

Ferris swallowed. He decided to put off the decision; instead, he turned the pages of the spell book. Some passages were obscure, and several pages were covered with fingerprints. Handling everything as carefully as he could, Ferris pored over his family heirloom, trying to get the spell into his head.

And then…

"…Should I go ahead and use the sacrament on this woman as soon as I can?" He deliberately avoided using the word *mother*, talking about her as though she were a stranger in order to maintain his equilibrium.

Bean's face lit up. "Yes, yes!" He nodded enthusiastically. "That's right, as soon as you can. Bring back my wife. And then the three of us can share a joyous reunion as a family!"

Ferris didn't respond to this but walked closer to the body on the bed. He reached out to the woman, who looked just as if she were sleeping, and let mana run into the lifeless body.

"When did she die? It looks like she's been here a while."

"More than two years ago. I've been periodically using magic to prevent the body's decay… The smell is the only thing I haven't been able to do anything about. But if you can bring her back, then there's no problem. She's not like the other corpses around here with their rotting flesh. The body itself is exactly as it was when she died."

Two years ago. That would have been the year of the birthday celebration for Crusch that Ferris remembered so vividly. That year had been a turning point for him, and apparently it had been for his parents, as well.

He let his mana run through every inch of the body, and found that Bean had been telling the truth. Other than the lack of functions necessary for life, his mother was so well preserved one would never have thought she was dead.

She truly was just as she had been at the moment of her passing...

"Felix. There is much I want to talk about, but I will restrain myself. For now, concentrate everything on what's before you. Is your mistress not precious to you? Don't fail her now. Or else—"

"Can I ask just one more thing?" Ferris broke in, touching his dead mother's forehead. He looked back at Bean, who had swallowed the rest of what he had been about to say. Ferris fixed him with a keen gaze.

"—Who was it who stabbed my mother to death?"

12

Crusch focused her attention as scratching footsteps came down into the basement. Her gaze found the cruel-faced slaver, eliciting a rasp from him.

"The poison should've worn off by now, hmm? Let's have a chat, my little princess." Miles smirked at Crusch where she was chained to the wall.

She sighed at his lascivious stare. "Not a very polite look you have."

"I can't stand arrogance. Many men enjoy seeing a prideful woman slowly brought to heel—myself among them."

"Not a very polite hobby you have, either." Her words gave no sign of weakness, but Miles seemed downright pleased.

It had been hours since Bean had left her in the underground room. By Crusch's estimation, Bardok, her military adviser, should already have the mansion surrounded. But she couldn't sense any such thing happening. Something seemed to have gone wrong.

"The Sacrament of the Immortal King—unbelievable. What better way to flout the kingdom's laws?"

"Heh! That's the duchess for you. Not many know about the sacrament."

"It's a secret spell that's largely kept out of public view, but there are records of its use during the demi-human war... I doubt you're the one who used it. It must have been Bean Argyle."

"Goodness gracious me. How do you think so keenly in this reeking chamber?" He scrunched up his face at the stench that drifted through the room, but nonetheless, this confirmed her suspicions. Crusch, of course, had only the awful smell in the underground room to go on; she had no idea whether the sacrament had actually been used. The hint came with Miles: He had brought undead warriors with him, as if to display them to her.

"If you're trying to intimidate me, then I'm sorry to disappoint you," Crusch said.

"Shouldn't a girl who sees a walking corpse just give a sweet little scream? Frankly, even I feel my blood run cold when I look at them."

"I'm afraid I left my girlishness behind long ago," Crusch said with the suggestion of a smile. Miles, accompanied by several of the zombies, looked at her in exasperation. But his expression soon changed, and he pointed to the ceiling above the bound Crusch.

"Well, my little princess, since you're ignorant of what's going on outside, let me bring you the news. A knight has arrived to save the captured princess. Though he hardly looked like one."

"—"

Miles was probably talking about Ferris. He was supposed to be in the capital—but for her sake, he had come back to the Karsten lands after just a short time. And Fourier was involved in it, she was almost certain. She pictured herself telling him that he could use his judgment if things went badly.

"I just can't outdo His Highness..." Her own ineptness had

produced this situation. She hated her foolishness, but she was also overjoyed that the two of them would go to such lengths to ensure her safety. She heaved a sigh.

Miles continued his gloating. "Bean had some demand for that knight. I don't know what he might do if the boy actually gives him what he wants, but I know it's nothing I agreed to."

"Oh, isn't it?"

"Think about it. Only people of a very specific bloodline can use this spell to raise the dead. Do you think I would let it slip through my fingers so easily? The moment people die, they become laborers with unlimited endurance."

"I see now. You were never in league with Bean philosophically. It was always about the slave trade for you. In fact…it's not even slave trading anymore, is it? You've stooped to simple grave robbing."

Miles only laughed, appearing unmoved by Crusch's barb.

So they had been wrong to suspect the House of Argyle of slaving. What Miles had been bringing them over the months were not slaves but a vast number of corpses. His role had been to procure the bodies that would be used to test the Sacrament of the Immortal King.

"Incidentally, the kingdom has no laws against the selling of dead bodies. It may not be the most reputable business in the world, but it's not a crime. You understand?" Miles said mockingly.

At first blush, it seemed like a good excuse. But for it to work, the country would have to close its eyes to one crucial thing.

"You're right," Crusch said, "we can't get you on charges of slave trading. But how do you expect to explain away what you've done to me? Kidnapping and imprisoning a duchess, not to mention the use of forbidden magic. Those are crimes. Far more serious ones than slaving."

"Yes, we do have a problem there. If I were to be arrested, I doubt I'd avoid the most terrible punishment they could pass down on me. So I have a request of you, my princess. I thought perhaps you and your knight could help see me safely back to my home country."

Miles looked like he might lick his chops as he made this suggestion. Crusch could sense confidence in his words, a strong wind that said this was not a bluff. That meant he believed he had some way out of this net.

"Frankly, it's not easy to take your word. You think you can get Ferris and me out through that battlefield?"

"Not easily, if you don't agree to cooperate. I won't do anything bad to you. Once I'm safely back in Volakia, you and your attendant can spend the rest of your days together. I'll negotiate it, don't you worry. I confess I fell for you at first sight, Princess."

"A hobby that's in very poor taste." She didn't believe his profession of love, but he was certainly looking at her with plenty of lust. She thought she could just glimpse a shadowy figure behind Miles's forceful actions. If she could only get him to tell her who was pulling his strings…

"If you won't do as I ask, I'll have to resort to less pleasant methods to get you to come along. But I don't enjoy hurting women, so I'll have to find someone else… Yes, I think your little friend will do nicely."

"—"

"That always works best with your type. Rather than hurting you, it's best to hurt someone you care about. When I get a good, clear scream out of him, I'm sure you'll—"

"Fool."

"Hah?"

Miles had brought Ferris up as his last resort, but now Crusch spoke over him. Miles frowned as Crusch stood up. He looked at her feet, where she should have been chained to the ground.

"Wait! How can you stand? You're supposed to be bound hand and foot—"

"Looks like you got distracted. Are you surprised? You should have been suspicious the moment you noticed my clear vision!"

"Feh! Damn. So it's straight to plan B, is it, Princess?" As Crusch shook her head, he sucked his teeth and set one of his undead warriors on her.

Crusch dodged the arms of the advancing creature. The last

vestiges of the poison made her slightly unsteady, but her burgeoning anger made her forget her infirmity.

"There are still some questions I want to ask you, but my patience has its limits. I will overlook your incivility to me and even your violence. But threatening Ferris—my knight—that I will not forgive."

"Oh, won't you? And what exactly will you do with your thin, womanly arms and your hands chained?" Miles glared at Crusch, who he had backed up against the wall, and gave a hideous smile, seeing that he once again had the upper hand.

But as he spoke, Crusch raised her hands. The cuffs fell away with a click.

"Wha?!"

"It would have been no more of a problem for me if they had remained bound—But regardless, let me show you what I will do."

Although her hands and feet were free, Crusch had no weapons—but she took up a fighting stance anyway. The underground room was dark and thick with stench. But to Crusch's eyes, everything shone clearly through that fetid air. She didn't miss the slightest gust of wind. She entrusted her swordsman's spirit—her mana—to that breeze, and she lashed out with her vision.

"—"

She spoke no words, but the body of the undead warrior advancing toward her suddenly buckled. And not only the one approaching her; the same thing happened to all the zombies in the room. The same wound appeared on all of them, as though a massive sword had sliced across them, and their briefly resumed lives succumbed once more to death.

This was what had allowed her to deal so easily with the Giant Rabbits, the technique that had earned Duchess Crusch Karsten the nickname "the Valkyrie." The technique One Blow, One Hundred Felled. After her exceptionally high-level attack, Crusch clenched her hand to dissipate the blade of wind she held and looked around the basement.

"That's…the end for Miles, I believe." Most of the corpses had already been dead when she used the technique, but she spotted Miles among them. He was soaked in blood and not so much as twitching. In an undefended moment, he had taken Crusch's blow and shared the same fate as his zombies. Crusch closed her eyes, acknowledging her own inexperience and her failure to take him alive.

"When he mentioned Ferris, I lost my cool..." Remembering what had brought this on, she shook her head. But soon she recentered herself. She had to find Ferris; no doubt he was only a short distance away upstairs.

"—Duchess of Karsten, are you here?!"

She heard footsteps on the stairs, and a long shadow stretched into the basement room. It was followed by a man in the uniform of the royal guard, who blinked with astonishment and relief when he saw her. The moment she looked at him, she knew whose orders he must have come on.

"I'm fine. You're a servant of His Highness Fourier, aren't you? Good work finding this underground room."

"Thank goodness you're safe. I'm Julius Juukulius of the royal guard. His Highness told me of this room... He thought you might be confined down here."

"I see. I shouldn't have worried him so." It was relief, more than surprise, that Crusch felt at Julius's words. She smiled gently, and a look of empathy came over Julius's face, but he quickly shook his head.

"I don't mean to rush you when you must be exhausted, but getting you out of this mansion is my priority. We must hurry."

"You seem impatient. Is there trouble above us?" She detected a whiff of fretfulness from him, and it suggested that all was not well. In response, Julius looked at the ceiling.

"—The building is on fire. We have to get out before it comes down on our heads."

13

"—Who was it who stabbed my mother to death?"

Bean was visibly shaken by Ferris's question. He had held himself in check as he descended into his world of madness. Nothing Ferris had said had made any impression on him, but this question drew out an obvious reaction.

"S-stabbed her? What are you...?"

"There's no point trying to hide it. You're actually pretty good at preserving dead bodies. Everything looks just like it did the day she passed...including the cause of death."

It was impossible to defy the laws of healing magic. The basic principle of Ferris's discipline was to encourage the body's natural healing abilities, helping the body to become more capable of helping itself. But of course, a dead body had no natural healing capacity, which was why it was technically not possible to heal the wounds of a corpse—although there were exceptions.

"My mother was stabbed—repeatedly. Over and over, so many times. This... Even I feel bad for her."

His heart hurt. Although Ferris felt nothing for her as his mother, no one deserved to die in such a cruel way. But another thought accompanied this one: Such a homicidal rage was unlikely to be the work of a passerby, a stranger. If there was anyone in the past several years who had hated his mother enough to kill her, it was...

"What's that expression? ...What a way to look at your father. What—what are you saying I did?!"

"I'm not saying anything at all."

"You are! Your eyes say it! Do you think it was wrong of me? Do you, too, think I was mistaken? Looking at me with those critical eyes every day—! Who could blame me, knowing I'd been betrayed by the one I loved?! I swear it was not my fault!"

Ferris didn't have to try to pry the truth out of his father. Bean confessed it practically of his own free will.

Ferris didn't know what had happened in the Argyle household since the Karstens had taken him away. But clearly, his parents had had some kind of falling out. And things had been done which could never be undone. His mother's corpse was proof of that.

"Is it guilt that makes you want to bring her back? Because you want to apologize?"

"Do you mock me?! I want the one I love to live, to live and live! Doesn't everyone?!" Bean was frothing at the mouth. He tore at his head, ruining his carefully styled hair. "When you lose something precious to you, you'll understand! No, your mother is dead! Do you feel nothing?! You must want her back…! Don't you want her back? Can any child abandon the love of his parents? Quickly, now! Return her to life! Or—or don't you care what happens to your beloved mistress? Do you need her to die before you understand—understand how I feel?!"

"—"

In the face of Bean's onslaught, Ferris realized talk would do no good. A faint blue light shimmered around his hands, and he quietly transferred it to his mother's corpse. Somehow, the moment looked almost sacred. And then the corpse's eyes drifted open.

"H—Hannah! Oh! Hannah!" Bean was ecstatic as the body shifted, sat itself up. He nearly shoved Ferris out of the way as he took up a place at the bedside. Ferris watched as his parents shared a reunion, even though one of them had been dead only moments before.

"Hannah! I've been waiting for this moment! For us to be like this again—"

"—"

With tears in his eyes, Bean supported his wife as she sat up, but she said nothing. She stared into the face of her husband. She gently raised her hands and placed them on Bean's cheeks. He smiled at the feeling of them, and Hannah, too, smiled faintly. It was a reaction that would not have been possible for a mere moving corpse, like one of the undead warriors.

And then…

"H-Han…nah…?"

Suddenly she was wringing the surprised rasp out of Bean. Her hands were around his neck, which creaked under a strength that the dead woman's thin arms should not have had.

"Whh—at is-s…? Feeli—x…!" He looked to his son, his eyes begging for help.

"Go see the person you love, wherever she is. That's what I'm going to do," Ferris responded quietly. Bean's face went rigid with shock, but Ferris showed not a hint of a reaction. "I won't let anyone take her from me. Especially the people who stole everything from me. She gave me something, and you'll never have it from me. I'll never give you any of the things I got when I became a person."

"Hrk... Hrrk..."

"Laying a finger on Lady Crusch was your first mistake— If you hadn't, I..."

He had his hand to his chest, but he couldn't bring himself to finish his sentence. He closed his mouth.

Even if he could have said the words, Bean wouldn't have heard them. The strength had already left his arms and legs, the light was gone from his eyes and the soul from his body. This was death, the absolute separation about which even Ferris could do nothing.

"...You should've just sent a letter."

Ferris spoke into the limitless emptiness, and it was the truest thing he said. Maybe he would have torn it up. Maybe he never would have accepted it. But just maybe, he wouldn't have done either. Just maybe, they would have had a chance to talk to each other.

With a gentle sigh, Ferris looked at Hannah. She looked back at him, still holding the limp form of the husband she had strangled, and smiled again.

Then her smile fell—literally—as she crumbled into a pile of powdery dust. A moment later, all that remained was a mound of his mother's ashes, the corpse of his father buried among them.

As Ferris looked at his father, dead, and his mother, vanished, a voice devoid of emotion spoke to him.

"—Master Felix. Is this what you wanted for them both?"

It was the maid, who had remained with them throughout everything and kept silent until the very end.

Ferris shook his head. "...It's not just that the spell book is incomplete. It was never a question of power as a spell caster. Using an awful spell like that—forcing a body that's stopped to start again—of course it was going to break down right away."

Surely Bean had known that. He was perfectly aware of the problem with the spell itself; that was why he hadn't brought his wife back on his own. Why had he wanted Ferris to do it? Had he really hoped for something more? Or did he just want to pass off responsibility for what would come of it? Now, Ferris would never know.

"So what caused the Lady to…strangle the master?"

"I can't say. All I did was bring her back to life using a flawed spell. Maybe it was lingering hatred from before her death that made the corpse do what it did."

She had been stabbed to death, after all. The soul didn't actually reside in the resurrected corpse, but perhaps the pain of it remained. Another thing Ferris didn't understand.

"…Maybe the lady simply couldn't bear to see the master live on in disgrace. She really did love him, you know." Against Ferris's gloomy assessment, the maid had another interpretation. It was perhaps too pretty an explanation for what had just happened.

"Come to think of it, what about you? Who are you, exactly?" There was one more thing Ferris didn't know, but it was an answer he might be able to get.

He had no idea what position the maid was in. Had she been in league with Bean? But she hadn't done anything to stop his death. And she didn't seem hostile to Ferris now.

As Ferris stood frowning, the maid smiled at him for the first time. It was a terribly lonely smile.

"I'm just a servant. I owe much to the master and his lady… I even held you in my arms many times, Master Felix."

"…Huh…"

The story didn't quite click with him. He couldn't imagine such a familial scene had ever taken place in this house.

"But never mind. I have to help Lady Crusch. Is she really all right?"

"You've no need to worry about that. I unlocked her chains. I think she's quite capable of getting away on her own." Then the maid gestured down the stairs, and Ferris immediately understood where

Crusch had been held. She had been shut up in that hideous basement room.

"That place again…!"

"Indeed. The master was rather set in his ways."

Ferris burned with anger, but the maid, for her part, continued to smile, still as lonesome as before. The expression didn't leave her face as she slowly approached the bed and the two corpses.

"I'm going down there," Ferris said. "You won't try to stop me?"

"Please, do exactly as you wish. I shall see the master and his lady on their way."

After all this, Ferris found he didn't have the slightest idea what the maid was thinking. But when it came to giving funeral rites to his mother and father, he thought it was more appropriate that this servant do it, rather than a boy who felt nothing for the people who called themselves his parents.

"I'll let you handle it, then. And I'll speak to Lady Crusch about you." There was no chance the maid would go unpunished, but perhaps he could gain her some clemency. With that thought in mind, he hurried out of the bedroom. As he rushed down the hallway, he heard something behind him.

"—Good-bye, my dear Felix."

"Huh?"

Then there was the sound of a door closing and a click as it locked. Ferris stopped in his tracks; that click gave him a bad feeling. He had no good reason for it, but his intuition said the sound marked something from which there was no turning back.

"Wait! Why'd you lock the door? What are you going to do?!" He went back and pounded desperately on the door, but there was no answer. Eventually, though, a response came from the far side that was more matter-of-fact than any reply could be.

"—That's hot!" The burning sensation made his hand jump off the doorknob. At the same moment, he caught another smell mingling with the stench of rot in the house: something burning. *Fire.* A fire had been set in the room he had just left, by the maid who had locked herself inside.

"What do you think you're doing?!"

But still there was no answer. Only immense heat told him what the maid intended.

He was aghast at how quickly the fire spread. It dawned on him that the plan all along had been for the entire household to die together. He kicked the door viciously.

"I hate this place! And everyone in it! All of it, all of it! I hate you—!!"

He should never have come back. He wished he had never seen his father or his mother, or that maid.

He dashed through the hallway, shoving aside undead warriors who stood dumbly, making for the stairs. The fire would take the whole house, and the remaining undead warriors would be cremated along with it. But so would Crusch, in the basement room.

Ferris went down the stairs, heading for that vile room underground. He was on the first floor. Where should he go to get to the room? He was in his own house, but he didn't know. He knew nothing. It was infuriating, so infuriating.

"Why does this place keep tormenting me…!"

He hated his legs for not being able to run any faster. He hated his memory for its failure to help him find the basement room. He hated his parents, who had never spared him a second thought. He hated the maid who had chosen to accompany his parents into death. It was as if everything here, all of it, every inch of this house, existed only to cause him suffering.

"Ferris!"

But just as he was about to burst into tears, he heard a voice from downstairs. His soul resonated with the sharp, resounding timbre instantly.

"Lady Crusch—!"

Even framed by leaping crimson flames, even in a place thick with the smell of rot, Crusch was beautiful. Ferris found her in the great room, rushed to her, and clung to her without a second's hesitation. She held him tight in her arms.

"Thank goodness you're safe," she said.

"Th-that's my l-line..." he said.

"I guess it is. I'm sorry for worrying you. But I'm all right, thanks to His Highness's plan."

Ferris looked and saw Julius, presumably there at Fourier's behest, standing beside Crusch. So he was the one who had saved her. But there was no time for Ferris to express his gratitude now.

Crusch looked up, narrowing her eyes as she confirmed that the source of the fire was above them.

"Ferris, are your parents...?"

"Get—! Get me out...now...!"

"Ferris?"

"Get me out of here! Take me away, just like before...! There's nothing here! If I stay here, I won't be me anymore...! Make me... human... Keep me by your side. With you, Lady Crusch, and His Highness...!" he begged her, stumbling over his words.

Emotions ran through Ferris that seemed alien even to him. Julius's face clouded with confusion, and he looked to Crusch as if for guidance.

She, in turn, answered, "—All right. Let's put an end to this time of injustice you've endured." She held him close, patting him comfortingly on the back. Ferris was surprised how relieved the gesture made him feel. "Julius, take the lead. I'll bring Ferris."

Julius nodded and set off in front of them. He easily pushed aside the undead warriors who stood mindlessly in their way, while others were swallowed by the flames. In the burning corpses, Ferris saw himself in this house. Burning, burning to the ground.

The terrible memories were swathed in fire, the origin he had so long suppressed turning to ash in a mantle of red.

"Lady Crusch, you're all right—!"

Almost before he knew what had happened, they were out of the mansion. A military official was rushing up to Crusch, who still held fast to Ferris's shoulders. They said something to each other, and Crusch kept Ferris's hand in hers the whole time.

"Look, the undead warriors—!" someone called out.

All the zombies had begun to move at once. Moments earlier, they had been attacking anything that got close. Now they all shuffled toward the mansion. They filed into the burning house, and one by one were reduced to motes of soot and dust.

Only the spell caster, or someone given authority by the spell caster, could control the zombies. With Bean dead, the warriors were merely awaiting their end.

"Perhaps even corpses don't wish to defile themselves after death," Julius said. His uniform was soiled with pus, and he watched the undead warriors march to their own destruction. There was no reply. All they could do was watch until the unstoppable conflagration consumed the house and all the undead had returned to ash.

14

"Damn her! Damn that woman...! This is serious. She'll pay for this!"

Miles spat and cursed as he tried to staunch the blood flowing out of him. The wound ran from his right shoulder to his back, and he couldn't treat it by himself. He had crudely wound some clothes around it, managing to stop the bleeding enough to cling to consciousness.

—Miles had survived the blow that cut down the zombies.

He'd always had a sixth sense for when his life was in danger. It had saved him today, but things couldn't get any worse. Not only had Crusch escaped, but Miles hadn't even been able to spirit away the spell caster who had used the Sacrament of the Immortal King.

In the distance, he could see the Argyle mansion wreathed in flame. The remaining undead warriors were incinerating themselves. Their suicide was a little distraction Miles had cooked up to buy himself time to escape. Bean was supposed to have overall command of the zombies, but since nothing was stopping them from carrying out Miles's orders to destroy themselves, he surmised that

Bean must be dead. Puppets and puppeteer alike were completely useless.

"All that work, and my only reward is a copy of his spell book... Blasted! These are my just desserts? What am I even going to tell them back in Volakia, returning like this...?"

"—Oh, you won't have to worry about that. If you land quietly."

No sooner had he let out his angry mutter than Miles was startled by a reply. It was only natural, considering where he was: up in the sky, far above the ground. So high up he could look down on the clouds. No one should have been able to speak to him there. And yet the owner of the voice continued calmly.

"I never expected a dragon rider. I nearly missed you. You're quite the capable spy—which is why I recommend you land quietly."

The red-haired youth who casually rode upon the winged dragon seemed to be doing his best to press Miles's buttons. The boy had the sun at his back, making it impossible to see his face, and that left Miles to imagine the worst.

The flying dragon was something Miles had brought from Volakia to give him a means of escape if necessary. He had a tunnel from the basement room in the mansion to the outside, and he had intended to bring Crusch and the spell caster with him, using the dragon to escape the net of undead around them. It was humiliating to flee home alone, his plan in tatters.

"There aren't supposed to be any dragon riders in Lugunica!" Miles yelped.

Unlike water and land dragons, flying dragons were proud and would not readily submit to human control. Even in the Volakia Empire the knowledge was hard to come by; beyond the Empire's borders, it shouldn't have been known at all. And that Lugunica, a nation that called itself the Dragonfriend Kingdom, should try to tame and train them—it would be a terrifying task. The skies were supposed to belong to the Volakia Empire alone.

"Surely they haven't broken that unwritten law—?"

"No, you're quite right. Lugunica has no dragon riders. I just stowed away."

Miles gasped. "Im—impossible!" His anger at finding someone trespassing on his domain so high up in the sky was intensified by the young man's nonchalant answer.

The slaver, his eyes bloodshot, ordered the dragon to make a quick about-face. They were flying almost level with the clouds; who could simply "stow away" at that altitude? In this world of fearsome winds, Miles and the dragon were one. It was his pride as a dragon rider, as well as the bond of trust forged with the creature since they had both been young, that made such flight possible. If they could throw the boy off in an unguarded moment, it would be over.

"I'll warn you again," the young man said. "Just bring the dragon to the ground. I can't permit you to leave the country."

"That's enough out of you! You'll die before I land this dragon!"

"...A shame."

Miles, on the ragged edge of consciousness from blood loss, caused the dragon to slow down very suddenly. He gritted his teeth against the ensuing force, which slammed into all his wounds at once and made his bones creak.

The boy, however, had no chance. With nothing to hold on to, he went tumbling from the dragon's back and fell even as Miles watched.

That was it. He would be reduced to bits of quivering flesh when he hit the ground, and good riddance to him.

"Wh-what the hell was that boy, anyway...? It doesn't matter. Right now, I have to..."

Miles was lucky not to be spitting blood at this point. He gripped the reins tightly. His injuries had begun to bleed again. If he didn't rest soon, he couldn't be sure he would survive.

"—!"

No sooner had he had this thought than he felt his intuition prickle. It was the same feeling he'd gotten before Crusch attacked, the one that said he was in mortal danger.

It was born of an instinct deeper than thought, one that sought to preserve life and limb above all else. It had saved him more than once. But this time, in this instant, Miles found his arms and legs unwilling to move. And why not? After all, there was no point in trying to run from the overwhelming sense of death rising up from beneath him.

"...Ah."

Miles hardly had time to speak before he was engulfed in light. The dragon and its rider vanished into the sky, leaving no trace.

And then there was nothing.

15

"We had someone on the inside. We made contact with that maid during the two months we were watching for the slaver. I believed we had to do more than just watch if we wanted things to work out in our favor."

As they stared at the smoldering remains of the Argyle mansion, Crusch explained to Ferris what had happened in his absence.

She gazed at the debris. "When I was poisoned, I started to worry that her cooperation with us might have been a sham. But she did away with any doubts when she snuck away from our two criminals to unlock my manacles in the basement."

"Why would she go out of her way to get involved?" Ferris said. "It seems so dangerous..."

"During our investigation, I started to have questions about the slave trader who was visiting the house. I would have liked to take him alive—that's my fault. Personally, I think he may have been an agent of the Volakia Empire... But I'm sure if we asked them about it, they would play innocent."

Crusch seemed to have a good grasp of the players involved in this plot. The only thing she didn't appear to have figured out was what Bean had hoped to achieve with the Sacrament of the Immortal King and why he had needed Ferris. Really, only a peek into Bean's mind could have answered those questions.

"I...I just got in the way, didn't I? I overstepped myself, in a lot of ways..."

Even if Ferris hadn't come back, Crusch would have gotten

herself out of her prison and stopped Bean's plan. Perhaps the house wouldn't have burned down, leaving everything a pile of ash.

"...If we focus on the hypothetical, our lives will be nothing but regrets. Perhaps without you, I would be dead underground by now. If you and His Highness hadn't come, I might not be standing here safe."

"You're just saying that to make me feel better."

"It's true, I am. But regretting your actions on the basis of what might have been is worse. It can only exhaust you." While Ferris stared disconsolately at the ashes, Crusch crossed her arms and spoke firmly. "You were worried about me, and with no concern for your own safety you came back to a place you had tried to avoid your entire life. When I heard that, locked up in that underground room, I cursed my own incompetence. But I was also...happy."

"Happy, Lady Crusch?"

"It must have been extremely painful for you to come back here. What was done to you in your youth hardly bears speaking of. I couldn't blame you for being unable to think about it or unwilling to approach. And despite that, you came here to rescue me— You must forgive me, but I was overjoyed."

Crusch knelt so that she could look Ferris in the face where he was crouched down, hugging his knees. Her amber eyes pierced him, cutting through the dark clouds that clung to his heart.

Why, how, did this person always make such warmth well up in his chest?

"Was I...able to help you, Lady Crusch? Will you allow me, even as I am...to stay by your side, and dedicate my life to you?"

"I stand by my answer."

"...Tell me again. With the words you used...back then."

She felt his emotions roiling—tremendous regret, and at the same time a yearning for happiness. If only he could break through all those things, if only he could find the strength to stand.

"—Raise your head and look forward. Don't let those dark clouds gather in your eyes. It may be difficult at first, but I'll help you. For now, just trust me."

He wanted her to save him, with the words she had used to lead him out of the darkness and show him the world for the first time.

"—"

Wordlessly, Ferris looked at Crusch, and then he looked again at the burned remains of the mansion. For some reason, he felt tears on his cheeks. And then he found he couldn't stop them.

Embraced by a pair of strong, slim arms, Ferris wept like a child.

16

—As she held the crying Ferris, Crusch thought back to what had happened in the basement room.

The maid had slipped away from Bean and Miles and come down to Crusch. She unfastened the restraints and manacles and removed Crusch's blindfold. Before the maid left, however, Crusch called out and questioned her.

"Whose side are you on? You poisoned me—but now you're abiding by our agreement and helping me escape. Your actions don't make sense."

"I apologize if you find me confusing. But I have my own goals in mind."

"Oh, do you? Is that the reason you continue to serve the House of Argyle?"

One of the reports to Crusch had stated that Bean and this maid had known each other for much of their lives. The relationship had apparently been long and quite close, much like that between Crusch and Ferris. And Crusch knew that if she were to go mad, Ferris would almost certainly stay with her rather than abandon her.

"Lady Crusch," the maid began, "have you ever been in love?"

The question caught her off guard. Crusch looked at the maid wide-eyed, unsure what she meant. The maid closed her eyes and shook her head, taking Crusch's silence for an answer.

"Then I don't think any amount of explaining would help you understand what I want."

"...The flow of this conversation makes it clear who your feelings are for. But there are too many things that it doesn't explain. Were you Felix's wet nurse?"

"—"

The moment Crusch said that, the maid's formerly expressionless face stiffened, and the wind picked up. No—it only looked that way to Crusch. In reality, it was a swell of powerful emotion. It was something like delusion. The same tumultuous feelings she had sensed in Bean resided in this woman, too. But that suggested...

"...Wait. Your hair. Your eyes..."

Looking at the maid's taut face, a spark caught in Crusch's mind. The remarkable flaxen hair. The clear yellow eyes and gentle expression. If she were to smile kindly, Crusch suspected her face would bear a strong resemblance to one she knew very well.

—She reflected that Ferris had met his fate because of the suspicion of infidelity.

"If you have the first thought of harming Felix..."

"I'm not going to do anything to Felix. You're the one who distanced yourself from him, aren't you? What I want has nothing to do with Felix...with that boy."

That was the last thing the maid said as she turned away from Crusch. With the chains unlocked, it would have been possible to stop her. But the commotion would have meant the end of everything Crusch had worked for. For a moment, the duchess found herself caught between her personal and official priorities. Then, still unable to choose, she called out to the departing maid.

"Hannah! Hannah Rigret!"

"If you're too loud, you'll attract Miles's attention. Now is the time to be loyal to your duty."

Crusch had no choice but to watch as the maid disappeared from view.

The taste of defeat bitter in her mouth, Crusch hoped she would have another chance to talk with the maid. Then she would discover the true connection between that woman and her knight.

But she would never get the chance. The flames consumed Argyle manor: the bodies of Ferris's mother and father, along with the maid, and whatever truth she was keeping.

Crusch was left with only her doubts and a secret, the only one she could never tell Ferris.

17

Overhead, the clouds that had crowded the sky were broken. Fourier quietly let out a breath. Before they'd left the castle, he'd ordered Marcus to put some insurance in place, and what happened in the sky was proof that it had worked. Although there might be some questions later about the use of a tactic that was normally forbidden so close to the country's borders.

"But I don't think we'll have to meet Volakia in force today. They don't want to contend with us any more than we with them."

Some outside agency had clearly been involved in the recent events surrounding the House of Argyle. Fourier had never met Bean Argyle personally, but the family's status and history convinced him that Bean didn't have the ability to do something like this on his own.

He thought about who might have played a part in this. Perhaps those within Lugunica who wanted to see Crusch fall from grace. Or perhaps an interloper from outside the country, someone with bigger goals in mind. He forced himself to contemplate the worst possible scenario. It was likely that what the Volakians had wanted from all this was to obtain the House of Argyle's secret spell that allowed them to control undead warriors. The current Volakian emperor was said to be a cruel man. Given the friction between Volakia and Lugunica, it had been necessary to prevent anyone else learning the forbidden spell.

"I managed to do everything I wanted to. Sometimes I impress even myself." Fourier's reading of the situation had been so perfect that he found himself bursting into spontaneous self-congratulation.

Fourier's intuition sometimes proved considerably sharper than average, but this time it had been especially brilliant. Then again, he had been focusing his full concentration on it ever since Crusch had spoken with him.

Granted, this sometimes left him with a pain in his head and a heaviness in his chest…

"But it's a very small price to save Crusch and Ferris."

Those two were now talking together near the burned ruins of the Argyle mansion. He dearly wished to join them, but it would have been a most impolitic time to break in. Ferris and Crusch shared a bond that was for them alone. True, Fourier had his own bond with each of them, but he knew that at this moment it was necessary to keep his distance for reasons he couldn't fully articulate.

"Of course, it's hard for me to let Ferris have Crusch all to himself right now, given how worried I was about her…"

"On behalf of your friends, Your Highness, let me thank you for your considerateness." The speaker was Julius, who rode with Fourier in the dragon carriage. He seemed to find recent events thought provoking in his own way. His expression looked different, somehow, from the way it had before they left the castle.

"I gave you your fair share of trouble, too, didn't I, Julius? Well done getting them both out at the very end there."

"You needn't thank me, Your Highness. Truth be told, today's events made me feel acutely how powerless I really am. I think I may have let being chosen for the royal guard make me forget what it truly means to be a knight."

"Another serious one! Knights should be more—well—gallant! Do some brave deeds, and you'll be knight enough. Yes, I'm sure of it."

Julius looked entirely taken aback by Fourier's pronouncement. But he composed himself quickly and smiled, then nodded. "You've surprised me more than once today, Your Highness. I, Julius, swear anew my fealty to you."

"I'm not quite sure how I feel about that, but I accept your loyalty. Devotion to the kingdom is truly valuable. Let your heart be bound not to me, but seek the prosperity of our whole land. Now… you think it's about time?"

Fourier leaned over to get a look at Crusch and Ferris. Ferris, who had been crying in Crusch's arms earlier, was now turned away, blowing his nose. It looked like things had calmed down some. He could call out to them soon.

"Maybe I'll go and join them, then." Now eager, Fourier stepped proudly from the dragon carriage and down onto the grass, ready to go over to Crusch and Ferris. But as he did so, his vision wavered.

"—Your Highness?" Julius's voice sounded strikingly far away. The next thing he knew, he felt an impact, and everything was sideways.

Fourier himself didn't know what had happened. Until so recently he had been filled with the sense that he could see everything that was happening in the world, yet now that feeling had utterly abandoned him.

"Ferris! Ferris, come quickly! His Highness Fourier needs you!"

Julius's panicked shout was the last thing Fourier heard as his consciousness slipped away. Everything went dark, the world grew distant. But just before it left him, he heard two beloved voices calling his name. Fourier clung to that sound as the darkness overcame him.

<END>

THE DREAM OF THE LION KING

1

Fourier Lugunica's collapse was paid comparatively scant attention in the Kingdom of Lugunica.

A member of the royal family had fallen ill, and it was treated lightly. Normally, such a thing could not have been imagined, but at that moment it was excused by a peculiar circumstance in the kingdom.

—Fourier was not the only member of the royal family who had been brought down by disease.

Rather, every single member of the royal family of Lugunica had fallen ill. Fourier's father, the current king, Randohal Lugunica, was of course among them. There were individual differences in the symptoms of illness, but simple guesswork could not be allowed with a disease whose name and origin no one knew. In its whole history, the kingdom had never faced something like this, and it shuddered with the encroaching crisis.

"So my probationary period is fiiiinally over and I get to be a regular member of the guard, but the captain is just the worst! He's acting totally different from before! What a bully!"

"Mm, I thought as much. Just when you think Marcus is as serious as he looks, he turns out to have a mischievous side. I figured you two would get along."

"Your Highness, are you listening to me? Ferri is getting bullied by a mean ol' superior in the royal guard. I'm looking for some comfort here!" His eyes watered and his voice shook, but this only caused Fourier to smile.

Ferris shook his head helplessly at Fourier's amusement. Then he brought some water to the prince's sickbed and held it to Fourier's lips. The young man sat up with some difficulty, and Ferris could hear the water from the pitcher running down his throat.

"I'm sorry for always putting you to such trouble. It's almost like you're my personal attendant these days."

"Don't worry, don't worry! These days it's meowthing but low-lifes trying to get Ferri to heal their training wounds just 'cause they think I'm cute. I would *much* rather be with you, Your Highness. And Lady Crusch hasn't been acting very friendly lately…"

"Yes, she must be quite busy. I haven't seen her for days, and I'm getting lonely. Perhaps it has to do with my frustration at being unable to move. This accursed illness."

"—"

Fourier wiped his moistened lips on his sleeve, then nestled into his pillow and smiled weakly. His smile showed his distinctive canines, as always, but there was no energy to it. It was a forced smile to hide from Ferris the sharp pain running through his chest.

Fourier was emaciated. His shining golden hair had lost its luster, and his eyes, red like the twilight sun, seemed somehow faint. He spoke without vigor and often succumbed to fits of coughing. Above all, he no longer had even the strength to walk around. For the last month, he had been completely bedridden.

—It had all started on the day of the trouble at the House of Argyle. After the mansion burned to the ground, Fourier had stepped from his dragon carriage, only to collapse. The sight had caused Ferris to put aside all his emotions and focus everything on healing the prince.

Fourier seemed to be in pain. Ferris had transferred life force to him, put him in the carriage, and returned to the castle with all haste. That was where they first learned the grim truth that the entire royal family was ill.

After that, all the patients, including Fourier, were confined to bed rest in the royal chambers. The illness went on without significant change, but its pathology remained mysterious—even Ferris couldn't figure out what was causing it. Even Ferris, who was second to none in the art of using mana to cure sickness.

There had been signs. Ferris himself had seen Fourier's coughing fits and occasional bouts of ill health. At the Karsten mansion, he had groaned in pain—but he had refused to let Ferris examine him.

At the time, Ferris had been so busy thinking about himself and Crusch that he had overlooked these things. And only now was he keeping close to the prince, trying to make things better now that it was more convenient for him. Ferris hated himself so much, he wanted to disappear from existence.

"Ferris, shouldn't you—? Aren't you supposed to be with my father, not with me? You're the heir to the kingdom's greatest healer. It's your duty."

"It's all right. I make sure I've done everything I'm supposed to before I come to Your Highness. Don't make the mistake of thinking I'm putting you ahead of the king."

"I see, it was simply my misunderstanding. How embarrassing—! Crusch is going to laugh at me."

Fourier's smile as he spoke Crusch's name was lonesome. People grow more prone to loneliness as their bodies weaken with illness. Even Fourier, the very epitome of enthusiasm.

"Lady Crusch..." Ferris took Fourier's hand in his, patting it gently, and whispered the name like a prayer.

He knew Crusch was immensely busy. She was one of the highest-ranking nobles, and with the entire royal family incapacitated, there wasn't a moment when her hands weren't full. And yet, even so, Ferris couldn't help thinking...

I wish she would come comfort this sweet, lonely, precious person.

He couldn't do it by himself. He was no substitute for Crusch. Ferris treasured Fourier so much, and yet once again, he was unable to give the prince the strength he needed. Powerlessness tore always at Ferris's heart, threatening to break it.

"...The heartsick look doesn't suit you." Fourier's voice found Ferris under his self-torment, and then self-reproach struck him like a thunderbolt. Mentally gritting his teeth, he mustered a smile for Fourier.

"Aw, I'm not heartsick. Ferri is feeling fine—just fine!"

Far be it from him to start crying. Not here, not now. He might be powerless, but he had his pride. He couldn't heal Fourier's illness, but he could manage a smile.

If that was all he could do, then he would do it come hell or high water.

"Gosh, Your Highness! If you just eat and drink and then go right to sleep, you'll get fat...!"

"And then...Crusch won't...like me anymore..."

All he could do was remind the prince of the everyday things, so maybe Fourier could revisit them in his dreams.

2

In the royal assembly hall, Crusch Karsten had found herself unable to think anything for a very, very long time. For several days now the powerful and noble of the realm, along with the Council of Elders, the organization that essentially acted as the kingdom's brain, had been discussing what to do about the turmoil that faced their nation.

Crusch was getting awfully sick of the meetings she was obliged to attend as duchess. They had been talking for so long that she knew even the smallest details of every attending noble's face.

They had to deal with rituals where the king's presence was expected, while trying to prevent any word of the current situation reaching the world's three major powers. They had to take care of all the duties each member of the royal family would normally have attended to, all while trying to figure out what to do about a disease whose origins remained obscure. And on top of all that, each of the nobles had the usual business of their domains to contend with. It led to a level of confusion and exhaustion that few of them could remember experiencing before.

But now, a month after all this had started, the royal family's condition finally seemed not to be getting any worse. This was what they had just begun to discuss when—

"First Prince Zabinel is dead, you say...?"

The tearful report brought by the spell caster from the Royal Academy of Healing was more than enough to throw the room back into near panic. First Prince Zabinel Lugunica had been the first of the confirmed cases of illness in the royal castle. Hence the condition afflicting him might have been the quickest to act...

"This is all too sudden! How can this be? How can His Highness have gotten so ill?"

"It's impossible! I met with him only yesterday, and he... He gave no sign of being so close to the end..."

Those who had been especially close to Zabinel mourned the sudden news of his passing. But they weren't the only ones left agape at the report. Everyone in the room was shocked.

One person had now died from the disease that afflicted the entire royal family. And still no one knew the cause or how to treat it.

"Highness..." Crusch, too, felt a pang at the news. She was usually so careful to stand up straight, but now she felt she might break in half with the anxiety tearing at her innards. She could only think of Fourier, lying in his sickbed and offering his weak smile when she came to see him.

"We must consider the possibility that His Majesty, too, will leave us." Even as she chewed her lip, Crusch heard a raspy voice. She looked up to find that everyone who had heard had focused on the center of the room, where Miklotov, the representative of the Council of Elders, stood.

"Sir Miklotov, a poor jest! His Majesty? Leave us?"

"Mm. The inevitable cannot be avoided, no matter how diligently we look away from reality. We cannot afford to be optimists right now. Or else we will not be able to fulfill the duties of the most precious seat in our nation. Am I wrong?"

"Ngh..."

"We see now how quickly the condition may turn—and that means that even tomorrow, we could find ourselves facing the worst. When it happens, it will shake the kingdom, and our role is to support the nation during that time. We must not turn our backs on the people."

Miklotov's pointed pronouncement put to rest those who thought he was being disrespectful. His words may have been unsparing toward the kingdom's leader, but this only made them all the more necessary.

Thus, Crusch was the first to put aside her personal feelings and speak on the sage's behalf. "Sir Miklotov is right. If anything should happen to His Majesty, the kingdom won't disappear. It will fall to us to do something about it."

Crusch was one of only a few present of ducal rank, but she had relatively little experience and hadn't established herself yet. Still, her speaking up helped the rest of the nobles start to feel the same way.

"I'm grateful for your endorsement," Miklotov said. "Naturally, I still hope and pray that His Highness and His Highness's family will come safely through this trial. Please don't misunderstand me on that point."

He moved that the assembly begin discussing what to do with the kingdom in the event that they had no king—and last of all, he shot a meaningful glance at Crusch. Perhaps he was expressing his gratitude for her being the first to support him. But she didn't see it; she had already collapsed into her seat.

With things the way they were, she wouldn't be able to drop in on Fourier. She had become so constrained by her noble duties that she didn't even have time to see him. She couldn't let this precious, limited time go to waste. That was what she told herself even as her duty compelled her to remain at the meeting.

3

"...Crusch, is that you?"

Crusch was somewhat surprised to see Fourier open his eyes as he sensed her entering his room. She had tried to walk as quietly as possible so as not to disturb his sleep. Not only could he tell someone was there, but he had even known who it was.

"You surprise me, Your Highness. I have the sense there's nothing I can hide from you."

"And...perhaps there isn't. That's simply how well we know each other. Even with my eyes closed, even in the depths of sleep, I know it's you... It's been some time. Have you been well?"

"I've been terribly busy, but my health is fine. Your color looks good today, Your Highness. That's a relief." Crusch sat in a chair by the bed and studied Fourier's face.

Her last visit had been only a few days earlier, yet he seemed even thinner now. And Fourier had never been the beefiest person around. He was through burning fat; now his body was consuming itself. His cheekbones stood out slightly. It was impossible not to see how the disease was ravaging him.

"Crusch...I want to...feel your touch."

"Yes, Your Highness. With your permission." She gently reached under the sheets and took Fourier's trembling hand. His fingers had always been slim, but now they were despairingly frail. She rubbed the palm of his hand and interlaced her fingers with his.

"Ah. The touch of your fingers is pleasant," he said. "A woman's hand."

"Your Highness's hand feels rather thin, for a man. One would never think you had practiced so long with the sword."

"The sword... Yes, the sword... I suppose I'm the only one who could possibly best you. Though I've neglected my training for many days now."

"Your Highness would surely recover from a few days of rest before long. Though they do say that it takes three days of work to make up for one missed."

"Are you telling me to work three times as long as I've rested...? Merciless!" And then, like so often before, he fell into a fit of coughing. Crusch hurriedly turned him on his side and rubbed his back gently until it passed. His breathing was so harsh, and his back seemed so small.

"Ah, yes, what about...? What about the Argyles? And Ferris? Is everything going well?" When Crusch said nothing, Fourier spoke as if a thought had just occurred to him.

Feeling saved by the change of subject, Crusch nodded and said, "Yes. Thanks to Your Highness's good offices. I'm glad to say what occurred at the Argyle estate hasn't gone beyond the few of us. The deaths of Ferris's mother and father are being called an accident. So Ferris—"

"Can safely inherit the Argyle name. Good. That's good. He may say he doesn't want it, but he can't throw away everything he was born to. He mustn't."

"Do you think he'll be able to accept it?"

"Of course—he is my friend, and your knight, after all!" Fourier half turned to her and smiled, showing his teeth. He almost coughed again, but he forced it down into his throat. It caused his eyes to water, but he kept smiling. Seeing it, Crusch found herself unable to form any words. But she mustered all the strength she had to smile back.

This had never been a particular talent of hers, but Fourier often wanted to see her smile.

"Mm... I knew...your smile was...beautiful."

She shouldn't have left all the good cheer to Ferris. She should have at least learned how to make herself smile. Crusch tried to live life without regrets, but this one thing she dearly wished were different.

4

Over the past several months, Ferris had found it increasingly hard to believe that he was one of the Knights of the Royal Guard. He had been going to the healers' academy to check on the royal family members, and to nurse Fourier. How was any of this the work of a knight? It seemed a lot more like what a spell caster of the Royal Academy of Healing would do.

"The third prince passed away last night. That's the seventh person..."

Another one had gone, all the healers' efforts in vain. Ferris didn't want to hear the name of another dead royal, but at the academy the news was going to reach him whether he wanted it to or not.

Seven victims, and still they didn't know the cause of the disease. All they had learned was that once the patient developed a fever and became comatose, they were beyond help. All this, and just one worthless grain of knowledge.

"___"

Grieved, Ferris left the king's sickroom after another day of trying various curative magics to no effect. He had always regarded this place with awe, but after spending so much time there, he no longer felt anxious about it. His initial emotion, something like a holy terror, had long ago given way to a sense of powerlessness.

Ferris carried a black book as he walked through the halls of the royal castle. It was covered in blood and fingerprints. It could have been called, in some sense, a gift from his father.

The Sacrament of the Immortal King...

A secret spell developed by a witch that could resurrect the dead, granting corpses the power to walk again. His father had not been able to replicate the spell successfully, but if it could be done, even those who were gone could be saved...

"His Highness... If anything happens to His Highness..."

Ferris thought of Fourier, who grew thinner and more infirm by the day and, not for the first time, pictured himself getting the sacrament to work. Fourier's death, among all others, was not one he could simply turn away from.

He would need a miracle to save the fourth prince. And he never seemed to get a miracle when he asked for one. The sacrament was the only other thing Ferris could think of.

When he entered Fourier's sickroom, the bedridden prince laughed weakly and said, "Ferris, the makeup worked beautifully.

Crusch thought my color was good... Ha-ha, we sure pulled the wool over her eyes. She's so trusting."

The makeup was something Ferris had applied so Fourier's pallor would look healthier. Fourier had begged Ferris not to let him look bad in front of Crusch when she came to visit. Ferris was painfully aware that this had nothing to do with Fourier's pride but instead his consideration for Crusch.

Ferris said nothing. Fourier spoke as if he could read the boy's mind. "Nothing...troubling you with the knights, Ferris? Don't forget to lean on your friend... Yes, on Julius. You try to take on too much by yourself sometimes."

There were times these days when Ferris wasn't sure who was comforting whom on these visits.

"My... My friends. You, Your Highness... You're my only friend. Aren't you? So when you aren't feeling strong, I end up...by myself."

"Certainly...not. Don't worry, Ferris. You're kind, and at heart you are strong. Everyone loves you...and will befriend you, as I have. I may have been your first friend, but you needn't let me be your last. Remember this: Don't force yourself to be alone."

"Your Highness..."

Why was he talking like this, like this was the end? It wasn't the end. And how could he seem so attuned to what Ferris was feeling? Fourier's words had held real power lately. Not worldly power, but the piercing power of truth. It made Ferris afraid.

"Your Highness...! Your Highness, if anything happens to you...I'll..."

"Bring me back to life? Please, don't say such things."

"—"

Fourier had read him like a book. He was lying on his bed and couldn't have seen the tome in Ferris's hand. Yet he had guessed exactly what Ferris had in mind and refused it.

"I am me, you understand. My life began when I began, and it should end when I end. For it to go on after I end—that isn't right."

"But…but why? Is it so strange that I want you to live? That I want someone who's so important to me to be alive?"

Only as Ferris voiced the words did he realize they were exactly the same as those his father had babbled beside the corpse of his mother. If not word for word, then at the very least the spirit was identical.

"Don't lament, Ferris. Your heart is precious. Be proud of your abilities… You have the kindest power in all the world. Count not the wounds you couldn't heal, but the things you were able to save. Don't try to look back all the time while you're walking forward… I won't allow it."

"Your Highness…"

Slowly, so slowly, Fourier sat up in his bed. He had wasted away so much that he could no longer stand under his own power, but he wanted Ferris to see the spark of life burn within him. The scarlet eyes regained some measure of their former strength.

"And anyway," he went on, "I may yet best this thing. I'm… Yes. I'm your friend, and the fourth prince of the Kingdom of Lugunica. I even defeated Crusch in a sword battle. A little illness should be a…walk in the park."

Fourier raised his hand and gave Ferris a gentle tap on the forehead. His touch was so light, but his finger was warm.

"Don't abandon your duty as a member of the royal guard… It was I who had you assigned as Crusch's knight. Don't betray the vow we made to each other. The promise we made…as friends." Drawing long breaths, Fourier smiled again and lay back down on his bed. "I've grown tired with all this talking. But I was able to smile with you for the first time in a long time. That's good."

Ferris hadn't smiled. All he had done in front of Fourier that day was weep. But Fourier never spoke wrong. What he said sometimes sounded mistaken, but always turned out to be true.

"It was fun, Ferris."

So Ferris did everything he could to work his frozen cheeks into a smile.

"Right. This was fun, wasn't it, Your Highness?"

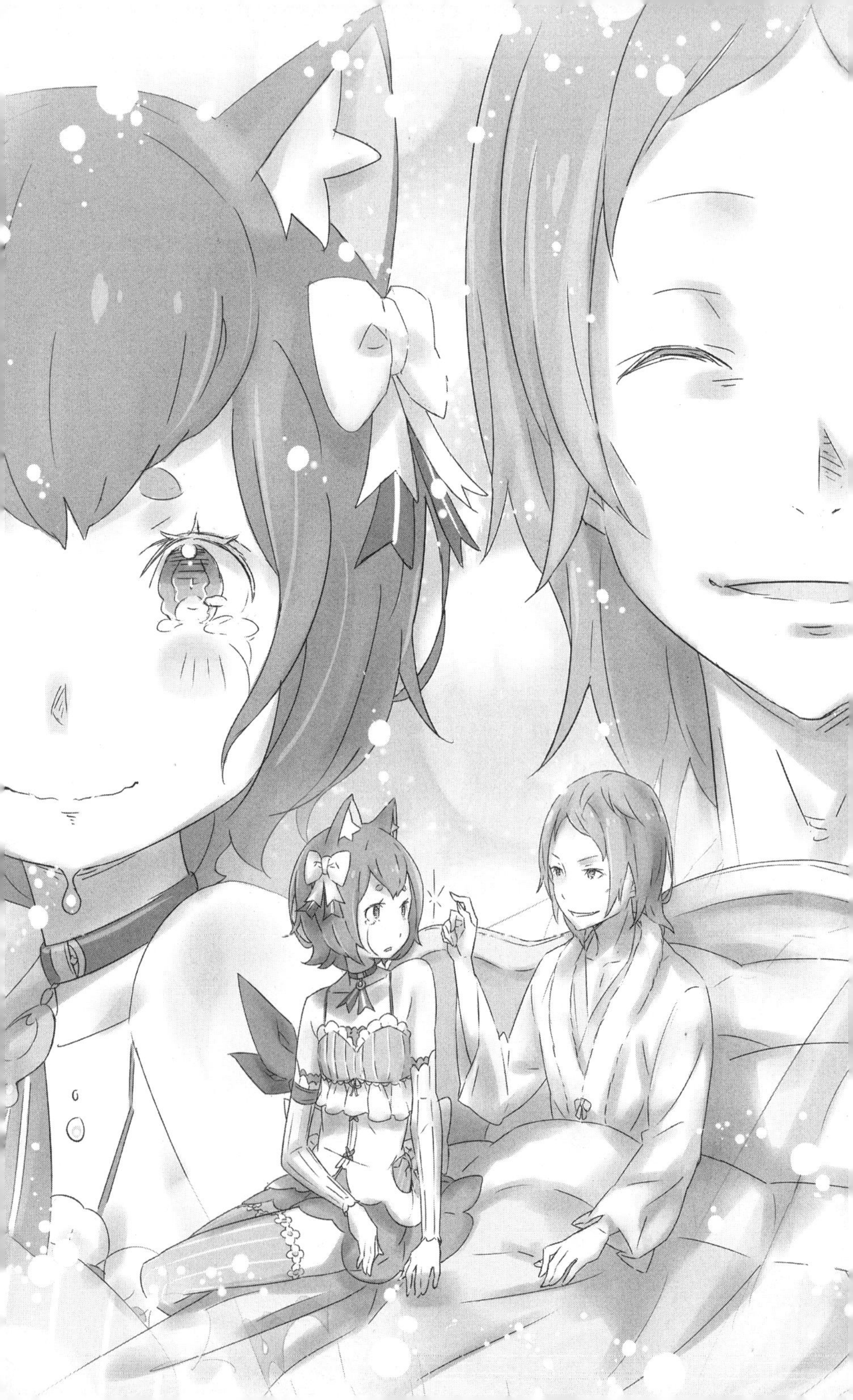

5

—The day was clear, but a breeze put a chill in the air.

"Crusch...I'd like to go outside for a while. Could you lend me your hand?"

"Of course, Your Highness. If you'll excuse me..."

"Oh! Carrying me yourself? Ha-ha! You are indeed a strong woman. I'm surprised again."

In the courtyard garden of Lugunica's royal castle, a profusion of seasonal flowers bloomed. But in the bustle and anxiety of the past several months, the colorful flora had found themselves rather lonely.

"Well, it's nice without a crowd. All the better to appreciate the blossoms—you can see them so much more clearly. Don't you think?"

"So you can. Your Highness is always so good at finding the bright side of things."

"I am, aren't I? I know quite a few good sides of you and Ferris, as well. In that, at least, I won't be bested by Meckart."

Crusch knelt in one corner of the garden, letting Fourier rest his head on her knees as the breeze drifted over them both. Fourier half closed his eyes sleepily, the garden floating in his fuzzy vision.

"You and I used to come here when we were young to view the flowers. Do you remember, Crusch?"

"I remember. I would accompany my father to the castle, and when I got bored, I would always come here...and you would always meet me. It was comforting to my childish heart."

"The first time I saw you..."

"I'll never forget it. You came tumbling out of the sky! I was shocked."

Their conversation about the past began to blossom.

Crusch smiled as she remembered, but Fourier shook his head gently.

"You're mistaken, actually. The first time I saw you was before that... I caught sight of you in this garden, from a distance. You were examining a young bud."

"...I didn't know. How embarrassing."

"Hardly. I was taken with you immediately. My heart beat faster, my cheeks got hot, and all I could do was stand there and look at you. After that, I would always look for you... Truth be told, our meeting was no mere chance. Heh-heh. I'll bet you were surprised."

"Yes, very much so."

Fourier's eyes crinkled, and his teeth showed as he laughed.

Crusch ran her fingers gently through the golden hair that rested on her knees, patted the pale cheeks tenderly.

"On the subject of surprising you, allow me to confess the awesome plans I have for the future..."

"Yes, Your Highness. Please, surprise me again. Please tell me."

"Very well. Listen closely. I... I intended to make you my queen."

"—"

"I would make you my queen, and Ferris would be our knight. And then—then three of us could always be together. It would be cause for contentment like no other. What do you think of that?"

"You... You certainly do know how to surprise me..."

Crusch found her voice catching, discovered she couldn't look at him.

Fourier, the gentle smile still on his face, listened closely to the note of joy in her voice.

"We've...been through quite a lot, haven't we? I so desperately wanted your attention... Heh! It led me to put you and Ferris to a great deal of trouble."

"...Your Highness. It was never a burden to do what you..."

"Tell me, Crusch... How did I do?"

"Your Highness?"

"Was I able…to be a Lion King worthy of your devotion…?"
"—"

They'd made a promise, once. They'd sworn by the pieces of the days they'd filled with laughter.
Crusch's breathing grew strained at Fourier's question.
"Your devotion was…precious," he said. "Something I cherished. Don't… Don't ever forget that."

Fourier smiled as if he were somehow proud of himself and raised his hand. He brushed Crusch's cheek, touching the hot tears that flowed down it, and traced his fingers along the line of her lips.
"Crusch."
"Yes, Your Highness."
"I…lo…"
"—"

There came a gust, a cold wind that tugged at Fourier's and Crusch's hair.
"Your Highness?"
"—"
"Your Highness, are you tired?"
"—"

"Your Highness, I know how you've worked and struggled. Please, rest peacefully."
"—"
"One last thing…"

The breeze continued to blow. But with her blurring vision, Crusch didn't see it, not even with her blessing. There, in the garden, Crusch held Fourier close and whispered.

"I wish I could have seen the future you dreamed of…"

6

The cruelty of it was that the death of Fourier Lugunica was treated almost as an incidental detail in the face of King Randohal Lugunica's passing.

The assembly was all that was left now, shrouded in depression now that its worst fears had been realized. Crusch, for her part, was plunged into a sense of loss and apathy. Fourier had been such a crucial presence to her that losing him was as much a shock and as much a torment as losing half her body.

Even now, when she closed her eyes, she could see his last smile. The image of him taking his final breaths was burned into her memory.

And at the last, the feelings he had been unable to finish confessing had vanished into thin air.

"—But we cannot sit around looking sad forever."

Miklotov was the first to cut through the thick atmosphere. The old sage looked each of the downcast nobles in the face, trying to rouse them.

"…That's right," someone said. "This isn't the time. His Departed Majesty would be sorry to see us this way."

There was a chorus of agreement. The sentiment spread, and Crusch found she had no choice but to look up and force herself to smile. To remain there with her head down would be the ultimate betrayal of what Fourier had wanted.

—She pictured his smiling face, remembered how he had always tried to look on the bright side.

"The royal bloodline has ended. We have lost our pact with the dragon. There can be no greater tragedy for the Dragonfriend Kingdom of Lugunica."

With those words, the image in her mind shattered.

Crusch looked up, doubting her own ears, while someone in front of her clutched his head.

"How can the *entire* royal family be gone? What will the dragon do? If we lose our pact, it will be a catastrophe for our nation. What with our relations with the Empire and the Holy Kingdom being as poor as they are right now...!"

What is he talking about...?

"There's also the issue of the preserved dragon's blood. There is always the possibility that its return will be sought. To guard against this, we may see fit to go ahead and use it..."

What are any of you talking about...?

Crusch stared blankly as she listened to the grim-faced attendees deliberate. Everything they were talking about came back to the question of what the dragon would do now that the royal family had been extinguished. The Kingdom of Lugunica had been under the dragon's blessing, saved from crisis more than once by the creature. Their fear was valid; Crusch was as aware as any of them that they were reliant on the dragon. But was that really the first thing they should be lamenting?

If they had wanted to debate the future of the kingdom, that would have been fine. If they had been worried about negotiating with other countries now that the king was gone, she could have forgiven them. But discussing how to manipulate the dragon—was that really the first thing on their minds?

With mounting disgust, it dawned on Crusch: None of these people were really unhappy that the royal line had ended. What they were worried about was the implications of it—whether the dragon would abandon them. They were terrified of being turned out from the cradle of the dragon's blessings. The death of the king, the end of the royal family—these were secondary considerations.

To them, Fourier's death is hardly a footnote.

The terrible thing was that if Crusch had not been so close to Fourier, she would no doubt be embracing the same fears as the rest of them. Her soul would be just as lukewarm as theirs.

That way of living, above all others, repulsed Crusch. She could hardly bear it as it cast a dark shadow over her heart.

"There is a matter I must share with you all."

The words cut through the furor of the assembly, and all eyes turned to the speaker.

It was Baron Lyp Bariel. He was not of high noble rank, but had been a favorite of His Majesty Randohal and much valued by the departed king. When Lyp had sufficient attention from the crowd, he made his announcement in a shaking voice.

"—There is a new inscription on the Dragon Tablet. The dragon has already revealed the fate of the kingdom."

This caused a fresh uproar in the assembly hall. The Dragon Tablet was a stone, a gift from the dragon and one of the kingdom's treasures. It recorded the future of the nation. A number of times in the past, the stone had warned the kingdom of threats to come, and they had been able to make preparations in advance.

No sooner had they been reflecting on how much they needed the dragon than they had been reminded in the most painful way of its power. Ignoring the feelings of Crusch and the others, Lyp began to read the inscription in a hurried tone.

"It says: 'Upon this, the end of the royal house, the kingdom shall find five candidates chosen by the Dragon Jewels, and with a new shrine maiden, the pact shall be made anew.'"

"The Dragon Tablet is telling us to choose a new king…? But how are we to find these five candidates?!"

"There are insignias," Lyp replied hotly, "jewels passed down by the royal house of Lugunica, which point to their pact with the dragon. The insignias bear those jewels, which will shine when held by one who is qualified as a candidate!"

At a gesture from Lyp, a cart was wheeled into the circular assembly room. Atop the cart were shimmering gemstones, the insignias of the Kingdom of Lugunica that bore the Dragon Jewels.

"If it recognizes you as a loyal retainer who can truly lead the kingdom, the insignia shall choose you. Does the Dragon Tablet speak false? Let each of you be tested in turn."

One of Lyp's assistants went among the people seated in the hall, putting the insignia before each of them. Some broke out in a cold sweat as they looked down upon it. Others gulped. If it were to glow in their hand, the path to the kingship would open.

The insignia was set in front of Crusch, as well. They said the dragon sought those who were loyal to the kingdom. If that were so, then surely she, as she was now, would not be chosen. But if…

"Then let us begin the test," Miklotov said. The Council of Elders went first, taking the insignia in hand. But there was no change in the darkened gem. There were some quiet breaths, and the slightest sounds of disappointment. So the test of the insignia began, working its way outward from the council. Disappointment after disappointment, and then came Crusch's turn.

The insignia was a triangular obsidian stone carved with a dragon design worked in gold. In the very center was the red gem called the Dragon Jewel, the stone that mocked the vain ambitions of those who were not fit to rule.

"The dragon? Who cares about…?" Crusch whispered, not letting the words out of her mouth as she grasped the insignia. She held it out in her palm for all to see. And then…

"—Oh, my…"

This came from Miklotov, whose normally placid face bore an unusual look of surprise. Everyone else in the room clearly felt the same way.

The insignia in Crusch's hand was glowing brightly.

"—So it seems even I, inept as I am, can do something for our kingdom."

She felt no shock. Her heart was too calm for that. As this registered with her, Crusch raised her head and closed her eyes.

—And in the darkness, she thought she saw Fourier's last smile.

7

When Ferris found out about the royal election, and that Crusch was one of those who had been chosen to stand, he combed the castle looking for her, until he arrived in the garden.

"—Lady Crusch."

Standing before the flowers, she looked so fragile that he had hesitated to call out. And no wonder. This was where she had spent those last moments with Fourier. It was the most holy place in Crusch's heart, the one place even Ferris could not enter.

He felt the pain of his own powerlessness as keenly as if a blade were digging into his chest. If only he could run to her, embrace her shoulders, and cast some magic spell that would heal her heart.

"Ferris, is that you? Well done, finding me here."

She spoke without looking back at Ferris, who bit his lip at his feelings of helplessness.

Now and again the wind gusted, picking up Crusch's long hair. Ferris watched her hair blow as he said, "I heard about the Dragon Tablet. They said you're one of the candidates to become the next king, Lady Crusch."

"Yes, so it seems. The dragon appears to have looked favorably on me."

Ferris could hardly have remained calm at this buffeting from the currents of fate. He had joined the royal guard, his mother and father had died, and he had lost Fourier, his bond with whom had meant so much. Now Crusch, his harbor in every storm, was caught up in some kind of royal election. Was there nothing safe or stable for him?

"What can I do for you, Lady Crusch? I don't know what to do…"

He didn't want to cause her any additional trouble, but he couldn't keep a quaver out of his voice. Ferris was too small a vessel to hold the emotions that roiled within him. Tears blurred his vision, and he wanted to run from the garden.

"Ferris, look at me." Crusch's voice made him jump.

He heard footsteps, and then two feet entered his downcast view. He raised his head and found himself looking straight at Crusch. The magic in her amber eyes captivated him.

"Ferris, let me vow to you before anyone else—I do wish to become king."

"Lady…Crusch…" Ferris caught his breath at her unhesitating declaration.

She was telling him she aspired to prevail at the royal election and ultimately take the throne. Ferris could not say anything further, but Crusch glanced around them and said, "The first time I met His Highness, it was in this garden. We often talked here and looked at the flowers together." She spoke gently; her eyes showed that she was remembering something long past.

Ferris didn't need to ask who it was she was remembering.

"In time, His Highness began to call at our mansion. I never told you, did I? Until I met His Highness, I always tied my hair back. Now I merely use a ribbon to keep it neat."

"I never knew. Why did you stop tying it up?"

"His Highness told me to be faithful to myself. So that was what I did. I chose the ribbon I gave to you, but...it began with His Highness."

Ferris unconsciously touched the white ribbon Crusch had given him, which he still wore in his hair.

She shared one memory after another with him, things he hadn't known—but one by one, they became memories he and Crusch shared. A bond so beautiful and so lively that he couldn't stop the flood of tears, or the ocean of smiles.

"Ferris, the time that we...that His Highness and you and I shared together...is something I cherish."

From the day Crusch had led Ferris from the Argyle mansion and first made him human, he had always been with her, and his circle soon expanded to include Fourier as well. A great deal of his life was made up of the two of them.

"But the existence of the dragon undermines that precious time of ours," she went on. "For many, His Highness existed only as a way of continuing the pact. They don't mourn his death, not really." Ferris stiffened; fire danced in Crusch's eyes.

What had she seen? What had happened during that time when Ferris couldn't be with her?

"But he did exist, enough to carve himself into my heart and yours. Fourier Lugunica well and truly lived."

With her right hand she touched her chest, and with her left hand, his. It was just a brush of her fingers, but Ferris thought the heat in them might burn his whole body. The fire of her resolve would swallow up every extraneous thought.

"The man who was my Lion King did live. I shall never allow anyone to say he didn't."

The pact with the dragon embracing the kingdom had protected the people for a very long time. But it had made their hearts weak, so much so that they were willing to ignore the death of this kind boy who had been loved by everyone he met. People's hearts had grown so frail that Fourier's death was all but forgotten in the face of the pact with the dragon.

"His death belongs to him. My Lion King is within me even now. I still dream the dream my king had—I alone can achieve it."

No one else saw how twisted the life of the kingdom had become. Everyone toadied to the dragon, begged favors from it, relied on its help, and in the process they had all forgotten how to walk on their own.

"No ruler but me will try to correct this, for nobody remembers those who sought to be true kings. So it falls to us to do it."

"Lady Crusch," Ferris whispered.

Crusch held out to him a dagger she'd taken from her belt. He took it and found that it was inscribed with the symbol of the Lion King. This was a precious heirloom of the House of Karsten.

"His Highness had a dream—of you, and me, and him, the three of us, building the future together."

"The three of us... Me, with His Highness, and you, Lady Crusch...?"

Faced with the striking weight of the dagger in his hand, Ferris finally realized what he had to do alongside Crusch and His Highness, to help in their resolution. Now, he had only Crusch. She was everything.

"His Highness loved this place," Crusch said somberly, "and it's where he spent his last moments. So I swear to him here: I will make you my knight."

At that, Ferris knelt wordlessly and offered up the dagger. Crusch took it and drew it, touching Ferris first on the left shoulder, then on the right, with the flat of the blade. Then she gave the knife back to him, completing the ritual of vassalage.

No one knew a knighthood had been bestowed there that day—except one, or perhaps two, Lion Kings who were present. And it was a beginning, and for the two of them, it was also the continuation of the dream of their Lion King.

Crusch glanced back over her shoulder. "We're going, Ferris. To reclaim our kingdom from the dragon and make His Highness's dream come true."

"Yes, Lady Crusch. Lead me, and I'll follow. We'll find where His Highness's dream takes us." There was no hesitation as he joined her. The first of the candidates for king, the one most strongly bound to her attendant, walked proudly away. The only ones watching were the flowers in that garden where everything had begun.

Bobbing gently in the breeze, a single bud waited tranquilly for the right moment to bloom.

<END>

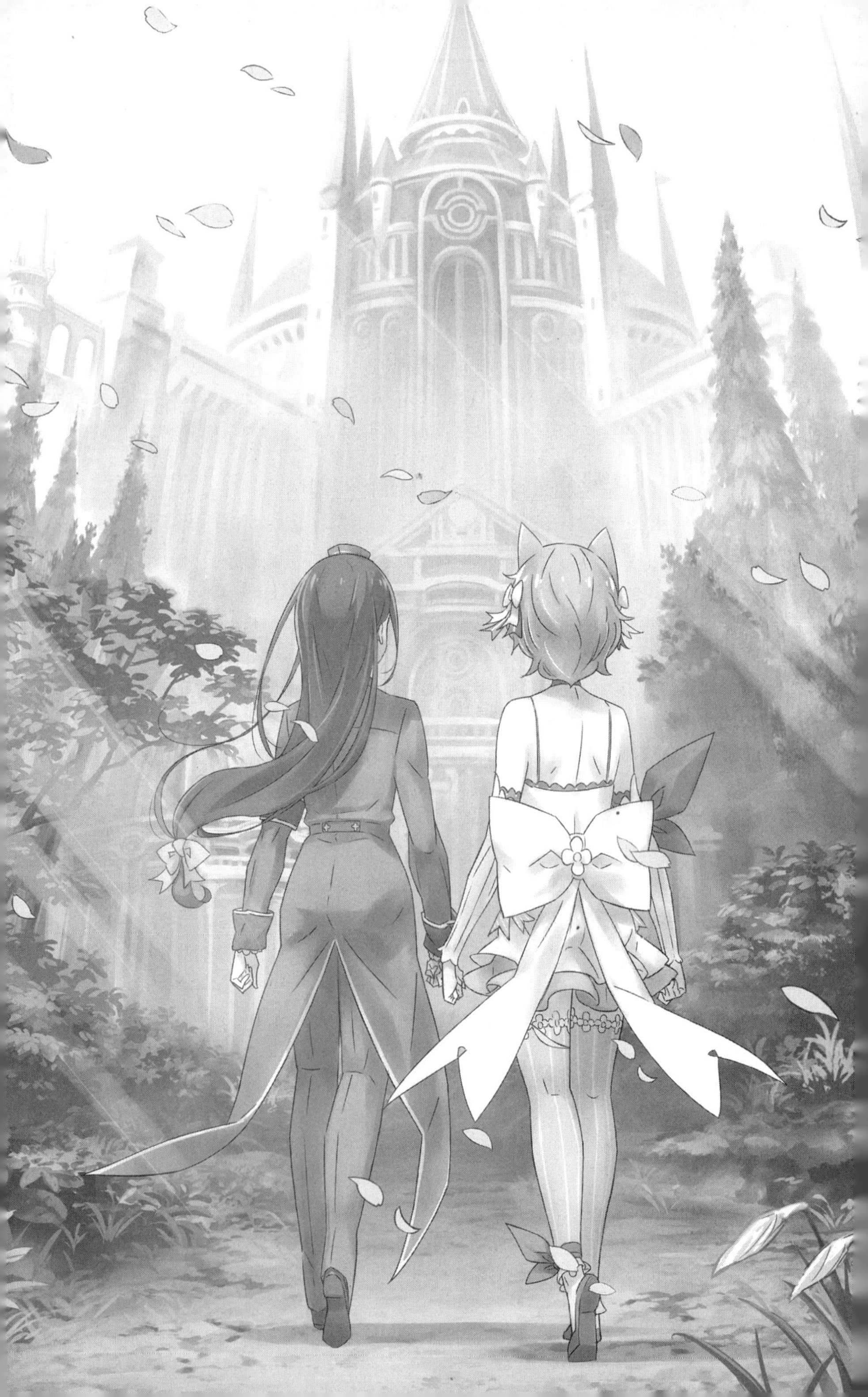

AFTERWORD

Hello! Always so good to have you here. This is Tappei Nagatsuki. Or, if you find it easier to imagine, a gray cat who goes by that name. Er, if that reference went over your head, just ignore it. Sorry.

This volume of *Re:ZERO* is a side story to the main plot. In the past, I've done short-story collections that get away from the events of the main series, but this time, rather than do another batch of vignettes, I decided to call this *Ex*.

I had actually intended to do this volume more or less in the vein of the other short-story collections, but during the planning stage, I found I had a lot of stories about how Crusch got her start, and then the suggestion was made that the whole volume could be devoted to that topic. So we found ourselves with the book you're currently holding.

None of the main characters from the regular series appear here; we're digging into the background of some of the rest of the cast. Some of the material is rather challenging, but I hope those of you who have read this far will see what Crusch and her friends have gone through and understand where her resolve comes from. I hope you've come to like them even just a little bit more, and that it will give you even greater pleasure in finding out what they get up to in the main story.

Having read the book, maybe you're wondering what's going on with the author. Well, I'm pretty obsessed with tabletop RPGs (I know I'm a little late to the party).

I knew TRPGs existed, but it seemed like there was a pretty high bar of entry for complete novices like me, and I could never quite bring myself to try them. But with some help from the people around me, I finally gave one a shot...and it's really something. They are super, super interesting.

People had told me that creative types tend to get caught up in TRPGs, and now I see what they mean: This is a kind of experience you don't really get with other games. You get to let your imagination run wild in somebody else's world. What author wouldn't love that?

There are all sorts of fun to be had here. I get to solve problems using only my wits, plumb mysteries with the guidance of my GM, drive my character nuts with my little mistakes, and lots more.

Publishing books like this has helped me make new friends and given me glimpses into worlds I had never known about before, where I've discovered other ideas and ways of thinking. Those are important experiences to have in life. I hope all my readers will challenge themselves—not just to try TRPGs but to do all kinds of new things.

For starters, you could recommend this series to people who don't know about it. Broaden your friends' horizons! I, personally, would certainly be happy if you did that. It's a way of bringing more happiness into the world, one person at a time. Try it!

I'm going to run up against my page count pretty soon here, so it's time for the acknowledgments.

I'm indebted as ever to my editor, I-sama. I'm grateful for your suggestion to delve into the backgrounds of some of these characters, including some who haven't shown up in the main series yet. Sorry for always making such ridiculous demands of you!

To my illustrator, Otsuka-sensei, as always, thank you so much for producing such wonderful illustrations in such a short time. I know I always ask for oodles of character designs, and I'm always impressed by how quickly you come up with them. For this volume,

I think you especially captured Fourier's slightly ridiculous side. Fantastic work.

To Kusano-sensei, my designer, thank you so much for all your work. This time the title was even longer than usual—in my head, I sort of thought of it as a challenge. *Even Kusano-sensei won't be able to fit all* this *in!* But it's a bet I would have lost. And I hope I'll keep losing those bets.

To everyone else in the editing and sales divisions, to all the proofreaders and the owners of all the bookstores, this book couldn't have taken shape without the cooperation of so many people. Thank you all.

And more than anything, my thanks go out to my readers, who picked up this book and came along with me on this story. I hope you'll stick around for the next one, too.

Okay, then. I'll see you for Volume 7 of the main series. Later!

May 2015
Tappei Nagatsuki
(Feeling deathly afraid of summer this year,
if the May heat is any indication.)

EVERYONE'S FAVORITE TIRIENA
Cute Tiriena!
Cute profile, too!
68"
○△X16
B: 59"
W: 59"
H: 59"
A little fan service. Big soft arms!
Mr. Nagatsuki,
Hope to see her again!
Shinichirou Otsuka
オオツカ
シンイチロウ

"Right, right, riiight! It's Ferri and Crusch, handling today's Message Corner! Now we can let everyone know just how great Lady Crusch is!"

"Don't get too excited, Ferris. I appreciate your thoughtfulness, but first we must fulfill the duty we've been assigned. You can only hold your head up high once you've met the obligations of your office. You understand?"

"Aww, Lady Crusch, you're starting out so cool, Ferri can barely handle it…!"

"What's wrong? Your face is red. Do you have a cold? If you're feeling ill, I can handle this…"

"Nope! Uh-uh! Not at all! Gosh, Lady Crusch, how cruel of you! Okay then, now Ferri's gonna dispel any concerns about my health by delivering the news with unbridled enthusiasm! First up, they're at it again! The beloved collaboration between Ministop and *Re:ZERO* is back! We've got some really lovely stuff in store for you this time."

"In light of summer bearing down on us, I gather there will be some wall scrolls showing Emilia and her friends in bathrobes, as well as key chains packaged with your favorite Ministop sweets. They are quite cute. You can use the Loppi terminal at any Ministop to preorder. It's a rather convenient device."

"It sure is. Oh, and, and! We have an announcement about the MF Bunko J Summer School Festival! The school festival is packed every year, and this year the events will include an autograph session with Tappei Nagatsuki, the author of *Re:ZERO*! Yahoooo, that's awesome! But is it going to go all right?"

"I'm sure the plans were made after due consideration. I have high hopes for that autograph session. Apparently there will also be announcements about merchandising and more at the summer festival. Details about the festival and the Ministop collaboration can be found on the *Re:ZERO* home page or MF Bunko J's home page."

"You're so thoughtful, Lady Crusch! You're wonderful! And on that note! One thing we definitely shouldn't forget is *Re:ZERO*, Volume 7! It should go on sale in September. Ta-da!"

"Subaru Natsuki has had his heart broken, but he starts off once again. With Rem's help, he opens negotiations with us—and then the biggest battle his new world has ever seen begins."

"If ol' Subaru's willing to help you achieve the kingship, Lady Crusch, I might actually have to admit he's got some good points. What a tragedy!"

"We can't be sure that's what's really going on. If we make the wrong judgment, we could find the carpet pulled out from under us. We'll have to be careful."

"A toe-to-toe fight with that dumb-dumb? …Ooh, Ferri just falls harder and harder for you!"

HAVE YOU BEEN TURNED ON TO LIGHT NOVELS YET?

IN STORES NOW!

SWORD ART ONLINE, VOL. 1-11
SWORD ART ONLINE, PROGRESSIVE 1-4

The chart-topping light novel series that spawned the explosively popular anime and manga adaptations!

MANGA ADAPTATION AVAILABLE NOW!

SWORD ART ONLINE © Reki Kawahara ILLUSTRATION: abec
KADOKAWA CORPORATION ASCII MEDIA WORKS

ACCEL WORLD, VOL. 1-11

Prepare to accelerate with an action-packed cyber-thriller from the bestselling author of *Sword Art Online*.

MANGA ADAPTATION AVAILABLE NOW!

ACCEL WORLD © Reki Kawahara ILLUSTRATION: HIMA
KADOKAWA CORPORATION ASCII MEDIA WORKS

SPICE AND WOLF, VOL. 1-18

A disgruntled goddess joins a traveling merchant in this light novel series that inspired the *New York Times* bestselling manga.

MANGA ADAPTATION AVAILABLE NOW!

SPICE AND WOLF © Isuna Hasekura ILLUSTRATION: Jyuu Ayakura
KADOKAWA CORPORATION ASCII MEDIA WORKS

IS IT WRONG TO TRY TO PICK UP GIRLS IN A DUNGEON?, VOL. 1-9

A would-be hero turns damsel in distress in this hilarious send-up of sword-and-sorcery tropes.

MANGA ADAPTATION AVAILABLE NOW!

Is It Wrong to Try to Pick Up Girls in a Dungeon? © Fujino Omori / SB Creative Corp.

ANOTHER

The spine-chilling horror novel that took Japan by storm is now available in print for the first time in English—in a gorgeous hardcover edition.

MANGA ADAPTATION AVAILABLE NOW!

Another © Yukito Ayatsuji 2009/ KADOKAWA CORPORATION, Tokyo

A CERTAIN MAGICAL INDEX, VOL. 1-13

Science and magic collide as Japan's most popular light novel franchise makes its English-language debut.

MANGA ADAPTATION AVAILABLE NOW!

A CERTAIN MAGICAL INDEX © Kazuma Kamachi
ILLUSTRATION: Kiyotaka Haimura
KADOKAWA CORPORATION ASCII MEDIA WORKS

VISIT YENPRESS.COM TO CHECK OUT ALL THE TITLES IN OUR NEW LIGHT NOVEL INITIATIVE AND...

GET YOUR YEN ON!

Yen ON
Yen Press
www.YenPress.com

WATCH ON crunchyroll

www.crunchyroll.com/rezero

Re:ZERO

-Starting Life in Another World-

©Tappei Nagatsuki,PUBLISHED BY KADOKAWA CORPORATION/Re:ZERO PARTNERS

Read the light novel that inspired the hit anime series!

Re:ZeRo
-Starting Life in Another World-

Also be sure to check out the manga series!

AVAILABLE NOW!

Yen Press
www.YenPress.com

YEN ON

Re:Zero Kara Hajimeru Isekai Seikatsu
© Tappei Nagatsuki, Daichi Matsuse / KADOKAWA CORPORATION
© Tappei Nagatsuki Illustration: Shinichirou Otsuka / KADOKAWA CORPORATION

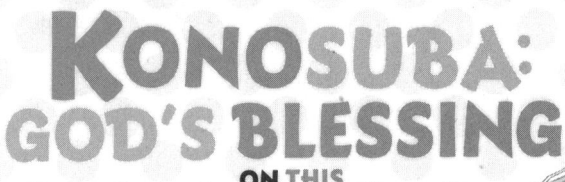